CLAN NOVEL:
LASOMBRA

RICHARD E. DANSKY

author	richard e. dansky
cover artist	john van fleet
series editors	john h. steele and
	stewart wieck
copyeditor	anna branscome
graphic designer	kathleen ryan
art director	richard thomas

More information and previews available at
white—wolf.com/clannovels

White Wolf Publishing
735 Park North Boulevard, Suite 128
Clarkston, GA 30021
www.white—wolf.com

First Edition: September 1999

10 9 8 7 6 5 4 3 2 1

Printed in Canada.

*Dedicated to Benjamin and Esther Cherdack,
and to the memory of Joseph and Sara Dansky.
Thank you for your love, support and encouragement
in all my endeavors, even the ones with fangs,
implements of destruction and things
that went bump in the night.
This one's for you.*

LASOMBRA

part one:
minuet

Morty never really understood the meaning of the term "meaty thump" until the very last second of his existence, not that the knowledge did him much good. After all, the thump in question was made by his body hitting the weed-split concrete of the sidewalk; and the meat, well, the less said about that part, the better.

From thirty-seven stories up, Lucita looked over the edge of the building dispassionately, her long black hair dancing in the strong breeze. The wind tugged at her loose sleeves and leggings, but less effectively, and the chill of the air failed to raise goosebumps on her olive skin. Once, a wind like this would have brought tears to her eyes, but no longer. She looked over the edge at the splatter pattern Morty's immortal guts had made on impact and tsked to herself. It was messy, too messy. She was getting sloppy in her old age.

Morty had been a warm-up, not even a paying job. He'd simply crossed Lucita's path a year or so previously, the last time she'd been in Philadelphia, and had made a profound annoyance out of himself. Lucita prided herself on keeping an even keel these nights (her sire, Satan roast his flabby, scabby soul, had constantly harped on her temper as something that would someday get her killed) but there were still a few ways to get a rise out of the dreaded Monçada's only childe.

One was to call her "babydoll," "sweetcheeks" or any other such "endearment."

Another was to try for a quick grope, though God alone knew why a vampire felt the need.

And a third was to resort to crude insults relating to Lucita's ethnicity.

Morty had gone three for three in the space of thirty seconds, which had to be some sort of record even among the sort of low-rent dirtballs Lucita ran with these nights. As a result, he'd gotten himself reclassified, moving from the list of "imbeciles who can be ignored" to "practice."

Two nights back, Lucita had agreed to a new assignment. The Kindred who'd arranged the deal had been a quiet sort who seemed to find the entire arrangement bitterly distasteful. Still, he'd been courteous and professional, and she'd found no reason to refuse the offer. The price had been right, the timeframe had been agreeable and she had been getting, not to put too fine a point on it, bored.

But it had been some time since she'd taken on an assignment of this caliber, and she didn't feel quite right about diving in immediately. Instead, she felt rusty. She felt unprepared. She felt like…she needed practice.

And thus it was that Three-finger Morty, one of the meanest sons of a bitch ever to run a pack through the streets of Philadelphia, ended up as a bloody smear on the sidewalk outside a brew pub.

Lucita sighed and hugged herself, more as a gesture of worry than as a way of warding off the weather. As warm-ups went, dealing with Morty had been barely worth the trouble. She'd be after bigger prey now, more powerful, more intelligent, and certainly more likely to be aware of her *modus operandi* than some street-level thug.

"This one," she said to no one in particular, "looks like it might actually be work." Then, without a backward glance, she opened the door to the stairwell and drifted down in its shadows, on her way to leaving the city behind.

Playtime, like Morty, was over. She had work to do.

Saturday, 17 July 1999, 10:12 PM
The Presidential Hotel
Washington, D.C.

Sascha Vykos sat on the edge of the immaculately made bed in her suite and angrily regarded a hand-written letter. The missive had been waiting for her this evening when she'd emerged from the haven she'd claimed. Formerly the Presidential Hotel had housed Marcus Vitel, the deposed Prince of Washington, D.C., but after he'd fled the city and Vykos had been confirmed as archbishop, it had seemed as natural to usurp Vitel's home as it had been to usurp his domain. She also maintained a suite at the Hyatt Regency Capitol Hill that, incongruously, the Sabbat had descended upon as its field headquarters in the nation's capital, the better to conduct cloakroom-style business on the fly; but whenever she could, she spent her days slumbering in Vitel's rooms. If nothing else, it was safer. After all, apart from her personal ghouls and bodyguards, no one knew precisely where she was havening. In theory.

That was why the presence of a cream-colored envelope sealed with wine-colored wax had been such an unpleasant surprise. None of her watchful ghouls had seen any interlopers during the day or early evening, yet there the letter sat on her doorstep, delicately arranged without even a smudge of dust. She knew who had sent the message. But messages like this were supposed to be conveyed by prearranged courier drop. Her haven was certainly not one of those drops, and that could only mean bad news.

The note was from her source inside the

Camarilla, signed "Lucius" as usual, for reasons that presumably had died with Caesar in the Forum. The brief message did not in fact contain good news. It noted that the conference of Camarilla elders in Baltimore had been reinforced by the powers-that-be back in the Old Country. Specifically, Ash, Vitel, *et alia*, had received as reinforcement Jan Pieterzoon, a Ventrue of some reputation as a strategist and schemer. Vykos was familiar enough with Pieterzoon's work, if not with the man himself; while he wasn't the threat that a member of the Inner Circle or one of their lapdogs might be, he was still a power in his own right.

The rest of the letter was less galvanizing, detailing the reactions of the various conference members to Pieterzoon's incipient arrival. There was the usual Camarilla-style backbiting and protestations of noble self-sacrifice, but the short version was that most of the delegates were torn between resentment over having to share the credit if they should happen to triumph, and secret relief at the desperately needed help.

Sighing, she re-folded the letter and tucked it back into the envelope. It was then that she noticed that the signet ring used to seal the wax had left an impression in the shape of the Camarilla's telltale ankh. It was a droll touch, and not one she would have expected of "Lucius." Either the spy had developed a sense of humor, or it was intended as a reminder that her whereabouts were known, and the knowledge could be passed along to others at any time. It was all dreadfully, unnecessarily complicated, but upon reflection, Vykos came to the conclusion that most Cainites of her age or older simply didn't know any other way to be. The simple and direct died simple and direct deaths; only the devious and elusive endured.

Carelessly throwing the letter on the floor, Vykos sighed. Pieterzoon's arrival was, to say the least, an unexpected complication. She frowned, crossed her legs and then uncrossed them, and found herself fidgeting restlessly. That would never do, not with the war council set to resume its so-called deliberations within the hour.

Suddenly impatient, she clapped her hands, twice. The door of the suite opened and one of her ghouls, a dapper, thin man with a hatchet face and a reddish beard that could best be described as "sparse," entered. "Yes, mistress?"

"Kevin, I need you to make a phone call for me."

"A phone call, mistress?" The ghoul's face and tone both registered his surprise. "Of course. Whom shall I call, and as to what end?"

"You shall call me, and you will do so when the circumstances demand that you do so." Kevin still looked puzzled, and internally Vykos debated whether she was doing the right thing by trusting even this simple task to him. He showed no signs of active disobedience, but precious few of competence, either.

Vykos sighed. Even if Kevin did not understand what he was doing, or why he was doing it, his expression should be one of rapt attention, reflecting a certain trust that all Vykos might ask of him would be explained to him properly. Confusion, when seen from that perspective, was a manifestation of distrust, and distrust was a form of disloyalty.

She would, she decided, do some work to make sure that Kevin's expression never troubled her again, if he succeeded in carrying out his instructions precisely. Otherwise, she'd express her displeasure more emphatically, and more permanently.

And then she told Kevin what she needed him to do, and when, and why, and she watched the light of recognition dawn on his face. It was, Vykos noted, possibly one of the most irritating things she had ever seen.

"Of course, mistress," he said, bowing and backing out of the room.

It took Vykos all of perhaps three seconds to decide that, regardless of how well Kevin performed his task, he wasn't going to see morning.

Life, even eternal life, was too short to put up with that sort of thing.

And in the air vent, something that looked almost precisely like a cat arched its back, then turned and scurried away.

Friday, 16 July 1999, 10:48 PM (local time)
Iglesia de San Nicolás de los Servitas
Madrid, Spain

The heart of the church was a huge, mostly empty room with a stone floor. In it, a fat man sat on a simple wooden stool, contemplating a chess board. A smattering of white pieces, including a handful of pawns and a single bishop, had been removed from play. So had a few black pawns, but that was all. White had castled and was concentrating on establishing a strong defense, while black was on the offensive but seemed oddly disorganized, and one of its knights was in imminent danger.

"It seems like a resignable position."

Cardinal Ambrosio Luis de Monçada looked up from the board, a beatific smile on his face. "Ahh, Sir Talley. It is good to see you in the flesh, my son. You are well? The trip was not too arduous? You have fed?"

Talley, as the templar called himself, nodded assent to all of his host's questions. "Your hospitality, Your Eminence, is as always impeccable." He eased his long frame down onto the stool opposite Monçada. Talley was bony and angular, with a face like a hound that has just seen the fox vanish once and for all. His hair was white, though his features made him seem no older than thirty. His hands were his most remarkable feature: They were long and slender, and the fourth finger on each was longer than the middle one. In his living days, Talley had once been accused of being a werewolf because of those remarkable hands; having dealt with any number of lupines in his time, he now found the recollection amusing. He wore a charcoal-gray suit, clearly hand-tailored by someone who knew how to accentuate the clean lines of the human predator.

By contrast, Monçada wore a simple priest's robe, and sandals that flapped against the floor as he tapped his foot, contemplating his next move. "Unfortunately, Don Ibrahim, my opponent in this game, is of the stubborn sort who will fight to the last angry little pawn." He looked up with an expression of mock concern. "And you seat yourself in his place! Truly, my son, I thought you were on my side in this matter."

Talley rose and bowed. "Forgive me. I shall, of course, repair to your side immediately, and beg humble apologies for my treachery."

Monçada chuckled, a thick, wet sound. "No, no. Sit. I just find that too many of the young ones these days have a dreadful tendency to get wrapped up in chess metaphors. It's lazy thinking."

Talley did not sit, but leaned over and picked up the black queen. "Mmm. Considering the chessboard, I'm not surprised the privileged few who see it are whipped into a tizzy by it. Lucita?" he said, indicating the piece he held.

Monçada reached a pudgy hand out for it. "Of course. The set itself was a gift from Vykos. He does marvelous work, do you not agree?"

"He?"

The cardinal shrugged massively. "He, she, it—it changes with its whim. I met Vykos first when he had his original form, and that is how I know him. He does me the courtesy of resuming it when he comes to visit."

"Ah. If it's all the same, I'll avoid the issue and keep this form for the foreseeable future."

Monçada gave a delighted laugh. "Your courtesy is greatly appreciated, and I trust you to keep the face that suits the one they call 'The Hound' best." He looked at the chess piece, then replaced it on the board. "Pity she was so reluctant to pose for this. Ahem." He looked up. "You would like to know why you are here, yes? The pleasure of your company is, while something I do not get nearly enough of, not sufficient to cause me to summon you."

Talley kept a poker face. "I trust not for confession, then? I'm afraid I've racked up quite a list of sins in the centuries since Jeffrey first brought me here; I must admit to having been a bit lax in my churching."

"We should make time for that soon, then, my little Hound. I have faith in you to perform the task I've set you without harm, but more faith in other things. God is merciful, but only if we avail ourselves of that mercy. And it is incumbent upon those of us who are irretrievably damned to pay careful attention to how we tend our souls. We are damned for a reason within God's scheme of things, but that does not excuse us from obeying those of God's laws that He has left to us."

Talley shifted uncomfortably. Unlike most of the Sabbat's archbishops and cardinals, Monçada actually had been an archbishop in life, and a pillar of the Church during years when faith was a palpable thing. Oddly enough, his belief had not deserted him upon the Embrace, instead twining around an ineffable belief in his own damnation. It was a curious combination, but a potent one, and Monçada's ability to draw upon the strength of his faith was one of the reasons he was so widely feared by even those who served him. Still, the cardinal's devotion to the sect did little to set those Cainites of little or no faith at ease around him. It was fortunate, then, that Monçada spent all of his time within the heart of his massive, mazelike cathedral haven. The cardinal did not journey forth into the world; the world, when he needed it, approached him humbly, and on bended knee.

In the distance, bells were tolling.

"Tut, tut," the cardinal said suddenly. "I trust you to keep your body safe enough to house your soul until you return, and then we'll shrive you. In the meantime, there's work to do."

Talley nodded. He was almost as old as Monçada, certainly faster and possibly stronger. But the cardinal had a presence, an aura of paternal wisdom and sheer power that made Talley feel like a child—a mortal boy—once again. He felt the need to garner Monçada's approval, to seek shelter and safety under the cardinal's beneficent gaze. It was most likely a trick, a side effect of some power or other that the cardinal didn't even realize he was employing, but the impact was devastatingly real.

Then again, according to Talley's great-grandsire Boukephos, Monçada had possessed that gift even when he was alive. It had been, said the ancient Greek, the deciding factor in Embracing Monçada, even over the protests of the Muslim members of the clan who were affiliated with the other side of the *Reconquista*. Now those self-same Cainites sought his counsel on matters temporal, if not spiritual.

"So what is this work you have for me?" Talley

had to force himself away from his contemplation of the cardinal, and it was clear Monçada was aware of his distraction. "I work better when I know what I'm actually supposed to be doing."

"You will enjoy this, I think. It's a bit of a change of pace. You don't have to hunt down and kill anyone, nor will you be walking to and fro in the earth, and up and down in it."

"I don't have to kill anyone?" Talley's tone became one of mock indignation. "Then why call for me?"

"Because I've decided it's time to broaden your repertoire, among other reasons. How do you feel about protecting some of my servants against assassination?"

"Bored, actually. Why do you want me to do it?"

"I have my reasons." It was said with an air of finality.

Talley frowned. "I don't like this. Whom am I supposed to be bodyguarding?"

"An archbishop in our little escapade over in America. Shall I tell you the whole story?"

Talley's eyebrows shot up. "Please."

Monçada shook his head, slowly. "There is not much to tell, alas. The American plan is proceeding well, though the leadership of the operation is divided. Schismatic, one might say. There are three archbishops in place, now that Vykos has been elevated, and I'm sure Boukephos has educated you as to what happens to power-sharing arrangements of that sort. One or more of the three tends to fall by the wayside with a dagger in his ribs."

"Or back," Talley added mirthlessly.

"Or back." Monçada nodded. "And in this case,

it would seem that the wheels are already in motion. Someone has decided to remove one of my archbishops. Someone has decided to be very certain that this archbishop is removed. Someone has gone to very great expense to hire an assassin to do away with one of those who are doing my will. Naturally, I do not approve of this sort of thing."

"What happened to Vallejo? The last time I met with *Les Amies Noir* I was told he'd gone abroad to watch Vykos. Why not just expand his assignment?"

"My dear Talley," Monçada said wearily, "your lack of faith in my judgment is disappointing, extremely disappointing. I know the difficulties inherent in this matter intimately; they are why I sent for my Hound, whose heart and skill are sufficient to overcome them.

"Now hush, and listen. An archbishop is the target of an assassin, yes. Do I know which one? No; it is enough that I know that the hunt has begun. Do I care which one? No; though I would be most distressed to lose any of my three able and talented servants. Preventing the assassination would the preferable outcome, of course, but even that is not the most important thing."

Talley drummed his fingers on the table, careful not to disturb the chessboard. "Ah. I see. So I am to insert myself into this little game, protect whichever of the archbishops seems most likely to be removed, and hand you the assassin's head on a silver platter? Christ's wounds, Cardinal, it's a joke! Defend three potential targets, all arrogant as Hades and no doubt bound and determined to prove they don't need me? And it's not as if I'm any sort of—of bodyguard. Get someone whose business it is to tend others."

The cardinal closed his eyes for a moment and drew in a deep breath. Rustling noises echoed from the shadows in the corners of the vast chamber, and the very stones of the floor were suddenly cold as fear. For a second, Talley feared he'd gone too far, but if he had, it was too late to call back the words he'd spoken. It would also be too late to escape with his life; the cathedral was a deathtrap to any who did not enjoy the cardinal's favor.

"What I want from you is simple. I want *you* to tell me who is plotting this foolishness; Vallejo has been there too long and may be compromised. Tell me who feels he is above my commands and the necessity to prosecute the war with the Camarilla, above the demands of the sect and of God. I find such arrogance intolerable, and I will know the author of it, if it costs the lives of a hundred archbishops. I will sire armies, if it comes to that, to uncover this traitor. And you," he said, leaning in close, "you will be my instrument, my Hound on the scent of those who betray me. Go to America, Talley. Watch the archbishops, and watch them watch one another. See who makes the first misstep. See who falls." Monçada's eyes were open now, black as the shadows he commanded, and Talley found himself unable to look away. "Use the ruses you must—I do not care if you tell them you're there to watch over the lowliest pack priest or the operation as a whole. I have already sent word to Archbishop Polonia of your incipient arrival. They will wonder why I have told Polonia and not Vykos, who is perceived as my catspaw in all this. We shall see what they make of that; no doubt some enterprising souls will see it as me withdrawing my favor from Vykos; instead, it is a wedge driven between the two, to see if they react to trifles.

"And I don't expect you to 'get' the killer, Talley. One or both of you would end up rather badly smashed if you tried, and I'd rather you didn't run the risk until after I've seen to the state of your soul, and that of my childe. If worst comes to worst, just make a statement to my dear Lucita that she can't simply decide to knock over the pieces on my little chessboard after all."

Talley blinked. Twice. "Lucita?"

Monçada nodded. "Lucita. Now you see why I don't want you to 'get' her. I am," he sighed ruefully, "entirely too fond of you both." The cardinal turned his attention to the chessboard, a frown on his face. "All that you need is waiting for you with Hidalgo, in the blue chamber. You remember the way?"

Talley nodded somberly.

"Good. You are dismissed." The templar stood silently, turned silently, strode silently toward the door.

"Talley?" The cardinal's voice was calm and measured. "Talley, if you see Don Ibrahim on your way out, you may wish to repeat your advice on his game position. I don't think he'll take it, though. I don't think so at all."

Saturday, 17 July 1999, 11:15 PM
Hyatt Regency Capitol Hill
Washington, D.C.

Cell phones were the sort of technological marvel that the elders of the Sabbat distrusted. Mind you, the elders of the Camarilla distrusted the blasted things in precisely the same way, but mentioning that to a four-century-old Tzimisce with a variable number of arms was a surefire way to get oneself turned into the vampiric equivalent of saltwater taffy. Accordingly, younger members of the sect politely didn't use the things around those of their superiors who were likely to take offense, and made sure not to mock the old farts for being fossils until they were safely out in the field.

That was why it was such a shock when an audible chirp came from within the folds of Vykos's jacket. The war council had been proceeding in its usual fashion, (which is to say that two minor "dignitaries" had already been killed, and a third staked and put into storage because there was still some argument between Polonia and Vykos as to the man's ultimate usefulness), with much chest-pounding and little in the way of actual strategy, when the cell phone went off.

Instantly, the room went deathly silent. Vykos looked left, looked right, and slipped a pale hand inside the jacket of her conservatively cut blue suit to remove the anxiously bleating cell phone.

Every eye in the place was on her. She acknowledged such with an airy wave, flipped open the phone, and put it to her ear.

"Yes?" Her fluting tones wafted over the room as every vampire in attendance suddenly did his level best to look elsewhere, pretend disinterest, and eavesdrop for all he was worth. "You say he's arrived? Fascinating, yet not entirely unexpected." There came a pause, to which Vykos responded by nodding twice. "Excellent. I expect regular updates on his whereabouts, contacts and the like." There was another pause, and some agitated squawking that those sitting nearest to Vykos ("near" being a relative term in this instance) could almost make out a few tantalizing words. Vykos listened, frowned, and drummed a single slender, sharp-nailed finger on the tabletop. Finally, she interrupted. "No. That is not your mission. Do I make myself clear? Wonderful. I expect to hear from you tomorrow."

And with that, Vykos folded the phone up neatly and put it away. She looked around the room, aware of how intently the other Cainites in attendance were watching her, and let slip a small smile.

"I'm dreadfully sorry for the interruption, Archbishop." She bowed her head, as if in contrition, in the vague direction of Polonia. The archbishop made a small gesture, as if to dismiss the interruption, and almost succumbed to the temptation to roll his eyes. Around him, the others fidgeted, shifted in their seats or audibly grumbled. No one dared meet Vykos's gaze, however, or had the courage to voice a complaint. The Tzimisce elder almost tittered, but restrained herself. It was priceless, the way the lot of them were on tenterhooks over the phone call. They were all so anxious to salvage any scrap of information, the better to obtain the slightest of advantages on their rivals, that they'd do anything to learn what she had heard.

Indeed, she suspected most would gladly kill to have the knowledge of what the party on the other end of the line had been saying. After all, knowing that little tidbit would surely unlock the enigma that was Vykos, enabling one to learn the secrets of the ages, the truth about all of Vykos's plots, and probably the color of Cardinal Monçada's favorite cassock as well. It was astonishing, the importance the young and ambitious attached to every bit of trivia dangled before them. It was also amusing to be able to manipulate them into a veritable frenzy so easily. Here were easily two dozen of the finest war leaders the American Sabbat had to offer, hardened murderers and tacticians who'd ravaged their way up the eastern seaboard with admirable, sharklike efficiency. Yet here they were, anxious as schoolboys trying to read a note over a classmate's shoulder.

This, Vykos mused to herself, *is the sort of moment that puts the whole thing in perspective. And the best part is, I'm going to upset the applecart and tell them all what they want to know anyway. They'll all be so disappointed.*

"Oh, I should explain what that was about, shouldn't I?" She favored the glowering Borges with a winning smile and was rewarded with a poorly disguised snort of disgust. Around the table, others leaned forward in their eagerness, or sat back, feigning disinterest with a profound lack of acting ability. Only Polonia seemed able to maintain a truly stoic demeanor; it was entirely possible that he didn't care.

On the other hand, it was also entirely possible that he already knew what Vykos was about to reveal.

"It seems I have some news, information of importance. Jan Pieterzoon is in Baltimore."

The reactions to her announcement gave Vykos an excellent chance to gauge the level of the room, as it were. Borges and a few others showed varying degrees of alarm, interest and concern, though Borges's hood of shifting shadows made it as hard as ever to read the man. Almost none of the Tzimisce present showed so much as a flicker of recognition. And the vast majority of those present who were younger than a century looked variously confused, bored or just plain irritated.

"What the fuck is a Yawn Peckerzoom?" The voice came from the far end of the conference table, a section that Vykos had once heard Polonia refer to as "the children's table," and it belonged to a heavyset, perpetually disgruntled-looking vampire named MacEllen.

By the time Vykos glanced over that way, the man had half-risen out of his chair and planted his knuckles on the table, giving him a particularly simian appearance which his full black beard and sunken eyes did nothing to dispel. He was the leader of some roving pack or other that had done yeoman work cleaning up Camarilla resistance in captured cities, and who felt that having done so entitled him to an opinion on overall strategy. While the man was loud, obnoxious and deliberately crude, he was also looked on as a leader by several other itinerant "commanders" up and down the mid-Atlantic region. He was also a rival to Bolon, commander of the Tzimisce war ghouls now off mopping up the last pockets of resistance in the Sabbat's new Southern cities, for the succession to the late Averros as head of the Nomad Coalition. As such he was worth keeping alive as a way of controlling his putative followers—and as leverage on his competition.

Otherwise, it would have been a race to see who at the table could first gut him like a fish.

The man had stones, though. Even when Vykos turned an expectant stare on him, he barely flinched. "I'm serious. We've been sitting in here with our thumbs up our asses all night, Seamus gets his head turned into a fucking desk accessory when he interrupts someone else, and then what happens? Miss Manners gets a phone call, stops the whole thing dead, and announces that some Kraut ratfucker that no one's ever heard of is in Baltimore. Big fucking deal. We'll all drop by his place for crab cakes and then go see the aquarium. Fucking wonderful." MacEllen jutted his jaw aggressively forward and glared. His face was flushed and a faint sheen of bloody sweat shone on his brow.

Once again, Vykos had to resist the urge to laugh. Oh, MacEllen posed no threat to her or to anyone at the meeting who actually mattered, but if she failed to treat him with the utmost seriousness, the man was liable to do something foolish and the council would turn into a riot. That would mean lost nights while the casualties were straightened out, replacements were found and so on. It would be dreadfully inconvenient, and probably not worth the pleasure of liquefying the idiot's neck.

Fortunately, Polonia chose that moment to intercede. "*Mister* MacEllen," he said, quietly, though the effect on the room was like that of a whipcrack. MacEllen's supporters, who had been slapping him on the back and working themselves up to various antisocial behaviors, fell silent. A few surreptitiously moved their chairs away from where he sat.

MacEllen himself made a small noise in the back of his throat as the blood visibly drained from the big man's face. He'd wanted to score points off the bigwigs, not force a confrontation. Now he'd gotten more than he had bargained for, and the severed head that had belonged to the lamented Seamus and now served as a centerpiece was a mute reminder of what was likely to happen.

Vykos, pleased that she didn't have to dirty her hands dealing with the junior Lasombra, sat back and watched.

Polonia was on his feet now, slowly circling around the long table counterclockwise toward where MacEllen stood. "Let me see if I have your position correctly. You feel that, by taking a phone call that informed us that a potent and extremely competent enemy has entered our sphere of influence, the esteemed Archbishop Vykos has interrupted this meeting, to which your contribution thus far has been repeated shouts of 'Kill the fuckers.' Am I correct so far?"

MacEllen looked up; by the time Polonia had finished his recitation, he was standing right next to him. The older Lasombra was actually shorter than his adversary, but Vykos could tell that the contest of wills was profoundly uneven. MacEllen didn't stand a chance. Polonia had five hundred years' experience of commanding men and vampires, while his opponent could bully some rabble. This evening, the archbishop had eschewed the formal garb of his office for a simple black suit and white-banded collar shirt, but he wore them with a military crispness. MacEllen, by contrast, wore a sloppy black leather jacket with a zipper that had apparently been chewed off, relatively clean jeans, and a Skynyrd T-shirt that had clearly seen a decade's worth of better nights.

Also, Polonia had the advantage of knowing exactly what he was doing, while MacEllen was just trying to make some noise. Vykos pondered for a second, and supposed that the description of the situation as "cat and mouse" would only be adequate if the cat in question were a jaguar and the mouse were very small indeed. A sudden noise brought her back to the tableau; apparently MacEllen was speaking.

"…Not saying she's not important, but goddamn it, a cell phone in the middle of a war council? Those things can get tapped easier than a keg. And—"

Polonia cut him off. "I am quite certain that Archbishop Vykos has taken adequate precautions to ensure the security of both her communications and this council, MacEllen. Though I appreciate your concern for the well-being of everyone here," there was a ripple of derisive laughter at that, "you may wish that you had chosen a different manner of expressing your concern." He smiled, a friendly, open smile that a teacher might give a student who wasn't irretrievably stupid.

MacEllen warmed to it. "Well, yeah, I can see that, but you know, I was just trying, I mean—"

"Because," Polonia continued, dropping his left hand to rest on MacEllen's clenched right fist, "if you were to make such an interruption again, or were once again to suggest that the hand-picked representative of our beloved cardinal were that stupid, I would be forced to demonstrate my displeasure." Without changing expression in the slightest, Polonia began squeezing. MacEllen's eyes bugged out of his skull at the sudden pressure, and he began to struggle to break the archbishop's grip.

Polonia's voice remained steady, his tone measured. "Now I am quite certain that, were I to break every bone in your hand as an object lesson in courtesy to your elders and betters, you would eventually be able to heal the damage, provided I did not actually pulverize any of the bones. I have done so in the past, much to my dismay, you see. It's a matter of control, and when I get…irritated, my control sometimes wavers." His face took on a mock-doleful cast at that, prompting titters from around the room.

MacEllen's face turned red again, then purple, then blue. A vein bulged in his forehead as he tried to channel his blood into the strength he needed to break Polonia's grip. It did no good, as neither the archbishop's hand nor his tone budged.

"Indeed, once your hand healed, I think you'd be an even more valuable part of this war council, MacEllen." Audible popping sounds could be heard from beneath Polonia's hand, and MacEllen whimpered. "At the moment, however, you are a rude, loud, uncouth child who no more deserves a seat at this table than he does a pony ride." The pops became snaps, and MacEllen's whimpers descended into a low whine. Bloody foam flecked his lips. "Know this for a fact, MacEllen. The reason it is your hand and not your head that I am crushing is that your stupidity has not yet outweighed your usefulness. The instant that changes, I will gladly turn your skull into a drinking cup and let Vykos draw out your eyes for baubles; I'm told she accessorizes quite well. Should any of your followers seek to interpose themselves," and his gaze took in the room, "I will *personally* deal with them, and send whatever remains to Madrid in a small box with white ribbons on it as a present for His Eminence the Cardinal. Do I make myself clear?"

None of MacEllen's followers would meet Polonia's eyes. The archbishop nodded, and the faintest hint of a frown crossed his face. A crack like a gunshot split the room, and MacEllen collapsed, gibbering. What could be seen of his hand was a bloody, misshapen mess, and splinters of bone angled off in all directions. Polonia smiled, and squatted down to pat MacEllen's head. "So, are we all through interrupting? Wonderful." The archbishop straightened up and caught Vykos's eye. "Now, our honored friend, I believe you were about to explain to all of us why precisely Herr Pieterzoon concerns us, yes?" He gracefully took MacEllen's abandoned seat and propped his feet up on the fallen pack leader. "Please, the floor is yours."

The tension went out of the room like water. Suddenly there was background chatter again, and the sound of bodies readjusting themselves and the chairs they sat in. Vykos would have applauded, if she'd been the sort to applaud. She rose and spoke directly to Polonia. "Jan Pieterzoon is a Ventrue of considerable age and a most impressive lineage. He is, if my sources tell me true, one of Hardestadt's brood, and among the oldest and most dangerous of that line. He is not, as Ductus MacEllen suggested, German, but Dutch. Nor does he, I suspect, fuck rats. Pieterzoon is devious, efficient and more than skilled enough to turn much of the population of this room into a series of delicate piles of ash. His presence can only mean that the Inner Circle is about to take a direct hand in affairs here, which is a development we have been anticipating with concern for some time. Needless to say, his reports back to his sire and that worthy's peers will have a great deal to do with what sort of response we can expect. Therefore, it behooves us to eliminate him as quickly as possible, before he makes too damning a report, or takes the opportunity to interpose himself in our plans more directly."

Across the table, Borges frowned. "He's in Baltimore, which means he's caged like a rat. North is Philadelphia, south is where we stand, and west takes him nowhere. I say let him sit in Baltimore and make all the reports he wants. The jaws of the trap are about to close, and I for one would like to take this Dutchman home with me. Don Medina Sidonia would no doubt be profoundly appreciative of the gift. He's been waiting for Pieterzoon's head on a plate for a very long time." Around the room, rumbles of assent wafted up.

Vykos spread her hands in a conciliatory gesture. "If there were any other way, I'd be happy to allow you to capture him, but we simply do not have that luxury. If we allow Pieterzoon to gain his footing, to become comfortable, then he will become a most formidable foe, and he may be harder to subdue than you would think. Consider how the remaining Camarilla vampires will rally around him. Consider the personal resources he can bring to bear. Consider this, and you will realize that we need to destroy him while he's still uncertain, still off balance, still—"

"Jet-lagged!" called one of MacEllen's adherents. Polonia silenced the man with a look, but the rhythm of Vykos's speech had been broken. The room dissolved into shouted chaos. A fistfight broke out between a member of one of the roving packs and a member of Borges's entourage; the Archbishop of Miami turned to deal with it in his own savage way. Any hope there had been of keeping order vanished.

Vykos caught Polonia's eye and raised an eyebrow questioningly. The Lasombra gave the tiniest of head shakes, and, resigned, stood. "I think a short recess is in order. Those of you who feel the need to kill one another at this juncture, the basement has a concrete floor so the staff will be able to sponge up your remains easily. As for the rest of you, we shall reconvene in two hours."

Vampires and the occasional ghoul loped for the double doors that led out into the hallway, their exit punctuated by a loud snapping sound as Borges took care of his business. Within seconds, the room was empty except for two of the three archbishops and the still-moaning MacEllen. Polonia sighed. "Was that last mutilation really necessary?"

Borges shrugged and made a great show of dusting his hands. "Not particularly, but it was enjoyable.

"Your playmate MacEllen was right, in any case."

"Hmm?" Idly, Polonia kicked the pack leader's still-recumbent form, just to make certain he hadn't gone anywhere.

"Taking the call during the meeting was a bit ostentatious. The Nomads aren't much individually, but they're vaguely formidable when they're all pointing in the same direction, and consistently antagonizing them when there's no real need means that they may all end up pointing at the cardinal's pet. Mind you, I suspect that she could take care of the lot of them without excessive effort, but it's really much more useful to have them taking orders, is it not?"

Polonia made a show of thinking about it, stood and stretched. "Perhaps. On the other hand, they need some discipline if they're ever going to be a real fighting force as opposed to a rabble. Overwhelming some isolationist Toreador who's retired to Asheville to take up basketweaving is one thing. Dealing with a city with real defenses, one that's had some time for preparation—MacEllen and his friends will founder and be shattered, and I can't afford to throw them all away that idly."

"*You* can't," Borges repeated, half to himself. "Of course. I'll bow to your superior knowledge of Camarilla defenses, as you've spent so many years analyzing them in New York, yes? I'm sure you have a *very* good grasp of them by now."

If Borges was hoping for a rise out of Polonia, he was disappointed. The other Lasombra steepled his fingers and nodded. "Indeed. I know them quite well, which is why I respect what they're capable of, regardless of what we've accomplished so far. If you'd ever bothered to face them in the field, instead of pissing away Miami one block at a time to the Setite snakes, you'd have a bit of respect for them as well."

Borges purpled at that, and for a moment Polonia thought the younger archbishop would leap across the table and attack him. Then the moment of fury passed, and Borges managed a wan smile. "*Touché*, Archbishop. I look forward to partaking of your wisdom." He executed a perfect bow, pivoted, and strode out the room. The only evidence of the confrontation was the crushed and mangled back of the chair behind which Borges had been standing.

Sometime during the debate, MacEllen had stopped making noise. The only sound in the chamber was the hum of the air conditioning, which Polonia found suddenly annoying. He pursed his lips. Borges was a fool and a braggart, but he was right. Vykos's maneuver had been designed to antagonize the Nomads and other, less-organized types, and for once in his unlife Polonia had no idea why.

"My Cardinal," he whispered, almost as a prayer, "I sincerely hope you know exactly what you are doing in sending me this fiend. Grant me guidance, grant me strength and, if this madness continues, grant me the opportunity to explain myself after I tear the head off each and every idiot I am being forced to work with here."

Piety sated, Polonia walked through the double doors of the chamber. Behind him, a tendril of shadow reached back to shut them with a neat little click. And beneath the table, still clutching his ruin of a hand, MacEllen didn't notice at all.

Saturday, 17 July 1999, 12:09 AM
Iglesia de San Nicolás de los Servitas
Madrid, Spain

Don Ibrahim never felt quite comfortable entering Monçada's inner sanctum. Part of that was the positive explosion of saints' portraits that lined the walls of nearly every corridor; the iconography was deeply disturbing to Ibrahim's conservative soul. There was also the fact that every bit of wall space that was not covered in graven images was instead decorated with mirrors, which Ibrahim found unpleasant to walk past. Monçada had explained the latter, noting that they allowed him a perfect perspective on most visitors, while not allowing those visitors to see him; but even so the sheer number of the things was oppressive.

In addition, there was the fact that the two Cainites had tried to kill each other on any number of occasions stretching back to the early twelfth century, when Monçada was still a priest whose words moved thousands of worshippers, and Ibrahim was a blade in the hand of the princes of the *taifas*. Of course, both had sworn any number of times since then that the past was past, what was done was done, and so on. The truth of the matter was, however, that politics within the Sabbat made them allies, and if either still harbored a thirst for vengeance, that one simply didn't have enough other allies to afford to indulge it.

The centuries, Ibrahim noted with a rueful smile, *make for strange bedfellows*. Then he strode into the cardinal's *sanctum sanctorum*.

Monçada was on his feet, ever the gracious host. "Don Ibrahim, how good of you to come." Ibrahim noted that the stone floor had been covered in rugs of rich weave, and that the cardinal himself was barefoot; both were expressions of respect. "I'd offer coffee, but we both know better."

Ibrahim executed a perfect bow. "It is a pleasure to see you again, Cardinal."

"And you, my friend. I must admit, I have been awaiting your return for some time."

Ibrahim strode purposefully over to the table holding the chess set, and seated himself on the stool behind the black pieces. "Oh? Don't tell me you have been that starved for conversation."

The cardinal laughed, politely, and maneuvered himself into the opposite chair. "Not at all. I just have a new stratagem that I thought might be effective against your defenses. I was anxious to try it out."

"Indeed?" purred the Moor, his glance flicking over the board. "Are you so confident of victory that you can afford to experiment?"

Monçada gave an almost bashful shrug. "Truth be told, my most recent guest expressed some doubts about the tenability of your position."

Ibrahim pursed his lips, his curling beard almost brushing the tips of his king and queen. "Oh, no doubt. But are you certain that your guest was not merely saying so to appease you?"

"I doubt it," replied Monçada quietly. "It was Talley."

"Talley!"

The cardinal nodded. "Talley. He was supposed to mention something to you on his way out, in fact. Hmm. Your move, I believe?"

"Talley…" The Moor pondered his position and, after due deliberation, advanced a pawn a single space. "Why, if I may ask, did the Hound grace you with his presence?"

"Because I asked him to, of course. Talley knows better than to visit me uninvited. I think his first visit scared him entirely too much for him ever to be comfortable around me." The heavyset man sucked on a fingertip contemplatively, then advanced a bishop. "I had work for him."

"Of course you did." Another pawn moved forward, blocking the bishop's clean line on the pawn protecting a rook. "What service could the estimable Englishman Talley provide you that one of your other, less notorious servants could not?"

"Are you sure you want to make that move? I'll let you retract it, if you want." Ibrahim just stared, and after a moment the cardinal moved a rook onto a more-or-less clear file. "Ahem. I want Talley in the Americas. Something there displeases me."

"Oh?" Ibrahim picked up a white rook, looked at it. "Would it be obtuse of me not to have noticed before how cleverly this piece mimics your dear templar?"

"Oh, not at all, not at all. Most of my partners never notice at all, nor do they notice the other faces."

Ibrahim grunted an acknowledgment, and continued looking at the set with new eyes. "That bastard Medina Sidonia, Chardin, Muntz…is that Skanderbeg? Hmm. And why is Lucita now my queen? When we began play, her face was on your half of the board. Why the change?"

The cardinal made a small, almost embarrassed sound. "When Vykos made the set, I had him make two queens. A...moment of weakness on my part, I must admit. The side she plays on depends on my mood, and the latest report I have of her exploits. Sometimes," and he heaved his bulk into laughter, "she stands on both sides."

Don Ibrahim picked up his queen and examined it closely. The Lucita between his fingers was tall and slender, with high cheekbones and an arrogant cast to her features. Her gown was long and flowing, something that Ibrahim privately doubted she'd ever worn in life, and her hands were folded demurely at her waist. "The likeness is remarkable," he said. "Why has she now joined the ranks of your enemies?"

"The same reason I needed Talley, in truth."

"Don't tell me you're siccing the Hound on your childe. Surely she can't have done anything so terrible." Ibrahim replaced the queen two ranks forward. "And your bishop is threatened."

"Why, so it is," the cardinal replied, moving it back one space and over. "And Lucita has apparently gotten herself involved in something that could stagger the progress of the campaign that Vykos and Vallejo are engaged in. I've received word that someone feels that assassination is an appropriate way to deal with a disliked archbishop, and I strongly disapprove of such things. Lucita is, at this time, a tool of those working against my interests. I dispatched Talley to defend her potential targets. Oh, I don't expect him to succeed, necessarily—neither he nor Lucita holds a clear advantage in the matter—but the fact that he's present should provide sufficient reason for whoever's behind Lucita's hiring to perhaps think twice. I, too, can dispatch assassins when I must." There was silence for a moment, then the cardinal added, "And I will have your queen in three moves, my friend."

Ibrahim stared at the board. "I don't think so," he said softly. "You'll take her in three moves with the rook, but you don't want Talley to have her."

Monçada sat up, perplexed. "Perhaps not."

Ibrahim moved his queen back to safety, behind a screen of pawns. "Do you have any idea who might be behind this complication?"

"None at all. I suspect, of course, everyone." A knight made a cautious advance. "There are a great many players with an interest in that game, Don Ibrahim, and some may well be concealing their true allegiances. The best I can do is move to protect my interests, and those of the Sabbat. Beyond that, it is as God wills."

"*Bismallah*. Still, Allah helps those who help themselves. You've invested much in this matter. Are you leaving yourself too thin on the ground?"

"With God's grace, all will be well."

"You know more than you're telling, of course."

"Of course. Come. I've had a repast prepared for us. You will share a meal with me, as we are now friends?"

"Of course. Shall we return to the game after we finish?"

"Certainly. The game will always be there."

Ibrahim rose. "Alas, my friend, I fear you are exactly right."

Sunday, 18 July 1999, 12:29 AM
Hyatt Regency Capitol Hill
Washington, D.C.

The room was small, with wood paneling and thick carpet on the floor. The furniture was of mahogany, and surprisingly good quality for a hotel. Whenever possible, Vykos preferred staying in places like this when Fate forced her to visit North America, at least when there were not more solid accommodations to retreat to. On a vague level, she was still uncomfortable with the sheer newness of the entire place, but surrounding herself with competent craftsmanship at least let her avoid thinking about the transience of most of the continent's construction.

The meeting had, of course, been a fiasco. She hadn't expected any differently. After the first few easy victories, the Nomad Coalition (she could barely contemplate the name without laughing) had gotten almost completely unmanageable. Unfortunately, they still had to be invited to each and every council session. If nothing else, it kept them off the streets for several hours a night, and she agreed with Vallejo's assessment that, if they ran around unsupervised in a single city for a week straight, they'd probably do more damage to the operation through sheer stupidity than the Camarilla would be able to do through stubborn resistance. The curfew that had been established in the city was proof enough that a lack of discretion had its consequences; there was no need to pour more kerosene on that fire.

That being said, she still found dealing with the Nomads and others of their ilk wearisome.

There was a gentle knock at the door. That was odd. She'd given the ghoul standing guard in the outer chamber of the suite strict instructions that she not be disturbed. On the other hand, assassins—her dear Parmenides excepted, but he was in any case off assisting with the siege of the Tremere chantry—rarely were polite enough to knock. "Yes?"

Polonia spoke from outside. "A thousand pardons for the intrusion, but I was wondering if we might conspire for a moment before the meeting reconvenes?" The man was ever courteous, and about as harmless as a knife to the kidney. Of course, it was better to get an idea of his thoughts before the meeting began than otherwise.

"Of course. I'd been hoping you'd come by. Do come in."

"You are too gracious," the archbishop replied, and the door swung open of its own volition. Polonia strode in, noted Vykos's position in the large chair behind the desk, and made the decision to remain standing. Behind him, more tendrils of shadow pulled the door shut, and at his feet a pool of inky darkness that bore a suspicious resemblance to a cat paced silently.

"I was under the impression the hotel had a 'No Pets' policy, Archbishop."

"It's just a little toy of shadow I take with me on occasion. I find it soothing. Also, it's remarkably effective at catching mice."

"Mice?"

"I misspoke: vermin. Mice, rats—all sorts. Besides, if we were enforcing the 'No Pets' policy, where would that leave your ghouls?"

Vykos let a ghost of a smile cross her lips. "Indeed. But I can't help taking in strays."

Polonia chuckled. "For purposes you don't immediately share, no doubt. But let it pass, let it pass. How goes it with the siege? Have the Tremere seen fit yet to run up the white flag?"

"No change. It's just a matter of time." Vykos made a throwaway gesture and stretched languidly. The effect was entirely lost on Polonia, who'd bent down to scritch his shadowy cat between the ears.

"I suppose that makes some sort of sense. Please do keep me informed when there is progress."

"Of course."

Polonia straightened back up. "I appreciate your courtesy. As for the other matters at hand, I am curious as to why you went to such lengths to irritate MacEllen. I'm really not in the mood to play at tutor with a naughty child, Vykos, and I would hate to think you were putting me in that situation deliberately."

"Tsk tsk, my dear Archbishop. You wound me. The call was important, you know."

"I'm quite aware of its importance, and of who Pieterzoon is, and how much any number of my acquaintances in the councils of my clan—"

"*Les Amies Noir* ?" Vykos threw the name out carelessly, knowing that no one not given the blood of the Lasombra should know of *Les Amies'* existence.

If she was hoping for a rise out of Polonia, the ploy failed. The man ignored her interjection completely. "Any number would dearly love to take the man apart sinew by sinew. I'm also aware you received a letter from an unknown source before the war council began, and had the knowledge of Pieterzoon's arrival in Baltimore all along." His voice was gentle, almost scolding. "Are you deliberately trying to make this difficult for me?"

"Not at all. MacEllen just needed a bit more prodding to get to a point where you'd feel compelled to reaffirm his place in the—how shall I put this?—pecking order."

"I'd really rather prefer not to have to kill the lot of them, Vykos. I know the Little Tailor is working quite hard to recoup our losses from Atlanta, but you and I both know that whatever he comes up with won't be nearly as effective as what we lost. If we lose all of our seasoned irregulars as well, that's going to push the timetable on the entire project back, and somehow I don't see that prospect pleasing the esteemed cardinal."

"Perhaps. Though you and I both know you won't have to kill MacEllen. The reason he's alive and Averros is not is that MacEllen will back down when he's outclassed. And you, Don de Polonia, outshine MacEllen as clearly as the sun outshines, mmm, the lesser of Mars's two moons."

Polonia laughed in spite of himself. "I'm disappointed in you, my dear. I'd heard you were a better flatterer than that." He coughed, once. "Actually, I think I've simply made him angry enough to loathe me in silence rather than disrupt the council any longer. He'll be looking for an opportunity to take his anger out on one of his own followers, just to salve his ego. Still, either way, it's an annoyance or two less at the meeting."

Vykos nodded. "Indeed. An annoyance or two less. I'm so glad I could be of assistance in the matter."

Polonia smiled, humorlessly. "Your assistance is,

as always, appreciated. If you will excuse me?" Vykos made no protest, and Polonia walked to the door. The cat followed a few leisurely steps behind. The archbishop placed his hand on the doorknob, then paused and turned. "Oh, I almost forgot. I thought I should warn you. The Camarilla's not the only one getting a bit more company from the Old Country."

"Oh?" The word contained rather more surprise than Vykos would have liked to have let slip.

Polonia nodded. "Yes. Apparently someone's gotten concerned about the safety of our finest generals, or some such. There have been rumors of assassination attempts and similar foolishness. As a result, we'll be receiving a bodyguard. The man has rather impressive credentials, and a most fascinating lineage."

"Really." Vykos's self-assurance was back in place, seamlessly. "And when does this paragon arrive?"

The archbishop made a great show of consulting his watch. "In about half an hour, if traffic is good. Which will give me plenty of time to introduce you to him before the war council resumes." And with that, he turned and walked out. The cat, arrogant as its master, followed.

Sunday, 18 July 1999, 1:07 AM
Hyatt Regency Capitol Hill
Washington, D.C.

The tone of the war council changed completely when Polonia reconvened it. For one thing, MacEllen had fewer supporters, but those who did stick by him were united in a sullen hatred they directed down the length of the table to where the author of his humiliation sat. Borges seemed agitated, but didn't speak, instead drumming his fingers incessantly against the dark wood. Past him, Vallejo, who'd been absent earlier, sat ramrod straight and radiating obvious disdain for the rabble to his right. Vykos was, as ever, unreadable and cool, though Polonia thought he detected some pleasure at Borges's discomfort. And to his own immediate right was the thin, supremely bored-looking Talley. The man had clearly endured an uncomfortable journey, and was looking forward to the remainder of the meeting with all of the joy of a nun faced with a Tarantino film. *Ay me*, thought Polonia. *The sooner I begin, the sooner it ends and I can bid good night to this walking ghost.*

"My friends," he said, flowing to his feet. "I have a profound honor; namely that of introducing a most illustrious addition to our efforts here. Cardinal Monçada"—and Vykos's iron control wavered visibly for a moment—"has seen fit to grace us with the presence of another guest, the most esteemed Señor Talley, who holds the exalted rank of templar among the cardinal's servants. He is here to ensure the success of our work by protecting those of us who are most at risk of cowardly assassination."

Vykos frowned at that. Polonia noted it, but decided to plunge onward. "We've already had one such attempt, on our beloved Vykos. None of us want to risk a loss of that magnitude again, nor do we wish to see anyone else become a secondary target. Would you not agree, Archbishop Borges?"

The Archbishop of Miami nodded sharply, with the look of a man being told that his son is not his own. "Of course. We should take every step to protect Vykos from another such attack."

Polonia smiled blandly. The trap was about to close.

"Oh, I have communicated back to the cardinal that Vykos needs no further protection," said Vallejo. "Talley is here to protect all of us, my dear Archbishop."

Borges, Polonia noted with some satisfaction, now had the expression of a man who'd discovered that none of his children were his own, and that his wife had trouble remembering his name. Not only had he been told that he was going to be watched very closely by an extremely powerful vampire who looked like death warmed over and who brooked no nonsense whatsoever, he'd been maneuvered into a position whereby his refusal to accept that surveillance would be seen as disloyal.

And if he refused, and an accident occurred that deprived the operation of his services, well, *que sera, sera*, or however the damnable song went.

Borges stammered something or other that was perfectly incomprehensible, while at the end of the table, MacEllen's supporters whooped their amusement at seeing one of the high and mighty taking it on the chin for a change.

"Enough." Talley had a low voice, a whispery one that undercut all other voices it came in contact with. "Archbishop Borges, I have been assigned by my cardinal, as a token of his esteem for all of the assembled commanders, to serve as protection for certain among you. It has come to the cardinal's attention that there may be an attempt on at least one of the archbishops assembled here, as a method of derailing our operations while the Camarilla buys time to consolidate its defenses. I am here to make sure those attempts fail.

"Just because you draw my attentions does not mean that you in particular have been specifically targeted for anything other than my presence for an evening. If my conversation displeases, rest assured, I'll soon move along to someone else. Otherwise, don't read anything more into it than you absolutely must, and remember that I did not achieve my current title by being less than effective at my chosen tasks." He surveyed the room for a moment. "Now. Everything I have heard tells me that this operation has been proceeding exceptionally smoothly, and I trust the planning meetings have been just as smooth. My Lord Polonia, I look forward to observing. You must forgive me, however, if I abandon this seat of honor and instead take up my duties. The cardinal was most insistent that I begin immediately." And he stood and walked over behind where Borges sat, flushed and angry. "Please, Your Excellency. Pretend I'm not even here."

The meeting, Polonia thought, was proceeding in a most satisfactory fashion. Talley's presence was sufficient to unnerve Borges, which kept him from making too much noise. Vykos still didn't seem over-joyed at the templar's presence, but Polonia chalked that up to the notion that she was displeased that the news had come to him first. And Talley himself? The man might as well have been a piece of furniture, or a sculpture.

Business had proceeded with remarkable alacrity, and now only two items remained on the agenda: the presence of the accursed Pieterzoon, which he'd decided to hold off on until now, at the end of the council; and another matter that would require a certain amount of delicacy. The former was going to be profoundly unpleasant, so he decided to open with it and get it out of the way. Ghouls brought in refreshments and removed debris. Polonia's dislike of the creatures was far less pronounced than most of his clanmates'; he just cordially loathed them and everything they stood for. The head of the unfortunate Seamus had left some time ago, leaving only a bloody smear on the table, but Polonia preferred a relatively clean work area for council. After all, fewer body parts strewn about meant fewer distractions for the hungry.

"We're nearly done with the night's planning, I am most pleased to say. I know many of you are feeling restless, and I'll be as happy as you are when we finish. Now, I believe the matter of Herr Pieterzoon is next. Vykos?"

Vykos stood, graceful as always. Certain of the Tzimisce at the table chanted her name, but it was a half-hearted effort; in truth, everyone was too damn tired. In one of Vallejo's rare lighter moments, the man had claimed that he found the war councils three times the effort of actual fighting, and that he was sure he'd be bored to death long before the Camarilla found a way to put him down.

"As I was saying earlier, I would suggest to the council that we deal with Herr Pieterzoon immediately. As we can all see," she let a graceful finger pick out Talley from the crowd, "the stakes have just gotten higher. We simply cannot afford to wait any longer to deal with him, lest he rally the Camarilla forces effectively against us."

Borges grumbled discontentedly. "You said that already, Vykos. I don't think things have changed that much," he glanced up at the impassive Talley, "in the last few hours. So explain why and how we need to get this bastard. Do a good job, and I'm with you."

"Why, Archbishop, thank you for your words of support." Vykos's voice dropped to a dangerous purr. "Now, consider why Talley has been sent here. He is here because Europe has entered the fray, and because assassination has become a permissible weapon. Clearly, one of our great advantages thus far, besides the sheer will and ferocity you, the soldiers of the Sabbat, have brought to bear, is the small contribution made by myself, Commander Vallejo, the Little Tailor and others. We are here. We are settled. We are part and parcel of all that will be done. By permitting Pieterzoon to survive, we allow him to whittle away our advantage. And if he establishes himself here, how much longer before he brings in allies? Before the tide of our advance slows? No, we must maintain our advantage—any general in any age would tell you that. Narses, were he here, would laugh at our indecision."

She spun, then, and locked eyes with Talley. "As for the other reason…they think they can resort to the dagger because the sword has failed them. If we turn the dagger back on them, they will abandon it. If the architect of their assassination campaign—and make no mistake, this has Pieterzoon's stink on it—then their own efforts will crumble. And I am sure that is a sentiment everyone in this room who just might be targeted by the Ventrue's assassins can share.

"So, shall we do this thing? Shall we eliminate Pieterzoon before he becomes more of a menace—for he is one already, and becomes a greater one with each passing hour—or shall we allow our enemy to gain strength while we sit idly by and wait for the knife in the dark? What shall it be?"

The roar of approval that burst forth came from dozens of throats. Vykos bathed in it, drank in the adulation, gloried in it. Even Borges appeared convinced. Only Polonia, Vallejo and Talley seemed unmoved. Polonia shook his head. The die was cast.

It took ten minutes for the roaring to die down, as Vykos seemed to be in no hurry to let things settle. Finally, Polonia interrupted. "Well, the motion seems to have carried, Vykos. Now, how shall we go about implementing the will of the," he waved his hand to take in the room, "people?"

Vykos smiled poisonously. "For shame, my dear Archbishop. That's your responsibility. You're in command; I merely host this arrangement by virtue of being archbishop of the city. I wouldn't dare to usurp your authority. I leave the entire affair in your capable hands."

Polonia glowered at Vykos for a long moment, until the uncomfortable silence was broke by a heretofore silent member of the war council:

"I'll take it. Me and my boys—we'll take it."

Sunday, 18 July 1999, 2:01 AM
A subterranean grotto
New York City, New York

Something looked different. Calebros stared intently at the printout from SchreckNET that Umberto had handed him a few minutes before. The words on the paper—the actual physical manifestation of thought—were sharp and crisp. Calebros didn't like it. He remembered Umberto saying something about replacing a daisy wheel with a laser jet—or some such nonsense; none of it mattered much to Calebros. He preferred the solid weight of his typewriter. Umberto could keep his space-aged doo-dads. Maybe the world, Calebros pondered, would be a better place if people still used dip pens and ink wells. He shrugged. Maybe not.

The form of the message, of course, was less significant than the content. The report from Courier included a few choice morsels of knowledge. If only he had access to the Sabbat war council chamber itself! Calebros sighed. It was not to be. Besides, extrapolation could reveal much that was hidden. Time would reveal the rest.

Calebros spent several minutes integrating this new knowledge with that which he already knew, then reached for his trusty Smith Corona.

18 July 1999 **FILE COPY**
Re: Baltimore/Washington

D.C., Courier reports—
Talley arrived in U.S., meeting with
Sabbat war council.

Balt., Colchester reports—
J. Pieterzoon considering use of
"specialist"; Talley's presence may
influence that decision and the
eventual choice.

I know a likely candidate
to suggest.

file action update: Talley

Sunday, 18 July 1999, 2:11 AM
Sheraton Inner Harbor Hotel
Baltimore, Maryland

Lucita sat, cross-legged, in her hotel room and spread the paperwork her client had provided out in front of her. The dossier on her target was depressingly complete, covering everything from observed manifestation of supernatural abilities, favored weapons, companions, wardrobe preferences and affiliated ghouls on down to taste in music, common turns of phrase and feeding preferences. Also included in the file was a series of photos, ranging from irritatingly blurry surveillance camera shots to up-close-and-personal images that by all rights should have gotten the photographer killed.

She shook her head, long black hair swinging back and forth as she did so. Clad only in simple black pajamas, she looked pensively at the clock on the nightstand. Quite a few hours remained until dawn, so there was plenty of time to get familiar with the details of the target. She'd memorize all the material tonight and destroy the supporting evidence.

The room had already been lightproofed, of course—the curtains taped down, the door secured against both intrusion and the cleaning staff and so on. She'd also covered up the lengthy mirror on the wall opposite the bed by hanging a spare bedsheet over it; the older she got, the less she wanted to see empty mirrors where her face should be. Lucita briefly considered sleeping in the tub, a tactic commonly used by younger vampires on the road, but dismissed the notion. After all, if trouble came for her, it wasn't going to be stopped by the flimsy bathroom door. For that matter, the sheetrock of the walls wasn't going to do much good against the sort of opposition she usually encountered. There came a time where you just had to stop worrying, and get on with your nightly business. That was a lesson dear old papa had never learned, squirreling himself deeper and deeper into his poisonous tomb in Madrid.

He'd tried to make it her tomb, too. He'd called her home and informed her of her duty as a loyal childe. Told her how he expected her to remain by his side through the centuries. Explained how she would help him, for the glory of God and the clan.

And then he had told her how very, *very* much he loved her, his only childe.

She'd lashed out at him then, with shadow and with steel. He'd laughingly subdued her, easily snapping the dagger she'd thought would prove the key to her freedom. Then he'd taken her hand and mockingly patted it as if to let her know what a clever girl she was.

She'd nearly torn her arm out of its socket to escape. He hadn't pursued her, hadn't sent any of his servants or beasts of shadow to retrieve her. All that followed Lucita into the night was his laughter, and a cheery farewell.

He was looking forward to seeing her again, he'd said.

She'd sworn she'd never go back, but every century or so something pulled her back to Madrid, to the dour stone building that the faithful and the damned alike flocked to. At one point she'd worried that it was a trap, that on one of her visits "home" the sect she'd spurned would be waiting for her. But it seemed that Monçada still loved his childe, and protected her from the wrath of his flock.

The last time she'd returned had been seventy years ago. To her surprise, her sire had not been alone. With him had been an old acquaintance and occasional enemy, the Tzimisce Sascha Vykos. Vykos had even been wearing his original skin, the one she remembered from their first, rather unpleasant meeting. She'd started to call the shadows to her then, but Monçada had intervened. Vykos was there at his invitation, the archbishop said, performing a special commission for him. Monçada, you see, wanted a chess set, a very special chess set.

And he needed Lucita to pose as the black queen.

"I'll leave the room, of course, my dear childe. Modesty forbids me from remaining." He'd turned and swept off, leaving her alone with the Tzimisce.

"If you please, Lucita," was all Vykos had said, and then there was nothing but silence and the rustle of fabric for the remainder of the night.

Lucita had risked the dawn to leave when the work was finished, rather than risk spending the day under her sire's roof. In her time she had killed hundreds, if not thousands. She had waded in blood and reveled in death, she had torn her enemies asunder with shadow and given their childer to the flame. But something in the house of her sire—and the sense of cold eyes on her as she posed—made her feel unclean.

Lucita shook herself out of reverie. "Focus, Lucita, focus. You're a professional, remember?" she muttered to herself as she gathered up the files to continue her studies. She wanted to be ready to dive into work first thing the next evening.

On the nightstand next to the bed, her cell phone bleeped merrily. "Damnation!" she said, and reached for it. "Yes? What?"

She recognized the voice on the other end of the line instantly. It was the vampire who'd approached her not so very long ago about her current contract. She wasn't certain for whom the man worked, though she had a sneaking suspicion that it was one of her target's putative allies.

"What is it?" she said, putting less heat into the question than she felt.

"My patron has requested that I maintain contact with you on the matter of our business dealings. I felt a call would be less disturbing than a visit. Have I erred?"

Lucita bit back her first three responses, which were "Yes," "Never speak to me again," and "Had you knocked on my door, I would have killed you instantly." Instead, she merely said, "I don't enjoy interference in my work. The timetable for the target is in place. He will be dealt with on schedule and as we agreed. Now, are you just trying to impress me with the fact that you found my number, or do you actually have anything useful to add?"

There was a pause on the other end of the line. "A thousand pardons. I, of course, know nothing of this sort of work." There was another pause. "If you are interested, I have some information that may aid your task."

"Yes?"

"We are in the process of arranging a…situation for your benefit, so that you will have a clear shot at the target. The date and time will be communicated to you as we draw closer to fruition." The vampire's distaste for this arrangement was obvious; Lucita suspected he thought he was being forced to watch an amateur.

"I understand. Is there anything further I should know?"

"Not at this time. Pleasant dreams, mademoiselle. Good hunting."

She hung up without responding, suddenly weary of the idiotic games and pointless fencing. All of the dancing around and veiled threats and *double entendres*, and in the end it would still come down to her skill, speed and shadows tearing the unlife from yet another unlucky bastard. That was what it was all about. Strip away the formalities and the rituals and the pointed little jabs designed to let everyone know who was cleverer. All of them were just ways of protecting her kind from its own savagery.

She preferred combat to talk, these nights. It was more honest, and honesty was one of the few virtues that remained to her after all of these years.

Several hours later, the information in the file memorized and the components themselves destroyed, she lay down on the bed and closed her eyes. Beginning to nod off, she had a sensation of vague discomfort, then realized she had rolled over onto the cell phone. She picked it up and looked at it curiously for a second. Her client's toady had used it to find her. Ergo, it was now compromised. With a minimum of effort she closed her hand around the plastic, and was rewarded with a shuddering crackle. The fragments of the device cascaded onto the floor, noiseless on the thick tan carpet.

As she closed her eyes for the day's slumber, Lucita smiled.

Sunday, 18 July 1999, 2:19 AM
Hyatt Regency Capitol Hill
Washington, D.C.

Peter Blaine had a great many nicknames, but none of them were complimentary. The kindest was "Lurch," for his uncanny resemblance to the comic butler, and it was the only one he'd answer to with anything less than obscenity. He didn't help his own cause, unfortunately; having a predilection for blocky, conservative black suits and shoes that could have started their own exterminator business. The fact that his face, shoulders, haircut and general build looked like the work of a lazy sculptor with a thing for straight lines didn't help matters.

Blaine was one of the poor cousins of the Sabbat, a Ventrue *antitribu* whose very heritage inspired snickers of derisive glee from the "true" clans of the sect. Furthermore, he didn't have the instinctive grace of the Lasombra or the sheer power or delicacy of the Tzimisce, so whenever he was in the company of a member of one of those worthy lines, he felt slow. Stupid. Awkward. Clumsy. Out in the field, when it was just him and his pack (which included one of each of the Big Two, but then again he knew how to keep Sonny and Terrence in line), then he felt like he was in command; but as soon as he got close to the big boys, the bottom dropped out of his personality.

Truth be told, the *antitribu* were the lower middle class of the Sabbat. Refugees from the tyranny of the Camarilla or descendants of same, they were relatively few in number and disorganized by temperament. If all of the *antitribu* had gotten together and demanded equal treatment, sure, there were enough to make a

richard e. dansky

difference. But the Gangrel *antitribu* were too busy snarling at the Brujah *antitribu*, while the Toreador tried to ignore everyone and embarrass their Camarilla cousins, and the Ventrue worked extra hard to convince the rest of the Sabbat that they well and truly belonged. Meanwhile, the Tzimisce and Lasombra just laughed up their sleeves about the whole thing and sent the *antitribu* out to die when they felt like it.

Frankly, the whole thing gave Blaine a headache when he thought about it too much. He'd come over to the Sabbat voluntarily to get away from the stultifying class system in the Camarilla. Slowly but surely he was starting to suspect he'd gone from the frying pan to the skillet, if not the actual fire.

Perhaps that's why he'd spoken up in the cold silence when Vykos and Polonia were having their staredown. Or perhaps he just wanted to get the hell out of the war council—he'd seen any number of other small-time war leaders abused, assaulted and decapitated, and figured that he really didn't want to be next.

In any case, in the silence after Vykos's challenge, Blaine's was the voice that was heard first.

"I'll take it. Me and my boys—we'll take it."

Archbishop Borges laughed. "Thank you so much, Captain…"

"Blaine. And me and mine, we'll take it."

"Well, Captain Blaine, this is not nursery school. We don't take volunteers here for important business." He laughed harshly, and a few of his followers laughed with him.

Blaine noticed, though, that neither Polonia nor Vykos was laughing—and they were the ones, he felt, who mattered. He might not be near the top of the ladder himself, but Blaine had a good nose for the flow of power, and right now it was obvious that power and Borges had little to do with each other in this particular council. And that knowledge gave him the courage to take a chance.

"I said, Your Excellency, that I would take my men and handle it. You don't know me, you don't know my pack, and you don't know dick about Pieterzoon. I do. You don't know what he looks like; I've worked with his childer and I've met him. I know how he talks, how he walks, and what sort of stupid poncy little things he's uncomfortable being without." Out of the corner of his eye, Blaine saw Polonia nodding slow approval, the archbishop's face a mask of impassivity.

"Bah. You say you know his childer? Wonderful. They'll identify your corpse." Borges's voice took on a mocking, whiny tone. "Oh, look, Percy, it's What's-his-name Blaine. He's dead. Isn't it droll?" Borges sat back, bristling. "We send you, we might as well not send anyone."

"I find your assessment of Captain Blaine's abilities intriguing," interjected Vykos smoothly. "And I am sure you have excellent reason for making that assessment, yes, Archbishop? You have seen Captain Blaine's pack in action, yes?" Borges flushed. "What? No? Then surely you've heard something of his inefficiency? No again? My goodness, what do you base this judgment of yours on?"

Coughs thinly masked snickers from various sections of the room. Borges looked around wildly at his tormentors, then up at Talley as if expecting the man to do something.

"I do not have to stand for this!" Borges finally roared. "And I am not going to let him botch things, this upstart, this traitor, this—"

"*Antitribu?*" said Blaine quietly.

"Yes, an arrogant *antitribu* know-nothing who thinks that because he once licked some elder's boots that he knows how to rip out that elder's heart!"

Polonia, Blaine noticed, had stopped nodding. The ground he was treading on had just gotten dangerous. "Perhaps. Or perhaps I know something you don't, can do something you can't, and don't need a lifeguard from around the world to keep me safe in my own hotel room. Scared of room service, my lord?"

"Why, you little son of a bitch!" Borges tried to surge out of his chair, got about halfway to his feet and then crashed right back into his chair as Talley's hand came down on his shoulder like a piledriver.

"Please sit down, Your Excellency," said Talley pleasantly. "Cardinal Monçada has asked me to keep you safe from any and all threats, and that does include the ones you bring on yourself."

Talley turned to Blaine. "Not that you're entirely blameless; be thankful that Archbishop Borges was not in fact seriously upset." His voice acquired the sing-song tone of a drill instruction. "So. Supposing the His Excellency had come across the table, what would you have done?"

Blaine showed teeth in a humorless smile and stood. "If he'd come across the table he'd have been an idiot, because by all rights he should be using shadow instead of putting himself in range for *this*." So saying, he reached down and snapped off the front right leg of his chair. Unsurprisingly, the chunk of wood had a jagged, sharp edge. "Been working on that off and on the entire council. Thought it might come in handy."

Talley tsked. "Interesting. What else?"

The *antitribu* made a show of moving the makeshift stake from hand to hand. "Not much, other than the fact that my people would have dog-piled the archbishop if I didn't manage to stop him on the first shot. And we've got a lot of chair legs down here."

Talley raised an eyebrow and nodded. "Crude, but potentially effective. However, you'd do better to show more respect for someone of the archbishop's power and position."

Polonia watched the display, pursed his lips and cleared his throat. "Passable," said the Archbishop of New York. "I approve of your forethought. Hmm. So, Captain Blaine, do you honestly think you and your pack have what it takes to deal with this Pieterzoon?"

Blaine hesitated for a second. He could still walk away, he knew. Pieterzoon was a tricky son of a bitch. On the other hand, the chance to watch that pudgy bastard Borges squirm…

"We can do it. What's the time frame?"

"As soon as possible." That was Vykos cutting in. "I wish you luck, Captain Blaine. My staff has prepared everything you will need to carry out the operation. I assume you can provide your own weapons and transportation?"

The *antitribu* nodded. "Of course." He paused, looked at his packmates. "Tomorrow night, midnight, you get Pieterzoon's head on a plate." He looked over at Borges. "You can come along and watch if you want, my lord."

"No thank you," said Borges tightly, and a warning flash from Polonia told Blaine he'd gone a bit too far.

"Right. If you could tell me where your staff has the information…?" His voice trailed off as he looked at Vykos. "Please."

"The material is waiting for you outside the conference room, Captain Blaine."

Blaine nodded once and walked out. His packmates, a nervous swagger infusing their stride, followed. The now three-legged chair that one of them had been holding tottered for a moment and crashed to the floor.

No one moved to pick it up.

The doors shut behind the last member of Blaine's pack, the hulking monoceroid war ghoul who'd spent much of the evening trying to carve its name into the ceiling of the room with its horn. Best estimates revealed that its name was "Jam."

"So, is that all we have for tonight?" Borges stretched and turned his head longingly in the direction of the door.

"Almost." Polonia somehow had a black cat made from shadow in his lap, and he stroked it absently. "There is one more question to be answered before we can adjourn."

The groans and complaints rose from around the room. "Oh, God." "What now?" "Can't it fucking wait?"

Polonia waited until everyone had shouted themselves out and it was obvious that he, at least, wasn't going anywhere. "It's a simple question, really, and can be answered in a moment, assuming that everyone cooperates."

"It is, is it?" Borges was clearly disgruntled.

"Think of it as a simple exposition piece, Archbishop Borges. So, Vykos, can you answer this one?"

Vykos looked unsurprised. "To the best of my ability, of course. Though I would prefer we hurried. I have a," and she gave a slight smile, "phone call to make."

"Oh, it won't take a moment. I just wish to know precisely how you are getting all of this marvelous insider information on Herr Pieterzoon and the like. After all, we're at least temporarily hanging our strategy on your *phone call*," the words carried a slight edge, "and before we send any more perfectly talented packs off to the hinterlands, I would prefer knowing on whose say-so they are acting, precisely." He placed the cat on the table; it sat there, motionless. "Blaine may not be an archbishop, but he and his are certainly a worthwhile asset. I would *hate* to think we had thrown them away on spurious information."

"I have my sources," said the Tzimisce quietly. "They are quite accurate."

"Ah, but there's the trouble. You have your sources. I," Polonia flicked a glance down at the cat, "have mine. Archbishop Borges has his. We all have our sources." The archbishop began pacing. "I would even wager that the noble MacEllen has a few of his own. However, that doesn't mean that all of those sources are accurate. Why, some might be better than others. And yours seem exceptionally well placed, which makes me wonder. Who are you talking to, Vykos?"

"Does it really matter, if the information is good?"

"If you don't tell me, I have no way of knowing if the information is good, now do I?"

"The cardinal—"

"The cardinal is not here. I am. And I tell you this, my Byzantine friend, not another pack, not another ghoul, not another bullet, not another breath goes out of here on your information until you release your sources. I am younger than you are, but I am old enough to know when something is entirely too convenient. It is entirely too convenient that you were the first one to know about Pieterzoon's arrival; it is entirely too convenient that you happen to have sufficient information available so quickly to hand to a strike force you just happen to need for immediate work. I do not like such coincidence. Am I making myself clear?"

Vykos scanned the room. There was a new edge there now, a faint charge to the air. Polonia had energized even the weary ones. She mentally counted allies and concluded reluctantly that she did not have enough on this particular issue.

"I understand perfectly, Archbishop. Better than you think. However, I hardly feel that revealing the name of my source to so many—any one of whom might be captured and forced to reveal what he had learned—is necessarily wise tactics."

Polonia swept into a deep bow. "Of course. I hadn't considered that at all. Then, shall we let the rest of these worthies go, and you can simply tell, say, my fellow archbishop, his bodyguard, and myself? No sense putting anyone else here at risk." He locked gazes with the Tzimisce, and, unbelievably, Vykos looked away first.

"Very well. Get the others out of here."

The others, to no one's surprise, left. It took surprisingly little time to clear the room. Within minutes, only Talley, Borges, Vykos and Polonia himself remained. Vallejo had left after a stern look from Vykos; Polonia and Talley both wondered what precisely had transpired there.

"So, what do we have, Vykos?" Borges's voice was weary, though he would have fought tooth and nail to avoid being excluded. "Share."

Vykos deliberately folded her hands on the table. "I will not give you the name of my source." She raised one hand to ward off the storm of protest. "The name is unimportant, and will do more harm to tell you than you will benefit by learning it."

"So why the charade?" Talley's quiet voice, as usual, cut to the heart of the matter. "I'm rather disappointed, after that buildup."

"Because, honestly, I don't have the energy to deal with yet another riot. And I will tell you all that you need to know, of course."

"Which is?" Borges was skeptical.

"Which is that my source, as it has been put, is a member of the Camarilla who is privy to the plans of the defense efforts against us. She, or he, is working to create windows of opportunity for us, as well as funneling me what information he, or she, is able. Beyond that, I cannot tell you more, and I caution you not to rely heavily on my source's goodwill. Loyalty, as we all know, is a fragile thing." She looked from face to face. "And with that, gentlemen, you will have to be satisfied. If you will excuse me." She rose and walked out of the room. Borges followed her, as did Talley. Only Polonia and the cat, re-emerged from some corner of shadow, remained.

"I am not at all satisfied, I am afraid," he murmured. "But it will have to serve, at least for now." And with that, he rose and walked out. Behind him a tendril of shadow darted out and turned out the conference room's lights.

The cat, abandoned by its master, gave its first and last sound, a plaintive yowl. Seconds later, it dissolved into the darkness of the room, as thoroughly as if it had never existed.

Sunday, 18 July 1999, 2:28 AM
Hyatt Regency Capitol Hill
Washington, D.C.

The elevator moved downward at a steady pace, its progress marked by a steady hum. Someone had torn out the ceiling speaker about five minutes after the war council had moved into the hotel. Now there was only the steady whirr of the machinery and the hiss of the air conditioning.

Five monsters and one manila folder were its only contents. One, the Lasombra named Sonny (Santiago, actually, but no one wanted to give him that much respect), did his level best to drown out the elevator noise by cursing a blue streak.

"Jesus fucking Christ, Blaine, what the hell did you just get us into? If half the 'When I was a Cub Scout in the Camarilla' stories you keep on telling us to keep us in line are true, this guy Pieterzoon's going to be harder to nail than any of the dickweeds upstairs, and that includes Miss Freaky Leaky Tzimisce."

"Shimishay," said Terrence, who was tall and lanky and wore John Lennon granny glasses that he never quite managed to get the blood off. "It's pronounced 'Shimishay'."

Sonny turned on him with the fury possessed only by the very short and self-conscious. "I don't give a rat's ass if it's pronounced Tzimisce, Goldfarb, or Your Mother, she's a fucking fruitcake, and you, Blaine, are a fucking stupid fruitcake for getting us put on this suicide mission, though the more I think about it the more I'd prefer suicide to another night spent listening to the assholes from New York and Miami snipe at each other and occasionally turn one of the little guys into a fucking blood-on-a-Trisket kind of snack—"

"Sonny," Blaine said pleasantly, "shut the fuck up."

"But Blaine—"

"Say nothing. That way, you're insured against saying something else that pisses me off. This operation is going to be hard enough without my having to stuff you into a mailbox before we start."

Sonny lapsed into sulky silence. No one spoke for a minute, and the doors suddenly opened on floor twelve. An elderly woman stood there, impatiently pushing the "Down" button. She took a step forward as the doors opened, then her eyes widened in fear. The towering war ghoul Jammer, his single horn sweeping up until it nearly scraped the ceiling, grinned out at her. She took a step backward, gasped something that could have been "Oh my sweet Jesus," and fell heavily against the far wall. A shriek of "Oh my God! Grandma!" could be heard from down the hallway as the doors whispered shut.

The Lasombra doubled over laughing. "Shit, that was beautiful." The others joined in the hysterics, and even Blaine found himself grinning. "Did you see the way her eyes got big when she saw Jammer? 'Oh Lawd Jeezus, preserve me from an elevator full of eeeevil!'" He completely lost it, wheezing with laughter as the elevator spilled them out into the lower level of the hotel parking garage.

The pack's van, a heavily modified Dodge with some fascinating innovations that weren't street-legal in most states of the Union, squatted ominously by the far stairwell. It was black, with fat black tires made from solid rubber, and heavily tinted windows. Blaine had thought about getting rid of it, because staties had developed a profile on serial-killer vehicles that made them zero in on suspicious-looking vans. The situation wasn't dangerous yet, but it was a pain in the ass, and Blaine had a soft spot in his heart for avoiding pains in the ass.

Except, of course, the ones he worked with.

"So do we have a chance in hell, Blaine?" That was Terrence again. Sonny was still too busy imitating the new cadaver on floor twelve, and the others were laughing along with him.

"Honestly? Yeah, we can pull this one off. I *have* met Pieterzoon. He's scary. Cold. Sneaky like you would not believe. But he's also a sissy bastard, and he hates fighting his own battles. That means he's going to be looking for a way out when he should be tackling us head-on, and that, in turn, gives us a small window of opportunity. Which," he said as he reached the van and opened the driver's door, "is a better chance than we stand with the assholes upstairs."

They climbed in, Terrence taking shotgun and the rest piling into the back. Sonny cursed at Jammer for sitting on his gun, and then the usual squabbling ensued. Blaine handed Terrence the packet he'd received from Vykos's ghoul upstairs. "There should be a map in there," he said.

The Tzimisce rummaged through the papers and extricated one. "Would you believe AAA?"

"At this point, I would believe anything," Blaine grunted, and threw the van into gear. Something, possibly a quiver of crossbow bolts from the rattling, fell over as he did so. "Right now I just want to get us to Baltimore and settled in by sunrise. Then tomorrow night, we worry about taking out Jan Pieterzoon and the dozen or so yesmen who are going to try to stop us."

"Any thoughts on strategy?" Terrence rolled down his window and licked his fingers so he could test the breeze. He did that before every trip, and Blaine found it oddly reassuring.

The *antitribu* nodded. "Jammer and Lox cause a ruckus and draw off his cover. You and I wade in and distract him for maybe ten seconds, and at some point during those ten seconds, Sonny pops up with his assault rifle he's so proud of and blows the son of a bitch's head off." He said all of this very quietly, to avoid letting Sonny overhear and get overexcited all over again.

The van roared out of the garage and turned north, heading for the entrance to I-495. Terrence blinked. "Got a better plan?"

"Honestly? Not yet. If that's what I still want to do tomorrow, then you can start worrying."

"If it's all the same to you, I'm going to start now."

Blaine grinned. "Be my guest. By the way, we're going to be stopping at, what is it, Chesapeake House, for gas and a janitor. Make sure you're not too hungry before we get started tomorrow. We're not going to have time to hunt, so this is the best I can do."

Terrence nodded. "And you claim rights to Pieterzoon's blood?" he said, his voice nearly a whisper.

Of course I do, Blaine thought, *You think I'm going to let you or laughing boy in the back get your claws on it? I'm the fucking pack ductus, after all.* But all he said was, "We'll let the survivors worry about it once we take the target down. No sense arguing until then."

"Of course," said Terrence. "No sense at all."

part two:
troy

The message at the front desk had been left by a Mister Schreck, which made Lucita roll her eyes. *Schreck* was German for "terror," as well as being the name of the actor who played the original cinematic vampire in the 1922 version of *Nosferatu*. In short, the note was simply an over-cute sewer rat's way of saying that he wanted to get in touch with her, and that he didn't mind having her know that he was Nosferatu.

Lucita graciously accepted the slip of paper from the desk clerk, made a show of reading it—*I'll call later*—and then tore it into shreds as she headed for the open elevator. She dropped the scraps into the ashtray as she entered the elevator car, which was blessedly empty apart from her.

The ride up to her floor was mercifully brief, which Lucita counted as a small favor. The fact that the Nosferatu had announced his presence meant business—well, either that or incredible arrogance, but that wasn't a trait most long-lived Nosferatu possessed. While she was already engaged on a contract—which was looking more complicated each night, as the Sabbat offensive washed over old havens and safe houses that she had spent decades establishing—she was by no means averse to lining up additional commissions. On the other hand, it might be that her coy contact had information to sell, which might well make her current job simpler.

The elevator slowed and halted, and Lucita

strolled out onto the fourteenth floor. Her room faced north, giving it the maximum protection from sunlight, and the "Do Not Disturb" tag still hung from the door handle. She unlocked the door and glided in. The room was immaculate, and she kicked off her shoes and lay down on the too-soft mattress to await the inevitable Nosferatu contact. She'd discounted the notion of a trap almost instantly. The Camarilla had bigger problems than her at the moment, and it simply didn't make sense for them to expend the sort of resources it would take to neutralize her. Lucita had long ago matter-of-factly assessed the manpower necessary to eliminate her; taking that kind of power out of the front lines would cost the sect another city, minimum. By the same token, the Sabbat had larger concerns. She'd received information to the effect that her sire was taking a very personal interest in the entire American affair, and that was another surety of her safety from at least those vampires who reported to him. Cardinal Monçada would not look kindly on anyone who destroyed his childe.

Lucita realized that such logic didn't protect her from assaults launched by the foolish, the ignorant, or the suicidal, but she was confident in her ability to protect herself from any and all of the above.

And if she was wrong? She'd been wrong before, very rarely, and endured. She'd endure this as well.

Precisely three minutes later, there came a knock at the door. "Miss? Room service," was the muffled call.

"Of course. I'll be right there." Lucita unwound from the bed and opened the door without looking through the peephole. She was eminently aware of who was waiting on the other side.

The young man with the dinner trolley looked distinctly uncomfortable in his uniform. "The dinner you ordered, miss," was all he said as he rolled the cart into the room. Lucita smiled without amusement.

"Please take that ridiculous disguise off—Mister Schreck? I would prefer that you were comfortable if we are going to conduct business."

The bellhop took a step back from the tray and bowed from the waist. When he stood back up, he was no longer a pleasant-faced young man, but a warty, bald man with a build like a linebacker's. He still wore the hotelier's uniform, which fit him about as well as one might expect, and the required cap sat jauntily on his bald and scarred pate. "Didn't want to scare the guests quite yet, miss. And I'll bet you say that to all the bellhops."

"The ones I have to dispose of later, yes. Are you volunteering?" Lucita sat herself down in a large chair by the sliding door to the balcony, leaving her "guest" to scramble for someplace to sit. It occurred to Lucita too late that the creature might sit on her bed and befoul it, but it was inconsequential.

"No. Not at all. And I'm not Schreck. I just work for him." The ersatz bellhop flopped down cross-legged on the floor. "I am, however, empowered to negotiate for him."

"That's good to know. So, how long were you waiting in the elevator for me?"

The Nosferatu was unabashed. "About an hour. Spent entirely too much time using the old heebie-jeebies to scare kine out of it to make sure I wouldn't miss you." He paused for a second and blinked. "Just to satisfy my professional curiosity, how did you know?"

"Elevators at rest for that long generally don't

have their doors wide open, for one thing. The muddy prints on the carpet were another clue. And then there's the smell. You're going to have to get better at this if you expect to survive."

The other vampire rubbed his lumpy chin thoughtfully. "Hmm. Hadn't thought of the door angle, and I stashed the cart up here to keep the cage clear. You'd be surprised how many times people ignore the other stuff, however. In any case," and he cleared his throat, "I'm here to talk business. I just thought you might appreciate the courtesy of a personal elevator." He grinned horrifically. "It's the little things that help close a deal, after all."

Lucita made a graceful gesture with her off hand. "Of course. But you're not here to play cage operator for me. What does Mr. Schreck have to offer?"

"Six million American, a copy of two pages of the Sargon Fragment, all the resources you need, the best protection from reprisal he can offer, transportation in the form of both air transit at your convenience and a vehicle of your choosing, incidentals, expenses, equipment and other sundries that are on the balance sheet but aren't worth mentioning here, and, if I read the fine print properly, a hundred free hours on AOL. The last is, of course, negotiable."

The only sign that Lucita was even vaguely interested was a slight lift of her right eyebrow. "The Sargon Fragment? Interesting. Mr. Schreck is certainly emphatic about wanting me to take this assignment. What does he want me to do?"

The Nosferatu shrugged. "What you do best. Return a few people to the sort of state dead people should naturally be in."

"People?"

"Our kind of people."

"Ah. Of course. Still, Mr. Schreck seems to be willing to spare no expense. Dare I ask what the catch is?"

To his credit, the Nosferatu declined to be ingenuous and ask what Lucita could possibly mean. "Mr. Schreck felt that a sufficiently large offer would impress you as to his seriousness and eliminate so much of that, and I quote here, 'troublesome haggling' that he finds distasteful."

Lucita stood up and began pacing. "A marvelous answer, and one that avoids the question completely. So what *is* the catch?"

"Time pressure, for one thing. The quality of the targets, for another."

"The fee isn't quite as impressive for multiple targets."

"Mr. Schreck is aware of your usual rates, and also notes that the offer is not strictly limited to cash. He also thinks that you may enjoy one or two of these assignments."

Lucita whirled and faced the Nosferatu. Part of her noted that he was clever; deliberately sitting cross-legged in an indefensible spot was about as good a job as a Kindred was likely to do of saying "I'm harmless." He'd also chosen the floor, not the bed or anyplace else that she was likely to use, and hadn't commented on the mirrors. All in all, he was well above the usual cut of messenger she dealt with, and as such, she found herself at least willing to listen to the meat of his pitch.

"Who?"

"Four targets. One archbishop, worth $3.4 million and the text. Another higher-up, whom I understand you may have met once. Two lesser warleaders who show some potential. They're worth a half a million each. We just need them done fast."

"For shame. You should never let your artists know that they have pressure on a deadline, little Nosferatu. You should also learn to use euphemisms better. Someone listening in, say, with a directional microphone might well pick all of this up and find a use for the information."

The Nosferatu shook his head almost imperceptibly. "Actually, I have a friend on the roof keeping the pigeons stirred up right outside your window. Should give anyone on a directional fits, and mess with microwave eavesdropping as well. You'd be amazed at how effective a wall of feathers is for that sort of thing. But I will take your advice to heart, and I thank you for it. Now, are you interested?"

Lucita pursed her lips. "Of course I am. But I'm not going to commit immediately. I'd like a bit more information, so that I might make an informed decision."

Inside, Lucita had already made her choice. The Sargon Fragment was something she'd been chasing for a very long time, and the opportunity to obtain even two more pages of it was not one she could lightly pass up. Besides, she was already contracted to deal with one archbishop; what was one more? And no prey short of an archbishop really concerned her. The fees for at least three of the four would be found money—but it never hurt to know more.

In response, the Nosferatu stood, his hands held palm outwards to emphasize the fact that he was no threat. He took two steps over to where the forgotten dinner trolley stood and lifted the lid from the metal tray that normally would have housed whatever delicacy the kitchen had produced. Instead, underneath were a number of folders, bound together with thick rubber bands. He lifted the tray and placed it on the bed. "All that you'll need is here, including terms for payment, what resources Mr. Schreck has placed at your disposal, and timetables on known enemy movements. Take a few hours. Read it over. If you decide you're interested, come on down to the lobby and sit in the chair opposite the elevators. Someone will come along to guide you to a place where you can meet with my superiors. The identification sign is simple: My man will ask you if perchance you read the latest *Blackwood's*. Seeing as the magazine's been gone for decades, it's not the sort of thing that's liable to get stumbled into."

Lucita frowned. "I would prefer another position. That chair faces some…decorations…that make my state rather obvious."

The Nosferatu chuckled. "We need our *bona fides* as well, Miss Lucita. Don't worry, we'll collect you fast. Incidentally, there's a decanter of lunch on the second level of the cart for you if you want it. Mr. Schreck likes to make people comfortable." He put the container on the dresser, bowed, and said, "Now, if you will excuse me?"

"Certainly." Lucita waved him out the door with the cart even as he shimmered back into his disguise. Her attention was already on the folders.

Suddenly, her so-called plate was very full indeed.

Contrary to what one might expect, the meeting was not in a sewer. It was, however, in a sub-basement that contained a leaky pipe, so the concrete floor was liberally spattered in puddles. Lucita assumed that this was so that her hosts could keep track of her movements by the sounds she made. Either that, or they were aware of the tricks she'd picked up from Fatima and were just playing to their own stereotype. Her guide had led her down here, cautioned her to wait, and vanished. Lucita probably could have tracked the man, but decided to play by the client's rules. To do otherwise would be rude.

The room itself was pitch black. She'd dealt with this Nosferatu before, however, and was reasonably confident in his sincere interest in keeping her alive. Still, it was always worth being cautious. She stepped forward.

"Schreck?"

The voice that answered her was rough and low, but unmistakably that of a woman. "Mr. Schreck was unavoidably detained, and sends his regrets. He does, however, want you to know that a quarter of your fee has already been wired to your account in the Caymans, per your standard instructions, as an earnest of his good will. If necessary, I can provide proof of that."

"I trust Mr. Schreck, though I must say I am disappointed in him."

There was a pause. "Mr. Schreck is a busy man. However, I have his full confidence and authority."

Lucita laughed. "So did the bellhop. Mr. Schreck is quite free with that."

The reply was a trifle strained, and Lucita knew she'd won a point. "Mr. Schreck trusts his valued subordinates. Now, business?"

"Business. Of course. So your Mr. Schreck wants an archbishop? It's quite a task."

"Yes, we want a particular archbishop, though if you decide to get greedy and take down multiples we won't be too terribly upset."

"You don't aim small, do you?"

"We aim for the necessary targets, regardless of size. Is the price acceptable?"

"For all four? Barely."

"It's more than you were paid for the last six combined, Lucita. Plus, I believe at least one of the four is someone you were considering putting out of his misery *gratis*."

"True enough. Excellent dossiers, incidentally."

"Thank you. We take pride in that sort of thing. Rumor has it we're good at it, you know."

"Rumor does indeed. Anything else?"

"A few. We've arranged transportation that we hope will be to your liking, and it's waiting for you outside the entrance you came in. The paperwork has, of course, been taken care of. It's yours now. Your guide is waiting outside this chamber, and will lead you there with due speed. When we receive more information on your targets' whereabouts and circumstances, you can rest assured that we will pass it along to you."

"Time frame on the first kill?"

"As soon as possible."

Lucita frowned. "That's rather vague, and a bit sudden."

Her opposite number laughed bitterly. "Believe me, we would rather have given you more lead time ourselves, but circumstances have changed very suddenly. Great things are afoot; every Sabbat war leader who's gone tonight is an offensive we don't have to counter tomorrow. And every pack priest who's looking into the shadows for you isn't keeping his mind on his job. That buys us time. Buy us enough, and you will find our appreciation made tangible."

"With this kind of time frame, I can make no promises." Somewhere off in the dark, a rat splashed through shallow water.

"Godspeed and good hunting, Lucita."

"You sound like my sire when you say that. It doesn't inspire confidence."

There was a quiet chuckle from the far side of the room. "We all make mistakes." Then came the sound of receding footfalls on wet concrete, and Lucita was alone in the dark once again.

She waited until the room was absolutely silent, and then retraced her steps. True to Schreck's representative's words, her erstwhile guide was waiting outside the door to the chamber, and graciously conducted her through a maze of tunnels and pitch-black corridors. Lucita felt that she probably could find her way back unaided, but accepted the assistance in the spirit in which it was offered.

After an interminable half hour of travel, the pair emerged at a fire door. The Nosferatu opened it for Lucita, then vanished back into the darkness. Outside on the city street sat a car that was clearly intended for her; there was no other reason she could conceive of for a BMW 325i to be parked there in particular. The keys were inside and the doors were locked, but that was no difficulty. She merely exercised her will on a patch of shadow in the coupe's interior. It snaked up and unlocked the door, then unlatched it and pushed it open. Lucita slid in and shut the door behind her. On the passenger seat was another folder, with a legend written in black Magic Marker. She ignored it; it would be her bedtime reading. A quick check of the glove compartment revealed a thick wad of bills labeled "For expenses."

Lucita took a second to reflect on the situation. It was not what she would have chosen, but it was what she had to work with. The pay was certainly good enough, and the client sounded desperate enough that she could no doubt extract additional concessions. All in all, it was far from unworkable.

The dashboard chronometer read 12:34. She had plenty of time to read the additional briefing material before the sun rose. Her employer had even been so kind as to provide two sorts of audio selections: briefings on all of her targets, and an extensive selection of classical music. She slid one of the former discs (home-burned and lettered in the same hand as the folder) into the player and started the car.

Friday, 30 July 1999, 12:53 AM
Sub-basement, the Wesleyan Building
Baltimore, Maryland

"A basement?" Banks of fluorescent lights flickered into life as the elevator shuddered to a halt and its doors opened. Jan Pieterzoon, scion of a noble Ventrue bloodline and survivor of a botched Sabbat assassination attempt almost two weeks prior, stepped out blinking in the sudden harsh light, and found himself squarely in the middle of a puddle of stagnant water. Beside him, his Nosferatu guide clucked concernedly.

"Actually, a sub-basement, Herr Pieterzoon. It's the sort of thing that's expected of our business operations, I'm afraid." The speaker was a short, squat Nosferatu whom Pieterzoon *thought* was a woman, though truth be told he couldn't be sure. "The water on the floor adds the required touch of sewer chic that people seem to demand when dealing with our little consortium. Really, it's a pity Monsieur Rafin isn't here; he gives a wonderful performance."

"Yes, yes. Wonderful. But a sub-basement?"

The Nosferatu shrugged. "It's secure, it's as defensible as your kid sister's virtue and it helps us get the second party to relax because she's dealing with 'typical' Nosferatu. They think they know what they're working with, they relax. And they don't think to look for toys like the swivel-mounted guns with overlapping fields of fire that Nigel controls. That's the guy over there behind the one-way glass on the south wall; he's a video game freak with fast-twitch like you would not believe. The slugs are birdshot suspended in Teflon with a steel jacket—same effect as opening the chest cavity up, pointing a shotgun full of #10 at the sternum, and pulling the trigger. Even your basic badass war ghoul tends to slow down when he's got holes in him the size of hubcaps."

"Ah. Very clever." Pieterzoon explored the confines of the mostly bare room, taking care not to step in the puddles. "Is that the only precaution?"

Pieterzoon's guide chuckled with a sound that Jan instinctively associated with the terminal stages of consumption. "Well, no. But I wouldn't want to bore you with the details."

The Ventrue closed his eyes and prayed for strength. He simply did not have time for this sort of thing, not with the Sabbat ravening up the coast like the plague given flesh. He had a great many things to attend to, and smart-alecky Nosferatu were nowhere on the list. "Wonderful," he managed at last. "So did the meeting at least go well?"

"Oh, perfect," the Nosferatu said breezily. "She waltzed in, gave verbal agreement to the deal, admitted to having read the packets that Claude had left with her, and went off to do her thing. Apparently she found the information satisfactory, though she was a little cranky about the time frame."

"Ahem. Yes, well, can't be helped. We simply don't have enough forces in the field at the moment—where *is* Parma when you need him? It's not like we couldn't use another strategist here—to do things any other way."

"Whatever." The hideous creature shrugged, or did something approximate. "Don't ask me; I'm scared of them all. But I can promise you this, Herr Pieterzoon: If they ever get down here, they're not coming back out." She (he was almost sure it was a "she") smiled hideously and tapped the concrete wall with a misshapen finger. "We're prepared."

Pieterzoon managed a wan smile. "Wonderful."

It was a busy night for the vampires of the Camarilla, especially those privileged (or unlucky) enough to be in Baltimore, nerve center of the sect's resistance to the Sabbat. Everywhere, Kindred and ghouls scurried about on tasks of greater or lesser importance. The threat from Gangrel Justicar Xaviar the previous evening that his clan would break with the sect was both a secret that could not be kept and a development that required no few adjustments to Camarilla strategy. Tucked away in his private suite, Jan Pieterzoon discussed new emergency tactics, as well as the other desperate plans already set in motion, with Marston Colchester, a Nosferatu ally.

Throughout the rest of the city, the strengthening of defenses was proceeding even without the direct supervision of Theo Bell. The archon of Clan Brujah was on his way personally to attend to matters in Buffalo, the city most imperiled by the defection of the Gangrel. No Kindred was unaffected by the dire turn of events.

In the midst of the frenzied preparations, one particular Kindred retired for the night, claiming a terrible headache. The others were very understanding, and allowed the Cainite to depart with only some more or less insincere wishes of good health trailing after.

Once "home," the vampire sat down and composed a brief letter on a remarkably expensive stationery, sketching out the entire Camarilla strategy for the defense of upstate New York, southern New England and so on. The sect's strategists had decided after vociferous argument that there was no way that every city could be held. The best thing to do, they'd then agreed, would be to concentrate the remaining force available. That meant evacuating cities, most notably Buffalo, and leaving behind screens of newly Embraced Kindred and ghouls to give the appearance of a strong defense. With any luck (and a judicious sprinkling of public appearances by higher-ranking Kindred every once in a while), the bluff would hold long enough to delay the Sabbat offensive and tie up Sabbat resources. That would buy time for the Camarilla to retrench, re-arm, and eventually, retake its lost territory.

Beyond that, the letter contained some inconsequential details about Pieterzoon's latest malapropism, and was signed "Lucius." The Cainite folded it, slipped it into an envelope and sealed it, scribbling "Sascha" on the outside. Such careless informality would infuriate its intended recipient. That sort of thing carried entirely too much enjoyment these nights.

All in all, the traitor reflected, the Camarilla had come up with a good plan. It might have done some of what it was supposed—if its details were not to be handed over to the enemy within hours of its conception. The vampire concentrated for a second, reaching out to summon a secure courier. The other would arrive in a matter of minutes, and would then take the letter off to Washington. There, it would no doubt have some very interesting effects on the Sabbat battle plan for Buffalo.

The Kindred, fiddling absently with the outstretched wings of a lapel pin, sat back in the chair and pondered the upcoming carnage with some satisfaction.

lasombra

Polonia hated parking garages. They were noisy, smelly, crowded, aesthetically displeasing and generally wet with noisome spills. On a more practical note, they were lit in a fashion that made it almost impossible to seize on useful shadows; they generated echoes that made judging distances by sound impossible; and they gave all sorts of idiots the notion that they'd make wonderful locations for ambushes. Polonia himself had been assaulted, not once, not twice, but three times in the past year alone by enterprising young Cainites. None of the attacks had come within shouting distance of success, but the affairs still left a bad taste in the archbishop's mouth.

Thus it was with some distaste, though no real trepidation, that Polonia stepped out of the elevator into the parking garage below the hotel. Thankfully, this level was mostly deserted. Only a few scattered cars were parked here and there, while across the way from the elevator doors was the van that MacEllen and his pack were engaged in loading. Cases, suspiciously bulging wrapped bundles, and various firearms were arranged in a semicircle around the van's back doors, while MacEllen and a short, heavyset vampire with a bowl cut and arms like lead pipes loaded various items with surprising care.

Briefly, Polonia considered walking over to where the others were, but he decided against it. MacEllen was just mad enough to risk doing something stupid, and in any case, it would be beneath his dignity. Let the man come to him.

It didn't take long for one of the other Cainites lounging around the van to spot Polonia as he stood, arms crossed, waiting by the elevator. A piercing whistle got all of his comrades' attention, including MacEllen's. The big man stared across the lot with undisguised hatred in his eyes, then began to lope across the expanse of concrete. A couple of the others drifted after him.

Polonia permitted himself the luxury of a smile.

"I have orders for you," he said, when MacEllen had gotten close enough to hear. "Important ones."

MacEllen spat. "Fucking great. What, are we being ordered to ride behind the rest of the army with a broom and a shovel now? Is that it?"

"On the contrary, the operation is yours. All of it."

For a moment, MacEllen was speechless, then hard suspicion masked his features. "This has got to be a setup. Why the change?"

"New information." Polonia reached inside his jacket and pulled out a small bundle of neatly folded sheets of paper. "This is for you. It details the operation, your objectives and your resources. You'll be getting another pack under your command, Einar's, and you'll be in charge of the assault on Buffalo."

"With two packs?" MacEllen was aghast. "Are you out of your mind?"

"As I said," responded Polonia coolly, "there is new information. Buffalo is your target; it will be only lightly defended. The Camarilla is withdrawing all but a token resistance force. All that you will encounter will be newly made vampires who have no notion of their potential, and the occasional ghoul. You should have no difficulty."

"Where did this information come from, Vykos's mole?"

"From the best of sources. The answers to all of your other questions," and he proffered the packet of papers, "are in here." Wordlessly, MacEllen took the bundle and tore it open. The others crowded around for over-the-shoulder glimpses. Polonia ignored them, and quietly reached behind himself to press the button to summon the elevator.

"You will have total autonomy in the field, MacEllen. I expect a complete and rapid success, considering the caliber of opposition you will be facing. If you fail, don't bother coming back. I'll find you to discuss your performance."

Right on cue, the elevator doors opened. Polonia turned on his heel and stepped into the car; the closing doors obscured him within seconds.

MacEllen watched him go with a mixture of hatred and fear. All around him, his pack members whooped and cheered as word spread from each to each that they'd be heading the Buffalo strike. But MacEllen wasn't so sure this was a good thing.

"Son of a bitch," he said, mostly to himself. "It's a setup. It's got to be." In his mind's eye he could see the arrangement: Forge new "intelligence," pick out the pack ductus who's getting a little too noisy and dangerous, hand him the news, and bundle him off to get chewed up by a meat grinder. The rest of his pack, and Einar's, too, would be sacrificed just to get rid of him. Vykos probably didn't even *have* a real spy.

But the only way out of the trap, he realized, would be to go straight into it and try to get out the other side. He couldn't run, or he'd have both sects after his balls. Hell, half his pack would probably jump his ass if he suggested cutting out now, just for the chance to be his replacement. No, he'd have to dive into whatever was waiting and kick *its* ass. Jaw set with grim determination, he turned back to the business of loading the van, a bit more carefully than before.

Monday, 9 August 1999, 1:34 AM
Guaranty Building
Buffalo, New York

"So I have to abandon the city?" Lladislas, Prince of Buffalo, Niagara and the surrounding regions, was mildly displeased. "One hundred and sixteen years of keeping this place free from Sabbat, breaches of the Masquerade, lupine incursions and the Canadian dollar, and now I simply fold my tent and leave my home? Bell, you're coming dangerously close to over-stepping your bounds here." Lladislas was a man of medium build, with short-cropped, sandy blonde hair that hadn't made up its mind how it felt about a widow's peak. He wore a suit that looked like it came off the rack at Marshall's, and which clearly wasn't big enough in the shoulders. Still, he was prince, and he had actually done a much better than average job of keeping his domain operating smoothly.

And that, in a nutshell, was why Theo Bell hadn't clocked him one yet. Besides, Lladislas was Brujah, and Brujah princes were rare enough that Theo didn't particularly want to lose this one. Lladislas had come up from the meat-packing plants, a Civil War veteran and early labor organizer. He'd risen to the post of prince with meteoric swiftness, first as the compromise candidate of a hopelessly deadlocked primogen council, and then through his own strength.

In short, Lladislas was a tough guy and a good soldier, and Bell really did hate to take his city away from him. That's why he was being polite. It was up to him, Theo Bell, designated asshole and bearer of bad news for the whole goddamned Camarilla, to get

Lladislas, his primogen, childer, hangers-on, and personal possessions out of the city. If all went according to plan, Buffalo would in fact remain undisturbed, and Lladislas's forces would be used more effectively elsewhere. Of course, Lladislas was not about to leave quietly for an assault that "might" be coming, so Theo was prepared to fudge a bit, or more if necessary, in stressing the imminence of attack.

Theo sighed theatrically. He was good for one more round of Mr. Nice Vampire, and then Lladislas was getting hauled out of here like the half-full sack of shit he was. "Prince Lladislas. For the last time, the Camarilla knows and values your service, and thinks very highly of the job you have done. That is why we are evacuating you and your subjects, instead of leaving you here for the Sabbat to use as a fucking piñata. Now, if you want to stay, you're more than welcome to, and when we come back and liberate the place I'll be sure to put up a nice little stone monument right over the greasy spot on the goddamned floor that would be all that we could find of you. Do I make myself clear? When the Sabbat shows up, you do not stand a chance against the sort of force that got brought to bear on Atlanta. Now you get your people together, you move them out, and you do it quietly."

Okay, Theo thought to himself. Maybe he wasn't feeling that nice after all.

Lladislas just sat there, wide-eyed. He opened and closed his mouth several times without saying anything. Clearly the man was on the verge of some sort of episode.

"No argument?" said Bell. "I like that in a prince. I'm going to scout around and get a good lay of the land. When I get back, we can talk about how we're going to handle logistics and what defenses you will leave behind. Oh, and for the love of God, get a better suit."

Lladislas was still gaping when Theo walked away into the night.

Some hours later, Bell found Lladislas at church, of all places. Specifically, the prince was outside St. Paul's Episcopal Cathedral, looking up at the edifice with a sad smile. Inside, a single light shone; a janitor making early-morning rounds, no doubt.

"I'm going to miss this place, Bell," Lladislas said without turning. "They built it while I was a boy. I remember everyone being so excited, one way or another. It meant work for a lot of men. It meant a lot of things. That was a hell of a long time ago, though. Wish it still meant anything at all."

"Saying good-byes?" Bell was always vaguely uncomfortable with moments of sentimentality like this; he figured that once you were dead, you shouldn't care quite so much any more. On the other hand, Lladislas's wistfulness over a church was positively petty compared to some of the manias he'd seen in Europe. It balanced out, he decided. It all balanced out.

The prince gave a laugh that had no humor in it. "More or less. It's either that or get my dander up, call you a prick, and let my temper paint me into a corner so that I have to stay and get myself killed all over again. Oh, you're right. We do need to leave. But don't expect me to be happy about it."

Bell walked down to the corner of Church and watched the evening's light mist make a halo around the streetlights. Cars zipped past intermittently, few even slowing down because of the slick streets. "No one expects you to be happy, Lladislas, except for a couple of the real thumbdicks on the council who no doubt will want you to kiss their boots because they noticed your little problem and sent me to fix it."

Lladislas grinned a crooked grin and looked over at the archon, who stood silhouetted by the light behind him. "They can be a bunch of right bastards, can't they?" Bell nodded assent. "But they're right this time. I've got eight, maybe nine Kindred who amount to anything here, plus about forty ghouls. We'd make a fight of it, but we just don't have numbers. Hell, there wouldn't even be anyone left to let the next city know we'd made a last stand." He spat blood into a sewer grate. "We have to go."

Bell stretched, the occasional popping noise from his back evidence that he'd been on his feet far too long. "I know. Believe it or not, I'm sorry. You did a good job here."

"Not good enough."

Theo rolled his eyes. "Stop with the self-pity bullshit—you sound like one of the clove-and-cape neonates. Let's talk about how we're going to get your people out of here."

"Already taken care of." The prince's tone was noticeably flat. "Like you suggested, we're going to have a couple of our youngest Kindred Embracing a small flock of gullible idiots who will fight to hold the city as a screen against our departure. The valuable ghouls are going to be evacuated. We've already started arranging transfers, job offers in other cities, relocations, visiting positions and the like. One of my bodyguards insists on staying behind. His name's

Haraszty, and he's going to be coordinating the defenses, such as they are."

"Stubborn. Not a good quality in a ghoul."

Lladislas nodded. "Nearly a fanatic. Channels it into sports, most of the time—I've caught him on TV during Bills games. He's one of the idiots who likes to paint himself blue. But he's a hell of a shot." The prince started strolling up Pearl Street. After a moment, the archon followed him. They made an odd pair, the prince preternaturally pale and formally garbed, while his companion was as dark-skinned as the Kindred condition allowed, dressed in a loose-fitting jacket over a red T-shirt and jeans. The archon had a massive pistol in a shoulder holster and a smaller one strapped to his leg, and both occasionally caught the light from the sickly globes atop the lampposts. The guns didn't do much against Kindred, but they did make meaty chunks out of most ghouls, even Tzimisce war ghouls.

Lladislas was unarmed. He was still prince here, after all.

"Any idea of when they'll get here?" he asked.

Bell nodded, though in truth he had no idea. Hopefully never, but "hopefully" had a way of turning ugly real fast, so Theo figured it was just as well to get things set up as quickly as possible. "A week at most. We've drawn the line at the Beltway, more or less, so they're stuck there. That means they've started swinging around to the west—through Wheeling, up past Pittsburgh and then on to here."

"And how much territory are we going to give them?"

They passed street lamps, mailboxes, parked cars. Nothing disturbed them. In the distance, an overachieving songbird let loose with the first frail notes of the day. Bell hesitated before answering. "That's up to the council. It's the usual backstabbing bullshit in there. That's why I like being in the field. It's cleaner." He suddenly grinned. "I'd give my right nut to have Parma over here, or one of the real heavy hitters from Europe. Or maybe my boss could just get off his ass and get out here before the roof caves in." The two shared a laugh at that. They walked on past the district courthouse, the run-down convention center looming on their right.

"Is it such a good idea to keep giving ground?"

Bell thought about it for a moment. "Yeah. Yeah, it is. Look at it this way: As things stand, we have a lot of territory to cover. That means we get spread thin on the ground. Say we've got a hundred Kindred over a thousand square miles, and ten cities in it we have to defend. That's ten Kindred per city, right? So let's say the Sabbat rolls in with fifty Kindred. Now, if we had all of our guys in one place, we could take them, right? We'd outnumber them two to one, and that would be that. But instead, we've got this ten-ten-ten thing going, which means that instead we have a whole lot of fifty-on-ten rumbles. And, since we're so badly outnumbered in each fight, they don't take diddly in the way of casualties. So we lose all hundred of our people, all ten cities and all of the territory.

"Now, instead, what we're doing is taking all our guys, pulling them back to the far border of that thousand-mile box, and planting them in two cities. Sure, we lose some turf, but now the Sabbat's got a choice of fair fights. Even better, if they hit one city with everything they've got—which at that point becomes the only chance they have—we can pull half the Kindred out of the other city and put a shiv right into their collective kidney."

Lladislas nodded. "Solid."

"It had better be solid, damnit. It's the only plan we've got, and if it goes belly-up, ain't nobody worrying about being prince of nowhere. There won't be anyplace left to be prince of. Not on the East Coast."

Lladislas gave a bark of laughter. "Hell, Theo, there's going to be no place for me to be prince of when this shakes down anyway. You think they're going to let me come back? Five will get you ten they hand over my city to some snot-nosed brat of a Ventrue 'as a reward for services rendered,' and I'm out on my ass."

"I can't promise anything, Lladislas, but I'll put in my word for you. But that's tomorrow, if ever. We've got more important things to handle, like the evac."

"True. Any thoughts?"

"A few. When you start bringing neonates over to soak up bullets, make sure they're fourteenth generation, thirteenth at best. I know it's tempting to do the job yourself, but you leave your childe behind, some Sabbat asshole's going to turn him into his personal six-pack and we've given aid and comfort to the enemy. No sense letting them have more to munch on than they catch themselves. Hmm. Another point. Keep the cannon fodder Brujah or Nossie. Anyone else, and someone's going to scream like babies with a load on about unfair representation, too many Tremere and shit like that. I hear it out of New York all the time, where the prince has them ass-deep in baby Ventrue. But our kind, they make the best fighters right out of the box and you don't have to deal with Gangrel noble-loner bullshit to produce them. And Nossies, well, no one cares how many Nosferatu you make; they don't play politics where the lights shine, so the Elysium crowd can pretend they ain't real."

The Prince of Buffalo snorted in amusement. "Beautiful. And so true!"

Bell grinned back at him. "Ain't it? We're fighting for our lives here, but the Ventrue and Tremere still have to piss on each others' shoes every chance they get, and all the Toreador want to do is critique the color of the stream."

Lladislas abruptly sobered. "Pathetic, isn't it?"

Bell nodded. "Pathetic indeed." He looked at his watch. "Damn. Getting early. Got a lot of work to do before the shit hits the fan. You have a ride?"

Lladislas nodded as the sleek black limo which had been discreetly pacing them rolled up to the curb. "Always. Rank still hath its privileges."

The car stopped and the driver, a heavyset man with a thick, bristling mustache, came around to curbside to open the door. Lladislas waved him off. He opened the door himself, gestured Bell inside, and climbed in after. With a minimum of fuss, the car rolled off toward Lladislas's favorite haven. In the east, the sky promised the first hints of dawn. To the west, there were clouds and a hint of thunder.

Tuesday, 10 August 1999, 12:22 AM
Interstate 270
Near Garrett Park, Maryland

MacEllen was not the sort of vampire who admitted to having any friends. That worked both ways, as not many vampires would have admitted to liking MacEllen. The ductus was feared, yes, and even grudgingly respected for his ability to win more fights than he lost, but even among the antisocial Cainites of the Sabbat he was regarded as a serious pain in the ass.

MacEllen did, however, have a real and serious affection for one member of his current pack, a Brujah *antitribu* named Tolliver. Tolliver was about five and a half feet tall and nearly that wide, and was built like a concrete sea wall. He didn't speak much, but when he did he got to the point as quickly as possible: Fully half his conversation was devoted to telling other pack members who were yammering to shut the hell up. In a fight, he was just as direct, dealing with whatever came at him with a combination of equanimity and brutality.

The latter was why MacEllen liked him so much, truth be told. MacEllen's temper was, to put it mildly, explosive, and he lost it on a regular basis. Indeed, "lack of self-discipline" was the reason given to him when he was passed over for admittance to the councils of *Les Amies Noir*; he was told that he simply couldn't be relied upon to keep his calm at moments when control was necessary.

He'd responded by doing his level best to wreck his sire's study, and it was something of a miracle that he hadn't been terminated on the spot. Still, MacEllen's notorious temper haunted him and all his doings, and it especially tainted his dealings with other vampires who knew enough to take advantage of it.

Tolliver, too, had the sort of temper that got talked about in whispers by those who didn't want their arms ripped off and then snapped in half. This was the common element that brought the two vampires, the blustering Lasombra and the sullen Brujah *antitribu*, together as friends. On this level they understood one another in a way that even their packmates never could quite grasp. Each had talked—or held—the other down from ruinous frenzy; each had seen the other go berserk in battle, and viscerally understood what the other was feeling.

And that was why MacEllen had decided to abandon Tolliver at a rest stop just north of Washington.

On one level, MacEllen conceded as he steered the pack's van along at what he considered a sedate pace, it was idiotic to weaken his force like this on the eve of battle. After all, the fighting was likely to be bloody and desperate, and Tolliver was the best that he had. On the other hand, if the gig was a trap—and MacEllen was damn sure it was—he didn't want Tolliver going down with him. It was cutting his own throat, he knew, but something told him he had to do it.

So, for the sake of his friend, MacEllen had spent the last night plotting ways to cold-cock the son of a bitch once he found a convenient place to leave him. He thought he had something good worked out, but the damn thing had better work or he'd have one pissed-off Tolliver coming after his ass, and God alone knew which way the rest of the pack would jump if that happened.

A sign on the right announced gas, food, restrooms and hopefully someone to eat two miles ahead. MacEllen bit his lip hard enough to draw blood, then announced that he was going to be pulling over for gas. There was the expected chorus of groans and cheers from the back; MacEllen didn't bother warning them not to be sloppy if they fed. It was pointless to do so.

"You've still got half a tank." Tolliver peered in from his position riding shotgun, a quizzical look on his face. His weapon of choice, a military-style automatic shotgun, was cradled between his knees. "Why are we pulling in now?"

MacEllen grunted in response and dropped the van over two lanes, nearly causing an accident in the process. "It's a hell of a long way to the next one. If something goes bugshit, I'd rather have a full tank available for making a run with." It was feeble, MacEllen knew, but rather than argue, Tolliver just made a noise that conveyed both disbelief and resignation, and looked out the window.

At this hour of the night, the rest stop was thankfully nearly deserted. A few cars were scattered in the lot, while eighteen-wheelers snored noisily further out. A lone attendant sat, bored, in the booth at the center of the gas station, while the lights in the nearby office were out. With expert skill, the ductus wheeled the van in and coasted to a stop. "Right, everyone out. Stretch your legs and don't make too much of a mess." Doors slammed opened and vampires poured out, loping across the tarmac and fanning out in the search for prey. MacEllen got out himself and watched them go with a surprising jolt of satisfaction.

Walking around to the other side of the van, he was pleased to see that Tolliver had not gone. Instead, the Brujah was squatting on his haunches outside the van, fingers laced behind his head.

"So what's this all about really? Just wanted them out for a minute?" Tolliver's tone indicated that he didn't believe a word of it. Head down, MacEllen began the laborious process of filling the van's tank.

"I wanted them away so we could talk. I don't mind telling you, Victor, this whole thing stinks."

Tolliver nodded and stood. "So it does. Smells like a trap. What's your plan?"

"Figure out what the trap is. Figure out who it's supposed to close on." With a hiss and a click, the flow of gas ceased. MacEllen yanked the nozzle out and stared pointedly at the readout on the pump. "Fuck. Twenty-three dollars for a lousy half tank?"

Tolliver ignored the digression. "And then what?"

"And then I get your ass out of the line of fire." With that, MacEllen brought the nozzle up with all the strength he could muster by channeling the power of his vitae, and cracked Tolliver underneath the jaw. The impact was enough to shatter bone and lift the vampire entirely off his feet. Tolliver landed fifteen feet down the concrete, his skull hitting the ground with an audible thump that made even MacEllen wince.

Cautiously, the ductus let the hose drop and stepped over to where Tolliver lay; if the Brujah were still conscious, everything would go to hell rapidly.

A smear of blood marked the spot on the concrete where Tolliver had hit; he seemed to be out cold. MacEllen looked back over his shoulder and didn't see the rest of the pack. Perfect.

With a grunt, he hoisted the *antitribu* over his shoulder and trotted over to one of the massive dumpsters. Almost effortlessly, MacEllen heaved his friend inside. The accommodations would stink, but they'd provide protection from sunlight until Tolliver was in shape to take care of himself.

Without so much as a good-bye, MacEllen jogged back over to the van. The others would have questions, of course, but he'd tell them that Tolliver was on special assignment or something. They'd bitch and moan and half-disbelieve, but they wouldn't argue. Adele could take over Tolliver's duties, and it would all work out. Somehow, it would all work out.

Tuesday, 10 August 1999, 10:14 PM
Guaranty Building
Buffalo, New York

"I can't do this, Lladislas. There is no way, no way in hell I can do this."

The speaker had one of the all-time great cauliflower noses, and that was his best feature. His skin was the color of a wet paper bag, except for the warty protrusions on his bald pate. Those were an impossible shade of green. His eyes were piggish and small, tucked into deep sockets and hidden by wrinkled skin. On his chin was a scraggly tuft of something that might once have been a beard, but now just served to hide a scabby wound that never quite seemed to heal. He wore a wide-lapelled blue coat over the ruin of what had been a perfectly good set of overalls and work shirt. Only his boots, knee-high and polished black, looked new. His name was Tomasz; he was the Nosferatu representative on Lladislas's primogen council; and he was profoundly displeased.

"I cannot, absolutely cannot go along with this, this *travesty* of a plan. I will not offer up my clan for the slaughter."

"For the last time, Tomasz, not your clan!" The prince slammed a blocky fist down on the table. Fine cracks spiderwebbed across the wood. "You and your childer and their miserable childer will get away scot free if you follow my instruction. If you don't, then so help me, I will leave you and yours here to die, and send a bunch of daisies to be laid on the grave of the Unknown Nosferatu every year. Damnation!" He picked up a half-full goblet and flung it against the wall; the blood the cup had contained made a jagged stain where it hit. Ghouls scurried in to clean the mess up, but Lladislas snarled at them and they vanished.

Tomasz picked up his own goblet, which was still full, and chugged noisily from it. "Temper, temper, Lladislas. Beating up the furniture won't impress me, won't impress me at all. Now unless you can give me something, anything, to convince me that this idiotic plan will work, I'm leaving and making my own arrangements."

"And just what the hell is that supposed to mean?"

The Brujah prince leaned over the table, his body quivering with barely repressed fury. Tomasz got a close-up view of the bigger man's fingers actually digging into the wood of the table, and decided that a conciliatory tack was in order.

"IIt just means that…I'm not convinced, not convinced at all that this plan is going to work, and was hoping you'd convince me."

Lladislas drew his lips back in a grin that showed entirely too many teeth. "I told you. It's very simple, and before you start complaining, it's not mine, so bitching to me won't get you anywhere. We are going to have to evacuate the city. No ifs, no ands, and no buts. I'm sure you've read the reports from Atlanta. As a matter of fact, I'm sure you have better sources than I do. You always do. And, having read those reports, what do you think our chances are against what's coming?"

Tomasz pursed his lips. "Somewhere between none and none."

"Exactly. And like you, I have no intention of getting slaughtered. I also don't intend to let the Sabbat profit from my city. I want this place to be a nail in their tire, a thorn in their side. I want them to waste so much time on Buffalo for so little gain that they burst blood vessels thinking about how badly they've been had. Does that idea appeal to you?"

"Of course it does. But I don't see how what you have in mind is going to do that."

"Bell's idea, actually, but I think it's brilliant. The brief version is this: We take your youngest neonate—what's her name, Ashleigh?"

"Phoebe Ashleigh, yes. What does she have to do with any of this?"

"She gets to live out many an elder's fantasy: near-unlimited right of creation."

"But that's absurd! She's barely survived any number of… I mean, why are you…" A sudden gleam of understanding slid into the Nosferatu's eyes. "Aha. Very clever."

"As I said, credit Bell. Ashleigh is just the most convenient candidate."

Tomasz shrugged. "What do you want to do with Phoebe? Just turn her loose? That strikes me as a poor, poor idea."

"Already thought of. We tell her to go to the clubs and pick out a half dozen—no, a dozen pretty boys and girls of the sort that she used to be. She gets to haul them back to a safe house I'll provide. She Embraces each and every one, and then a mysterious, shadowy figure—I had you in mind for this, actually, but I'll take it myself if you don't want to do it—can walk in and tell the babies that their only hope for being returned to human is to fight off the invasion of the monsters, and so on and so forth." He held up a hand to forestall the inevitable explosion. "What are you going to do, tell them the truth? Half will run away and the others will join the Sabbat. If we don't lie to them, they've got no incentive to fight for us, and every reason not to. Also, if we hold out the carrot of turning them back, we can also sucker them into abiding by the Masquerade. And so they're ready, willing and eager to fight."

"I was going to say," Tomasz interjected with a hint of acid, "that I wasn't sure they'd be in combat shape, if the assault is coming as soon as you say it is."

Lladislas's expression went ever-so-slightly cold. "Honestly, Tomasz, it doesn't matter if they are or not. They're not supposed to win this fight." More gently, he said, "They're not even supposed to survive."

"What if they do?" Lladislas just looked at Tomasz, and the latter looked away. "Ah. I see."

"There's no other way. All we need these Kindred for is to provide a speed bump. To make the Sabbat stop and look around and take a long time settling in here before moving on to the next city, so we buy time for our defenses. I will level with you, Tomasz. I don't particularly like you. Left to my own, I couldn't care less if you or Ashleigh fell down a sewer grate and got eaten by one of your mutant alligators. But I am prince. I have a duty, one that I take seriously. That duty is to take responsibility for this city and the Kindred in it, and for the moment, you are part of that responsibility. Once we abandon this place, that ends, at least temporarily. You'll be free to spit in my beer, puke on my shoes and tell the rest of the world about all the dirty deeds I've done. But for the moment, I am prince. This is what we're doing, because the prince says so, and because it's the only chance we have of getting the city back. Ever."

Tomasz looked up. "It stinks, you know that. It stinks to high heaven, and there are going to be a lot of pieces to pick up, even if it works."

"We've dealt with mass disappearances before, or don't you remember '96?"

"Eighteen or nineteen?"

"Does it matter?"

"Not really. But there will be an accounting for this."

Lladislas made a dismissive gesture. "Tomasz, we are Kindred. There is an accounting for everything we do, and an accounting for that accounting, and on into the centuries. You know that as well as I do. So make your mark in your ledger, and let Ashleigh make hers, and let the reckoning come when it may. And in the meantime, do what I tell you to or you won't have the time to make that mark." The Prince of Buffalo closed his eyes for a moment. "Mind you, even if you refuse, the whole thing goes forward. I've got Baughman lined up to do it as well; he's even agreed to stay behind and oversee the initial phase of things with Haraszty. I can do this without you. I'd rather do it with you. It will make the whole thing look better from the outside, and that would make my job easier. And right now, I really don't need anything that makes my job harder. Do we have an understanding, Tomasz?"

"An understanding, yes. A perfect one. If you will excuse me?" The Nosferatu rose to his feet and made for the door. As he reached it, he paused and looked back over his shoulder. "I'll deliver Phoebe to you in an hour. She'll have at least enough understanding of what's going on to be helpful, though I suspect she won't deal well with the shock of having all her childer slaughtered. You might have to put her down, too. For the good of the plan, of course." Tomasz strode out, his back as straight as he could make it. One of the waiting ghouls shut the door behind him, and Lladislas found himself alone in the room, with only the faint smell of spilled blood in the air to distract him.

He sat there for a solid quarter of an hour, until the ghoul at the door timidly knocked and stuck his head into the room. "Your Majesty? You said to tell you when Mr. Baughman arrived and, uhh, he's…" Lladislas turned around without bothering to disguise his expression, and the ghoul abruptly paled and stammered.

"Send him in," was all the prince said, and the ghoul bolted. A few minutes later, he returned leading a short, wiry Kindred in jeans and a shirt in a revolting shade of orange. Lladislas composed himself as the ghoul scurried out. "Mr. Baughman. Glad you could make it. I have a little job for you, one I'm hoping you'll find worthwhile. Mind you, if you're not interested, I understand; I've already spoken to Tomasz about handling part of it and he can certainly take care of the whole thing. But if you want in, there's a place for you. Frankly, this thing needs one of us Brujah to hold its hand, if you know what I mean."

Baughman looked back at the door, which had just clicked shut behind him. The ghoul was nowhere to be found. It was just him and the prince. The same prince, a little voice in his head noted, he'd spent fifteen years agitating resistance against. Of course, he'd come back to the fold and more or less settled in to the Camarilla routine, but this situation was looking awfully like a setup….

"Of course, Your Majesty," he said as he settled into a chair. "What can I do for you?"

It would have been a surprise to several of Buffalo's Kindred to discover that the haven of Tomasz the Nosferatu was not ankle-deep in sludgy water. It also was profoundly lacking in the smell of rotting garbage, any sort of sewage, or even the odd piece of salvaged, broken-down furniture. Tomasz may have had a face like week-old roadkill, but he liked his creature comforts, and his main haven reflected this.

The haven was in a storm drain, true, but it was a side chamber raised a foot off the tunnel that led to it. Arrangements of glowing fungi marked the corridor; some labeled traps that Tomasz had painstakingly set up over the years while others marked safe routes. Only he, and a few of his childer, knew which species of growth meant which. Farther out in the darkness, the watchful eyes of rat sentries gleamed in the faint light. No one, mortal, Kindred or other, could approach Tomasz's haven without Tomasz's learning of it.

Response time was something that was near and dear to the Nosferatu's unbeating heart, and he tried to make sure he always had enough of it. At the moment, however, he didn't have any, and he didn't like that one bit. And that was why he found himself entertaining company that even he found dubious in his haven.

It wasn't that Dustin was particularly ugly. By Nosferatu standards he was almost handsome, and could nearly pass for normal in bad light. Currently he was sitting on one of Tomasz's elaborately carved handcrafted chairs (brought over at great expense and difficulty from Krakow), being a perfect guest and paying rapt attention to everything his host said.

No, the reason Dustin had a somewhat shaky reputation among even his clanmates was that he liked to play with fire, and that was the sort of thing that made even other Nosferatu worry.

"I don't like this, don't like this at all." Tomasz paced up and down on a Persian carpet that was five decades old and showed not a thread out of place. Behind him, light sparkled on a collection of Viennese silver that had been lovingly acquired over a hundred years. "There is something amiss. Dustin, I need you."

The younger Nosferatu shifted uncomfortably in his seat. "Why me? Where's Phoebe?"

Tomasz grimaced. "She is on…other business. But Dustin, this is something more along your specialty anyway."

Dustin grinned, showing teeth going every which way. "Meaning you want someone killed, and sweet lil' ol' Phoebe ain't up to the dirty deed?"

Tomasz shook his misshapen head. "No, not exactly. I need you to watch for me. To kill if you have to, but mostly to watch."

"I don't get it." Dustin stood and took great care to dust off the chair, his movements just this side of exaggeration. "So you need someone to watch. Send your rats and leave me out of it."

Tomasz waggled a cautionary finger. "No, rats will not do for this. I need sharp eyes, and a good mind behind them. If you had studied more, you'd know rats are limited in some ways, some very important ways."

Dustin failed to disguise a look that conveyed a deep sense of "whatever," and took a step toward the exit tunnel. "That's nice. What now?"

"What happens now is that you stay when Phoebe and I go, and you keep yourself alive so you can tell me what really happens. I do not trust this."

"I take it refusing is not an option?"

"It is always an option, but part of that option is accepting the consequences of refusing."

"Ah." Dustin opened his mouth and closed it again. "Crud. Do I at least get to fight back if they spot me?"

Tomasz spread his hands in an expansive gesture. "Of course. You are of no use to any of us dead, so do what you must. Just remember what you are there for, though. You have a reputation for…too much enthusiasm. It will not serve you in this."

The younger Nosferatu chuckled. "Oh, don't worry. I like my skin, and I pack a few surprises these days. I'll make it out in one piece."

"You had better, Dustin. I am relying on you. And I think you will find the rewards for this task to be suitable."

"Oh really. Well then, we'll have to discuss those when I catch up with you. Have the rats tell me where the meet point is. I have some prep work to do."

With that, he loped off into the darkness. Tomasz muttered something that might have been a curse or a farewell, then set about packing. In the darkness outside his home, rats chittered to each other, softly.

Tuesday, 10 August 1999, 11:02 PM
Underneath Louisiana and Seneca Streets
Buffalo, New York

Unlike Tomasz's haven, Dustin's was quite literally a hole in the ground. More to the point, it was more a workroom than anything else. Dustin was a tinkerer, and he eschewed the "normal" Nosferatu hobbies of breeding monstrous ghouls, cultivating fungi and otherwise playing to stereotype in favor of building devices that left his clanmates leery of his company. He'd been a mechanic in life, and the bug to take things apart only to put them back together better was one that hadn't left him when he'd been Embraced. He'd just turned that interest to things that were more pertinent to his current condition.

It was one of those projects that concerned him now. It lay mostly disassembled on a workbench as Dustin took heated shears and cut lengths of plastic strapping. Whistling something that might have been an Offspring tune before he mangled it, he slid buckles onto the straps, folded over the plastic weave and used the flat of the still-hot scissors to melt a seal into place. On the workbench, a small gas flame jetted merrily into the air; a hose led from the burner to an ominously large tank. Most Kindred would have been climbing the walls to get away from such an arrangement, but Dustin was self-confessedly weird. On an intellectual level, he knew precisely the sort of damage open flame, especially the stuff flaring forth on his workbench, could do to him. He'd spent agonizing weeks regrowing the flesh on his hands after a couple of particularly nasty accidents, and he could feel the ravening, insane fear of flame that still lurked inside him every time he turned the gas jet on.

But that was nothing compared to the rush he got from seeing fire, from watching it dance and flicker and flare. In his rare philosophical moments, Dustin reflected that, on some gut level, he knew how a moth felt around the light.

There was a practical benefit to the whole obsession, too, however: Even other Kindred regarded Dustin as more cracked than an eggcup in an earthquake, and tended to give him a wide berth. That suited Dustin just fine, as he really had little interest in politics and less in being patronized by the pathetic quintet of Kindred who hung on to Prince Lladislas's coattails. Dustin liked being in the dark, he liked being left alone with his toys, and he liked making Tomasz's too-thin blood boil on a regular basis. Beyond that, everything in existence was gravy.

With a grunt, Dustin looped the straps through eyelets on the back of a large metal tank, then held the scissors in the flame for a minute to re-heat them before sealing the straps on. "Hope this damn thing works," he said to himself, and began strapping the aluminum tank onto his back.

Wednesday, 11 August 1999, 2:16 AM
Interstate 270
Near Garrett Park, Maryland

Tolliver had lived out of a dumpster for over twenty-four hours, and he frankly hated it. His jaw was still in three pieces where MacEllen, the bastard, had broken it. The back of his head ached, though at least he'd been able to mend the cracks in his skull and stop the bleeding. And to top it all off, he smelled like rotting fast food, old rainwater and vomit. All in all, it sucked, but he'd been damn lucky the dumpster wasn't emptied during the day.

As inhospitable as the surroundings were, he'd needed the time to heal, and he figured he'd hang here until suitable transportation came along. In the meantime, there was at least enough food and shelter, and he could be a patient sort of vampire when necessary.

Minutes ticked by. He hunkered down on top of the dumpster and watched for a suitable ride to arrive. Minivans came and went, as did broken-down Fords, dinged-up Toyotas and almost everything else imaginable. Finally, a perfect specimen rolled in.

The car was a black convertible, one of those squat little Beemers that had been all the rage a year or so back. The top was down so Tolliver could see the driver, a woman traveling by herself. She seemed utterly oblivious to anything except herself and her car, which meant that he'd be able to get close without a problem.

Plus, from what he could tell, she was a looker.

Soundlessly, he sprang down from his perch and

moved towards the gas pumps. Other cars whizzed in and out, but Tolliver ignored them. He'd be out of here so fast it didn't matter what anyone saw of him.

The driver was just getting back in when he reached the convertible. Her back was to him. It was perfect.

"Miss?" he said as he prepared to make a grab for the keys. "Could I beg some change from you?"

Lucita turned around, her eyes fixing on Tolliver's. "I don't think so. Get in."

"Oh, shit," he said weakly, and climbed into the passenger seat. His brain screamed at him to flee, but he couldn't. Lucita's will animated his limbs and forced him to sit meekly. Tears formed at the corners of his eyes as he tried to resist, but it was useless.

Lucita took the driver's seat, slammed the door and started the car. Beside her, Tolliver literally shook with hatred and the effort of resistance, but made no other movement. With a sniff of disdain, Lucita hit the accelerator and the car eased out toward the exit ramp and the highway.

There was silence in the car for a few minutes, then Lucita said casually, "What are you doing here?" Tolliver sat, silent. "You have another tenth of a mile in which to answer," she said mildly. "Otherwise, I'll be annoyed." Still, Tolliver said nothing. Unlamented, a highway marker whizzed by. "Fine. If you insist. Open the door."

Slowly, inexorably, Tolliver's hand reached the handle and pulled it. The door swung open for a second, then swung back toward closing. Helplessly, Tolliver struggled to hold it open. His eyes met Lucita's as he glared hatred at her, and too late he realized the mistake.

"Keep the door open. Take your right foot, and place it against the surface of the road. Hold it there no matter what. You may lift it when you decide that you're willing to talk to me."

Relentlessly, Tolliver watched his right leg swing out and his foot drop toward the highway. He was a brave man, and he had no fear of pain, but watching what was slowly, inevitably happening to him came near to breaking his nerve.

Then his foot started scraping asphalt at ninety miles per hour, and there was no more time for fear.

There was, however, enough time to scream.

Wednesday, 11 August 1999, 2:20 AM
The Sanctuary Club
Buffalo, New York

Phoebe hated the music they played at the clubs these days. It had no elegance, no style—just pounding beats that reminded her of men at hard labor, chained at the ankle and turning big rocks into small ones. By extension, then, she hated the beautiful people who came out every night to dance to that piledriver beat. They still had their beauty, the beauty that had been taken away from Phoebe because she'd laughed at the wrong man one night. They could still look in the mirror and not weep for what might have been, for the admiring glances lost and the hearts that Phoebe would never get a chance to break.

Small wonder, then, that she enjoyed hunting on the club scene almost to exclusion, and that she was a bit more brutal in feeding than many. But tonight, that hatred served everyone's purposes—Phoebe's, Lladislas's and Theo Bell's.

"Phoebe," the prince had said, all smiles and gentility, "I need a favor of you." Behind him had stood the giant of an archon, saying nothing and almost frowning, clearly there to play bad cop if Lladislas's attempts at persuasion went awry. Bell scared her the way big cats used to scare her, all muscle and grace that could uncoil with deadly speed. With an effort, she turned her attention back to what Lladislas was saying.

"So you see, there's absolutely no time to waste. I—*we* need you to start on this immediately."

"So let me see if I have this straight," she drawled. "I'm supposed to go out on the town and bring a half-dozen—"

"Ten," said Bell.

"—ten nice young men home and turn them into…into what I am, and then walk out the door and never see them again?"

"Exactly." Lladislas nodded with the urgency of a man who wants to get the damn meeting over with so he can get to either the golf course or the men's room. "Your pick. Don't worry about cover-up for the disappearance; I've got Haraszty already on it. We have a safe site in Lancaster picked out for the Embraces so you don't have to worry about that. The only pressure is time, which we have precious little of."

Phoebe crossed her hands in her lap demurely. "I'm certainly open to discussing the matter, sugar, but there's a little voice in my head askin' what I get out of this arrangement."

"The gratitude of some very important people," rumbled Bell. "Which is worth a lot more than you might think."

The Nosferatu smiled winningly. "Of course, but I was wondering if I could have a small token of more concrete appreciation?"

Bell shot Lladislas a glance, who returned it with a look approaching resignation. He sighed. "What do you want?"

"If I'm never gonna see these childer again, I want one I can keep. When this, whatever this is, is all over, I want to make one I don't have to leave."

Without even looking at Bell, Lladislas said, "Done. There's a car waiting for you downstairs. Tell Trietsch where you want to go, and he'll handle all of the transportation. Dinner's waiting for you out in Lancaster. I'll see you tomorrow night to hear your estimation of how it went."

"I'm going to need to go home and get ready. You can't expect me to go out looking like this, can you?"

"Fine. Whatever." Bell clearly sounded annoyed. "Tell the driver where you'll meet him. Just don't take too long."

And just like that, they'd dismissed her. The fact that Lladislas had given in so easily on her demand made her think she should have asked for more. Either that, or the prince had no intention of honoring his boon, but she tried to put that worrisome possibility out of her head. So here she was walking into Ash's (she supposed the title was a play on words; she despised that sort of thing), the latest in a long line of nightclubs to spring up, draw the crowds for a season, and then wither away. She had to be careful now; she'd already hit five other sites for recruits (she just couldn't call them anything but that) and didn't think she'd be recognized here, but you never could tell. Some nights the crowd along the rack was restless, and flowed from club to club like water. If someone had seen her at Gabriel's Gate, and then at Zoobar, and had seen her leave each club with someone…

She panicked briefly, and considered changing the face she wore to a new one—say, that of the McClemens girl she'd met on that trip to Savannah—but it was too late. She was already inside, and if she went into the bathroom to change faces without changing outfits, it might have been noticed, and, oh, damnation and hellfire. *Too late now, girl*, she told herself. *But after this one, I am definitely going home for a change of outfit and a change of face.* Squaring her shoulders and adding a little bit of sway to her walk, she plunged into the crowd.

It didn't take too long to find a likely recruit. He

was tall and thin, with hands that constantly fluttered as he talked, and a thin mustache. His hair was close-cropped, and he wore a red vest over a white shirt and gray slacks. Phoebe thought he looked like a waiter at an Italian restaurant, to be honest, and wouldn't have given him a second thought if he hadn't attached himself to her as she walked on by.

Not that she could blame him, Phoebe noted. She'd outdone herself tonight, giving herself perfect alabaster skin, an aggressively cut blonde bob, and a face with the sort of high cheekbones, piercing blue eyes and elfin features that would drive certain unsavory sorts of men to certain unsavory thoughts. The black outfit was perhaps a touch too severe, but it hadn't affected her success rate any. And now she had her touch on a string, and was slowly but surely leading him away from his friends and off into the night. At the moment, he was busy telling her all about himself, no doubts in hopes of exciting her admiration and desire. She found the whole thing laughable, of course—having seen five-century-old vampires crooning lullabies to tens of thousands of rats, she didn't find marketing executives for sports bars too terribly impressive.

Phoebe let him natter on as she drifted toward the door. When he paused for breath, she interjected, "Isaiah, sugar, that is absolutely fascinating, but I am afraid I cannot hear half of what you are saying in this," she made a gesture that took in the whole club, from the enclosed DJ booth upstairs to the crowded dance floor to the smoky haze of tables screening the bar at the back, "this dreadfully noisy place. But I'd so hate to end the evening so early. Would you mind…?" She let the statement trail off, and hooked a finger in her mouth coyly. "No, no, I couldn't ask that of you. It would be much too forward. You'd think terribly of me, I'm sure."

"Oh, no, no, no. Not at all. Ask anything." Isaiah leaned forward with almost feverish eagerness. Phoebe had noticed that when she'd made her little shrug, the boy had most certainly *not* been making eye contact. That, and the slight but noticeable pale band on his finger where a wedding band ought to have been made doing this a bit easier.

"I was thinking, mind you, that we don't have to end the evening now. If, of course, you ain't tired of my company?"

Isaiah licked his lips nervously. "Umm, sure. I mean, where would you like to go? I'd offer my place, but it's a terrible mess at the moment, I'm an awful housekeeper, I have to admit...."

...and your wife probably won't take too kindly to you bringing some blond thing home, sugar, she mentally finished the sentence. "Oh that's quite all right. I was thinking, perhaps, my place?"

Isaiah nodded. "Of course. And you have no need to worry, I don't think I could ever get tired of your company."

Across the street, Trietsch was waiting, silent and efficient, in the Town Car Lladislas had loaned Phoebe for the evening's work. The ghoul got out of the car and opened the door. "Good evening, Miss Phoebe." He glanced at Isaiah. "Sir.

"Shall I take you home, ma'am?"

"Why, that would be just lovely," Phoebe said. "Absolutely lovely."

Upon reflection, Lucita conceded that she probably could have simply forced the answers to her questions from Tolliver by the power of her mind, instead of resorting to torturing him, but Tolliver was the sort of vampire who invited that sort of thing. He'd been casually brutal and tiresomely vicious, and she'd lost patience with him upon their first meeting, years ago. Tormenting him was like tormenting a slug or a toad. One had no sensation that one was playing with anything even remotely human.

Oh, he'd broken after a couple of miles, babbling everything he knew. He'd mentioned whom he'd been traveling with, where they were going, whom they'd gotten their marching orders from and more. Apparently MacEllen and the rest had a haven set up for them thirty miles outside of Buffalo, a rendezvous point where Einar's second pack would meet up with them. Then they would trash the city, which apparently was only lightly defended. That was news to Lucita. She had quizzed Tolliver about other troop movements and so on, but the vampire had sworn he knew nothing. As he'd been worn down past the ankle by this point, Lucita tended towards believing him.

All in all, bumping into Tolliver at the rest area like that was quite the stroke of luck. Lucita hated to depend solely on intelligence supplied by the Nosferatu, so she'd been heading into D.C. to ferret out some information about her targets on her own.

After all, if she were going after Sabbat, it was going to be hard to avoid Sabbat territory. And then Tolliver had so kindly presented himself to her.

When he had spilled everything he was privy to, she'd slowed the car and shoved him out into the weeds along the shoulder. The sun would be up in a few hours and he'd fry. Or not. It didn't really matter anymore.

Lucita's car was pointed north as she pressed on into the night.

Tolliver hadn't moved much when Talley found him two hours later. A Sabbat lookout—they were stationed extensively along the northern arc of the Beltway—had sworn up and down that he'd spotted Lucita zipping past in a convertible, so Talley, after making sure the three archbishops were in secure locations, had gone to investigate.

After a bit of driving around, Talley came upon what a mortal would mistake for the results of roadkill dragged along beneath a car. The keen nose of the Hound, however, recognized Cainite vitae, even when it was spread in a bloody streak along a couple of miles of highway. Not too far beyond the end of the streak, Talley found Tolliver. The rotund and rather mangled fellow still survived, more or less.

Talley sliced his hand with the jagged edge of a muffler that lay discarded nearby. A few drops of blood revived Tolliver enough to mumble in answer to Talley's questions about Lucita. "Buffalo...and MacEllen's crew," he moaned during brief episodes of near-lucidity. "She wanted to know.... Buffalo...MacEllen's crew."

Talley wasted only a few seconds phoning for

someone to pick up the poor bloody bastard he'd found. The Hound himself was headed north. He knew an opportunity when he saw one. Lucita was going to Buffalo, for whatever reason. This was his chance, without the damnable, arrogant, impossible archbishops underfoot, to let her know that she needn't bother going after any of them; that he, the Hound, would not allow it. It was his chance, in accordance with Monçada's wishes, to warn her off.

It was *her* chance as well. If she didn't take advantage of it, Talley knew, he might very well have to kill her.

The house was a new one, in a new housing development that was up against the fringe of wetlands by some creek or other. The house was vaguely colonial in an impressionistic sort of way, painted white with blue trim. The porch light was on, giving the whole thing a weirdly cheery look. The hedges were neatly trimmed and the lawn was putting-green short. It was utterly suburban, if a bit masculine for a creature as frail and feminine as Phoebe supposedly was. Needless to say, Isaiah took to the place immediately.

Trietsch opened the door to the Lincoln and then vanished in the way good servants seem to have, leaving Phoebe and her victim alone on the walk. He'd tried to get frisky a few times on the way over, but Phoebe had playfully fended him off and pointed to the driver. "Soon," she'd whispered to him. "We'll be home soon."

And now they were "home"—someone's home, at least, and it would all be over soon indeed. She led him to the door and fumbled in her purse for the keys; he took the opportunity to try to steal a kiss. Laughingly, she fended him off and said again, "Soon."

The door opened onto blackness. Phoebe stepped inside and reached to the left, where she knew the light switch was. Isaiah followed her in, shutting the door behind him. The floor of the hallways was hardwood, and the overhead light gleamed off it. Slightly to the left, a carpeted staircase rose to the second floor, while past it the elegantly decorated living room stood mostly in shadow. Down the front hall was the breakfast nook, and past it a curtain hiding a patio door. The walls were painted eggshell white, and a landscape by someone who had taken at least a few classes hung on the wall to the right. Phoebe thought it was the blandest, dullest, most jejune thing she'd ever seen.

"Very nice," said Isaiah. "Did you decorate it yourself?"

"Why, no," Phoebe said, overcoming the urge to grit her teeth. "I had some people do it for me. The upstairs is much nicer, though. May I show you?"

"Of course," he replied. "After you?" He made a gesture that might have been considered suave by a girl with a few drinks in her. Phoebe just thought it crass.

"No, no, after you. I want you to be surprised when you get to the top of the stairs."

"If you insist." Isaiah started up the staircase without bothering to look for a light, his mind clearly on what he thought was waiting for him. Phoebe, who had no need of light, followed. As she watched him stump up the staircase, she found herself suddenly very weary of him, of his poses and transparent expectations, of his thinly veiled contempt for her and his elevated sense of his own attractiveness and prowess. It was going to be, quite frankly, a relief to kill him.

Isaiah reached the landing at the top of the stairs, his footfalls muffled by the carpet. Phoebe joined him seconds later. "Interesting," he said, "but a bit dim. So what did you want to show me?"

"That door, sugar," she said. "Leads to the bedroom, which I did decorate myself."

"Really?"

"Why yes," she said with a mischievous giggle. *God almighty*, she thought, *I am doing this man's wife a favor.*

"Step right through here, sugar." She opened the door and held it for him. He stepped past her, and she followed, shutting the door as she did. "Close your eyes. I want this to be a surprise when I turn on the light."

Obediently, he did so, going so far as to cover his eyes with his hands. Phoebe slid out of her jacket, undid her blouse and dropped her disguise, smiling all the while. She walked over to him, the only light in the room dim moonlight through the venetian blinds. Isaiah still had his eyes closed obediently, and his breathing had acquired a raspy edge. "Almost ready?" he said with a sort of pathetic hopefulness.

"Almost," she said, and placed her hands on his shoulders. "Now."

Isaiah opened his eyes and screamed. Phoebe just smiled. "How do you like me by moonlight, sugar?" she said, and forced him into a kiss. He struggled, but her hands on his shoulders drew him irresistibly forward. "How do you like me now?"

Isaiah screamed again, once, before she finished with him and dragged him down to the basement with the others. Two of them were starting to stir, but that was Tomasz's problem, not hers. She was just in human resources.

"Six down, four to go," she said to the air, and locked the front door behind her as she went out. Trietsch sat, waiting, at curbside. He opened the car door for her with impeccable courtesy, and then seated himself behind the wheel.

"You look lovely tonight, Miss Phoebe," he said as the Lincoln pulled away from the curb.

"Why thank you, sugar," she said, genuinely pleased. "But then again, I always do, at least in the right light. I always do."

It was damned dark in the basement, which was just the way Tomasz liked it. From his position at the top of the stairs, he could see that there were bodies on the floor. Some were moving and some were not; it was the former that concerned him. The latter had been tossed in by a few of Lladislas's bullyboy goons for the new childer to feed upon, otherwise they would have torn each other apart, rendering the whole exercise pointless. Briefly he wondered whom the victims had been. Homeless men and women, perhaps, or people whom Lladislas had wanted out of the way for some reason or other. It didn't much matter in the grand scheme of things, not anymore.

Tomasz had seen Phoebe when she'd returned from her last hunt. She'd looked weary, and there was no way she could carry on any longer. He was glad that she was done; less pleased that his part in this little drama was beginning. Still, *alea jacta est*, as Father Andreas would have said once upon a time, in the Old Country.

Tomasz looked down into the gloom, still cloaked in the shadows of the mind he could call to himself. He was used to the dark, used to spotting small details in it, and could see the tableau beneath him clearly. There were ten figures moving about, some more active than others. Two sat huddled in corners, rocking back and forth as if terrified. Others sucked quietly at the corpses on the floor, nursing like monstrous infants at a corpse-mother's breast. One pounded on a wall endlessly, senselessly, mindlessly. Another merely staggered about on his hands and knees, crying softly and promising anyone who might be listening that he would never do anything bad again. In the minuscule light available, they reminded Tomasz uncomfortably of worms, degraded and inhuman.

The sooner he got this over with, Tomasz decided, the better. So he let his mask of invisibility drop. Steeling himself in case the mob decided to rush him, he flicked the switch on the wall, and blinked furiously as the fluorescent bulbs on the basement ceiling flickered into life. At the sudden flare of light, all of the bestial things on the floor of the cellar stopped in their tracks and looked up at him. He could see fear in their eyes, and cold hatred as well. He had made no effort to disguise himself, so his full hideousness was on display. Hopefully it would be enough to frighten them into listening, or at least out of trying something foolish. The light showed the first warts beginning to blossom on the new vampires' faces, the first signs of monstrosity blossoming.

He sat on the steps and smiled as gently as he was able.

"Hello," he said. "My name is Tomasz, and I am here to help you."

They all looked up at him, sudden, terrible hope in their eyes. They believed him, Tomasz knew. They believed him because they had no choice but to believe him. Not to believe him was to embrace a truth too horrible to be borne. Not to believe was to admit that they had become monsters like Phoebe.

Or him.

He took a deep, unnecessary breath, and launched into the story that he and Lladislas had grudgingly cobbled together while Phoebe was out doing the prince's dirty work. It sounded clumsy to him, patchy and unbelievable, but he knew better already, and unlike the men in the room below, he was not desperate.

Desperate men will believe almost anything, after all.

Within a few sentences, Tomasz knew he had all ten in thrall. Part of him rambled on, but inside, he thought: *They will fight for us. They will die for us. And I cannot help but tell myself that it will be a kindness when they do.*

Dawn was not far off when Tomasz finished his tale, and promised the men that someone would return for them the next evening to help them. He told them that they were being kept in the basement to protect them from the fatal sun, and that they would slumber without dreaming. Then he had left them to sprawl among the other corpses, and locked the basement door. Two ghouls stood there with shotguns, presumably to keep the vampires within from attempting escape. He nodded to them as he passed, "I do not think you need to worry about them, no," Tomasz said. Upstairs, a bedroom had been sealed against the daylight when the house was built. Lladislas had graciously offered it to Tomasz, and sunrise was so close that he had no choice but to accept the invitation.

The room itself was comfortably furnished, with clean white sheets on a queen-sized bed and foil-wrapped windows. There was no other furniture in the room. Tomasz found himself drowsily disapproving of the decor as he locked the door behind him and lay down on the bed.

Tomorrow I gather Phoebe and my treasures, and we leave this place. And no one will ever know of this.

Thursday, 12 August 1999, 9:42 PM
Guaranty Building Parking Lot
Buffalo, New York

The Kindred of Buffalo, those few who remained, were leaving. All save Lladislas, Tomasz and Phoebe had left the night before. Bell had been on his way out of town when the first Sabbat sighting had come in. He'd seemed slightly surprised, never mind the fact that he'd been the one preaching doom and gloom since he'd arrived. He'd paused only briefly, to make sure that Lladislas would follow shortly, before leaving for Baltimore. Baughman was remaining behind, as was Dustin (though without Lladislas's consent or knowledge, in the latter instance). Ghouls were in place, leading the newly Embraced cannon fodder to strategic positions and arming them. Haraszty was on his headset, barking orders to his ghouls and pacing nervously.

Moving trucks had been leaving the city and heading southwest on I-90 all day, driven by ghouls and containing the evacuating vampires' prized possessions. Most would switch drivers at least twice before arriving at their final destinations; those currently behind the wheel had no idea where their cargo was ultimately going. Most didn't care: They were either well-paid or thoroughly conditioned not to be nosy. It made them better servants.

The few remaining vampires were escorted to chauffeured cars by heavily armed ghouls. More of the same took up places in cars that would pace the vampires' vehicles on the road out of town. Tomasz and Phoebe were headed to Syracuse, until Dustin could catch up, while Lladislas was going to Baltimore to join forces with the Camarilla elders there. The city's other Kindred of note had mostly elected to go into Ohio, at least temporarily. No doubt some would be returning east, while others would keep running.

Lladislas was about to climb into his Lincoln when Haraszty motioned him over. "Boss, we have another sighting."

"Oh?" Lladislas did not move, perhaps wisely. "How far out?"

"About twenty minutes on 90 westbound; they're better than I thought if they got that close without my people noticing. I've told the driver for the Nosferatu to cut down to US 20 and take that east instead. It's a weird route they're coming in on, but what do you expect?"

"How many?"

"Two vans so far. Probably advance scouts." Haraszty paused and looked around. "You should probably get going, sir. It's been a pleasure. I'll see you in Baltimore."

Lladislas nodded, suddenly uncomfortable. "Yes, of course. Thank you, Gustav. You know how much I value your service. Do what you need to do."

"I always do, boss. Have a good trip."

Without further comment, the Prince of Buffalo climbed into his car and slammed the door. His driver, Trietsch, waited a moment to see if his passenger was settled, and then pulled out. Three more cars, loaded with armed ghouls, pulled out after him.

The last Prince of Buffalo had officially abandoned his city.

Haraszty watched the cars go and suddenly felt very alone. He posed a few questions into the headset and got satisfactory answers. Baughman had been seen taking up his position with a few of his childer. The rest of the freshly made Brujah were in place in the downtown district, though one had insisted on positioning himself by the grain elevators. The Nosferatu had been more trouble, but the ghoul was convinced they'd fight better in the crunch. Most of them were in Delaware Park. Others were scattered throughout the city to give the appearance of a thriving defense. A few ghouls were placed strategically, both to get the baby vampires' asses in gear and to relay him accurate information.

Buffalo was as ready as it was ever going to be.

"And that ain't ready at all," said Haraszty to no one at all. The headset buzzed in response, and the moment of reflection was forgotten.

"Buffalo: 13 Miles," Adele read the sign with tangible excitement. "Beautiful."

"Shit, Mary, did you know Adele could read? I didn't know Adele could read." The van rocked with a general round of laughter while MacEllen's new second-in-command shrieked curses at her tormentor.

MacEllen glanced in the rearview at his pack. They were ready. They had their assignments—from steel factories to parks to churches. They'd even gotten a little bit of information on vampires they might be facing, the poor bastards liable to get left behind to anchor the smokescreen. That was his pack's target—the remaining vampires. Einar's was there to set up a ruckus to keep mortal authorities tied up, and to catch stragglers. Between them, they had just enough manpower to do the job right—if this was on the up and up, and not a screw job of the sort Polonia was famous for.

MacEllen was still convinced that the entire operation was a setup. However, he'd also convinced himself that even without Tolliver (and man, was he going to be pissed that he missed the fireworks), he just might beat the fix. If his team and Einar's did their jobs, they'd break the frame and come out smelling like heroes. Beyond that, he had begun speculating on what the night's work might net him. The Southeast might be overloaded with archbishops, but upstate New York was a hell of a long way from their jurisdiction. He would take Buffalo for a start.

The vans crossed into the city of Buffalo itself. Einar's peeled off, flashing its brights once as a salute. MacEllen smiled. It was too late to turn back.

The battle for Buffalo was about to begin.

Thursday, 12 August 1999, 11:15 PM
Exit N2, Interstate I-190
Buffalo, New York

"You don't want to be in that part of the city after dark, miss," was what the old man had said. He'd been friendly and polite, things that Lucita hadn't seen from a stranger in decades, and had actually seemed genuinely concerned for the welfare of a pretty young thing who was heading into a bad neighborhood. He looked about seventy-five, and was alone behind the counter of the convenience store-cum-gas station at a ridiculous hour of the night. Lucita guessed that either some local Kindred was protecting him, or he had an over-under stashed under the counter. Otherwise, there was no way he'd have survived long without getting mugged a few times and losing his sunny disposition.

Lucita had thanked him for his concern, paid for her gas, and left. Quickly, she climbed into the car and started it up. Normally she preferred a lower-profile vehicle, but something about this job told her that it would be wise to have a car that could flat-out scoot in an emergency. The engine purred to life and she pulled back onto I-90, heading north toward the center of Buffalo.

Younger Kindred often thought it was a big deal to steal stupid things just because they were vampires, but Lucita had found that it was the stupid things that most often led to trouble. Steal some gas and you piss off the station owner. Piss off the station owner and he calls the cops. The cops get called, they look for you, and all of a sudden feeding without complications becomes nigh impossible (because God knows that a cop would rather look for a gas thief than mix it up with someone likely to be packing, or interrupt a domestic disturbance). And so it went, and it was just easier to pay the twelve bucks and avoid complications. If the situation had demanded, she would have had no compunction about killing the old man and putting his blood to good use, but since the situation didn't warrant such, there was no point to causing trouble for herself. After all, normal young ladies who did normal things tended to fade from the memory of those who saw them—and Lucita didn't like to be remembered.

That was the whole logic behind the damn Masquerade, to be honest. It wasn't because there were any vampires out there who were "good guys" (though some folks spent years, decades or even centuries trying to play the role) and the Masquerade was some great and altruistic thing done for the sake of humanity. No, it made working easier. It made feeding easier. And it meant less competition and fewer hassles from kine with torches and shotguns. So few Kindred on either side of the fence understood that. It wasn't about kowtowing to the Antediluvians or keeping the world safe for poor fragile humanity.

It was about getting things done with a minimum of extra effort. There was no idealism involved. Lucita just liked avoiding unnecessary complications.

The top on the Beemer was up, but even through that and the sound of the engine Lucita could hear sirens wailing. A pair of pillars of smoke wafted upwards on the skyline ahead; no doubt the Sabbat was breaking things to distract the gendarmes while the local Kindred were rousted and put to the sword. It was all part of the basic *modus operandi*. Distract the mortal authorities, and it gave you a clear field to go Kindred hunting. The locals would have to protect both themselves and the Masquerade, and sooner or later their resources would stretch too thin. One or the other would tear, and then the city's Kindred hierarchy would get eaten alive.

"Simple, but effective," Lucita said to the night. On the passenger seat, the dossier on tonight's target sat open. A head shot proved that he was unattractive by any standards but a Nosferatu's or a mother's, with a piggish, heavy face and a scowl that was almost petulant. He had thick black brows and thick black hair and a thick, bullish neck. The picture had apparently been taken at a point when the subject was in the midst of some sort of shouting fit, because his mouth was open and his lips were flecked with spittle.

The name at the bottom of the picture was Roger MacEllen.

Hell, Baughman decided, was built entirely out of abandoned steel plants. And the one at the very heart of the whole thing was clearly modeled after the monstrosity he was currently wriggling through. Bethlehem had abandoned the place years ago, but it was simply too big to tear down. They'd left it sitting there, an open invitation to kids looking for trouble, gangs, dealers and of course, vampires.

Baughman had, like every other Anarch-wannabe Buffalo had ever spawned, havened in the plant at one point. This was before he realized that Prince Lladislas and his advisors kept the place standing as somewhere the rebellious teens of the Camarilla could go to perform the vampiric equivalent of smoking dope behind the garage before coming home, growing up and getting a respectable job manipulating the local media or some such.

However, at the moment it was a deathtrap. Baughman was sure of it. He'd been suckered—*How exactly did I get talked into this again?* he found himself wondering—into remaining behind with the skeleton force that was to hold the city after Lladislas and the big guns pulled out. In other words, he was there to get killed noisily and take out as many of the enemy as possible in the process, just to keep the Sabbat from realizing that they'd been had.

The situation, he concluded after due reflection, profoundly sucked.

Unfortunately, it was too late now to do anything about it. He'd heard the others enter the building a few minutes ago, and that meant that there wasn't any way out any longer. He'd also heard a few of his so-called support troops going down noisily and quickly, and that didn't exactly help his mood either.

Instead, he wriggled closer to the edge of the platform he was on and carefully got his AK-47 in line to cover the entrance to the room. The gun was a Chinese-made piece of shit, but it was all he'd been able to get his hands on when the orders came down. It was about as accurate as the local weather forecast, but once he hit someone with it, they tended to stay down, at least long enough for him to make sure of the job. He was positive he didn't have the personal firepower to handle one Sabbat badass, let alone a whole pack, but a really big gun, as his sire had been fond of saying, was a hell of a way to even the odds.

The room itself was a jumble of catwalks, walkways, abandoned blast furnaces and other, less identifiable things. Once upon a time this room had housed planning meetings, parties and the like for Baughman and his friends; now he'd come back to it because it had more potential escape routes than anywhere else in the building.

Voices in the next room snapped Baughman out of his reverie. Someone, no, two someones were coming, and they were arguing.

"...Could have sworn I saw him duck in here," came a male voice, damaged by cigarettes and whiskey.

"You'd better be right. We're behind schedule as is, and there aren't enough of us on this ride to afford unexpected delays." The response caught Baughman by surprise. He'd been told that the city was going to be swamped by waves of Sabbat. If what he'd just heard was true, then there weren't that many Sabbat in the city. In that case, there might actually a chance of holding them off.

More to the point, the fact that there weren't that many in place for a supposedly major offensive against a big target was a sign that someone's intelligence wires had gotten crossed somewhere. Either the council advising Lladislas had vastly overestimated the force lined up against him…

"Or we've been sold out. Son of a bitch." He cursed himself for speaking as he heard a scramble down on the floor. While he'd been lost in reverie, the Sabbat vampires had entered the room and crossed out of his field of fire. And now they'd heard him speak and knew where he was.

Well, the hell with it. What he'd figured out was more important than taking one or two shovelheads with him as he went. His first order of business was to escape; his second to bring word to someone, *anyone* higher up in the Camarilla to let them know that the whole operation had been compromised. He eased to his feet silently while his pursuers stomped about, backing toward a patch of darkness that he knew concealed a fire door to a stairwell with an outside exit. If he made it to the stairs and out the back, he could find a car to steal and run like hell. Quietly thanking God that he didn't have to breathe any longer, he silently lifted one foot, then the other, taking minuscule steps to avoid making any further noise.

The two downstairs sounded like they were still bickering. Perfect. The door was only a few feet behind him, hidden in the shadow behind a massive column of machinery. For the first time since he'd been thrown to the wolves, he dared to hope.

And that's when the shadow Baughman had been easing into decided to expedite the process, and swallowed him whole.

"Oh, fu—" was all he had time to say before it was over. The AK-47 clattered to the metal of the walkway, alerting the two vampires down below. They looked up, laughed, and walked out.

MacEllen was right on schedule, and so were they.

Friday, 13 August 1999, 12:58 AM
Baltimore Street
Buffalo, New York

Sheldon and Mary walked down Baltimore Street without a care in the world. They were hunting Camarilla vampires, and they didn't care if the whole city knew it. Sheldon was tall and thin, with a runner's build and a computer geek's complexion. He wore camouflage pants and shitkicker boots, and had a motherfucking big pistol jammed into his waistband. His head was shaved but his arms were hairy enough to make it look like he could lie down in front of a fire and play bearskin rug.

Mary was, by contrast, short and stocky, and looked like she'd done time in a car crusher in the not-too-distant past. She dressed like a preacher's worst nightmare of a drugged-out earth mother, and was dragging a baseball bat behind her on the asphalt. Her partner looked anxious and gleeful; she just looked pissed off.

"Goddamned sonnovabitch has got to be around here somewhere," muttered Sheldon. "Briefing said the ugly little bastard holed up in this part of town, so we just have to find whatever hole he's in and plug it with this." He took the pistol, a battered Desert Eagle, out of his belt and waved it around.

"You can be such an asshole," his packmate replied without heat. "We're chasing a Nossie. Fucker probably heard you coming two blocks off, ducked into the sewers and is halfway to Cleveland by now. All because you had to haul your metal-plated dick out of your pants and wave it around. Dipshit."

"Who you calling a dipshit?" Sheldon stopped, turned on his heel, and stared down at Mary. "MacEllen put me in charge of the team, so if you call me a dipshit again, I'll blow the top of your ugly head off."

"Try it and I'll rip your balls off."

"You can't reach that high."

"She's right. You are a dipshit."

The voice came from a point about five feet behind where Sheldon stood, and from a figure who hadn't been there a minute before. He had a face like the business end of a dumpster, and a massive bulge rose beneath the back of his tatty tan trench coat. His left arm stuck out at an odd angle, and in his right hand he held something that could only be a Zippo.

"Well hello, little ratboy," breathed Sheldon. "We've been looking for your ass, and now that we've found it, we're gonna stomp it flat." Mary fanned out to his right, while Sheldon brought the Desert Eagle in line with the Nosferatu's head. "Just hold still and this will only hurt like hell."

"Idiot," said Dustin very clearly, as he squeezed the trigger on the nozzle of the plant sprayer that he'd run up his left sleeve. With his right hand, he flicked the lighter into a blaze and brought the flame into contact with the stream of diesel fuel jetting out of the plant sprayer's nozzle.

The jet of flame it produced was impressive. The effect the wash of flame had on the two vampires it played over was even more so. Sheldon had no time for a scream; Mary barely a half-second more in which to try before the fire turned her face to a ruin and washed down her throat to crisp her from the inside.

Dustin swept the flame over the two writhing figures dispassionately for another minute, until he was sure they weren't getting back up. "Darwin would have loved you two, you know?" he said, and loped off into the distance to find more targets.

Friday, 13 August 1999, 2:12 AM
Outside the General Donovan Building
Buffalo, New York

"So what do we have here?" MacEllen jabbed down at the map with a long-nailed finger. His face was flushed and red, and his shirt collar was wet with beads of blood sweat. He'd just finished his sweep of the Bethlehem steel plant, and could barely contain his nervous energy. The scouting report had been absolutely perfect. The city *was* being held with a screen of recently Embraced neonates, a few slack-ass ghouls, and one or two real vampires who were being hung out to dry to sell the thing. Somewhere Hell had frozen over, because Polonia's info had been spot on. Of course, that didn't mean this was easy. There were a *lot* of the fresh-faced bastards, and they fought like demons. Once he caught himself missing Tolliver, but there was nothing to be done. The battle was being fought here and now.

Adele, her face covered by a fine sheen of bloody sweat, laid a talon of her own on the map and pointed to an area not far from where they stood. "We've got some kind of trouble here. Scaz said he saw, if you believe this, a Nosferatu with a flame-thrower. Whatever's over there, though, we haven't heard from Sheldon and Mary in half an hour, and that was where they were supposed to be."

"Flame-thrower, huh." MacEllen scratched his right armpit absently. "You'd think toting around fire would drive him apeshit."

Adele tapped the map, twice. "I'm not sure I believe the report. Scaz is also prone to eating bugs and throwing himself off of buildings to see how much it hurts. On the other hand, assuming the information's good, I suspect it's a lot easier to be brave about fire when the big fat nozzle of flaming death is pointed away from you." She stared at MacEllen until he took his finger off the map, then lifted it off the table herself and folded it. "Other than that one setback, though, we're sweeping the city. Resistance is stiff but incompetent, just like we'd been told it would be." She listened to the headset she wore for a second, and then nodded. "Okay, Delaware Park is cleaned out. Three babies with three big guns. They jumped out of the trees screaming, and Einar took them out, no mess." There was some crackling from the headset. "Hang on. Watts wants you to know that it took him all of ninety seconds, and that you owe him something that I really don't want to think about. In other words, it's all under control except this one little area."

MacEllen grunted something that might have been distracted approval. Losing even two vampires on something that was supposed to be a milk run, after all, would not help him look good at the next war council. The problem, even if it was just Mary and Sheldon dicking around, needed to be resolved quickly and cleanly. Otherwise (and he could just hear that sanctimonious weasel of an archbishop saying so) it would reflect...poorly...on his leadership capabilities.

Well, screw that. Time to go deal with the situation, whatever it was.

"Right. Let's go."

"Go where?"

"Either to find what's left of Sheldon and Mary,

or kick their asses for dicking around on the clock. If they're okay, that's great and we do mop-up. If Scaz saw something real this time, then you actually get your hands soiled." Adele had a reputation for letting everyone else do her dirty work, and MacEllen liked calling her on the issue. He didn't want her to get crispy-fried quite yet—she was too damn useful and he could get what he wanted out of her with a minimum of flak—but he'd be perfectly happy to see her have to charge in and mix it up with some bruiser, and get her pretty little ass handed to her in the process. She was just a little too satisfied with her self-appointed position on the fringes of things. She needed to learn that no one was safe, and that her prissy little act wasn't going to play here.

"Whatever." Adele was clearly pissed off, and that suited MacEllen just fine. They trotted west, toward the lake and the trouble spot on the map. "So what's your brilliant plan, assuming this guy is real? Or do we just rush in, screaming, and hope that Scaz was snacking on winos again?"

"It's simple. You attract his attention. I pop behind him and kill him. Flame-throwers are bulky as all hell, and there's no way he can turn fast enough to fry both of us. Any other stupid questions?"

Adele stopped in the middle of the street. "Yeah. What happens if he gets to me before you get him?"

MacEllen never broke stride and didn't even look back at her. "Then you duck." As she spouted a stream of curses at him, he just laughed and kept going.

Friday, 13 August 1999, 2:15 AM
Intersection of Scott and Washington Streets
Buffalo, New York

Talley had decided that he loathed Buffalo approximately two minutes after setting foot in the place. It reminded him unpleasantly of some of the Midlands cities, plain girls trying to tart themselves up for tourists by hiding all their dirt and grime.

MacEllen had no idea that he was there, of course. Letting the angry vampire know that someone was watching him would make him utterly unmanageable. So the templar had merely shadowed the operation, observing MacEllen's tactics, lending a small incognito assist on occasion while waiting for Lucita to show herself. Talley couldn't imagine anyone else on the attack squad besides MacEllen who Lucita could be interested in.

On the whole, Talley decided, MacEllen's work tonight had been brutal if uninspired. It wouldn't win him much recognition from those higher up, but on the other hand it was damn difficult to argue with success.

Now MacEllen was pelting off somewhere personally, trailed by his weed of an assistant. With a curious frown, Talley thought about making his presence known, but decided against it and instead walked from shadow to shadow in their wake. Neither looked back, so he went unobserved. Finally, they turned a corner and left him behind for a second, which for no accountable reason filled Talley with alarm.

Something painfully stupid was about to happen, he was certain of it. Either something had gone unexpectedly wrong or, more likely, MacEllen had decided that he needed to make a big show of how much he was doing personally to win this fight.

Abruptly, the night was interrupted by a scream, and a faint whooshing sound that made the hair on Talley's neck stand on end. He could hear MacEllen cursing, and then the sound of gunfire. The screaming, however, continued.

Stepping up his pace, Talley headed for the source of the noise. This might be just what—and who—he was waiting for.

Dustin was hot under the collar, and that wasn't necessarily a good thing for a Kindred toting around several gallons of diesel fuel on his back. After he'd toasted the two goons who'd been looking for him, Dustin had gone looking for more fun, but none was to be had. All of the tissue-paper troops that Lladislas had commissioned had been stomped flat by this point. He'd seen some of the corpses of the ones Phoebe had made, and he didn't have high hopes for the Brujah he'd heard were to the north and west.

He checked his watch. It had been four hours since the assault began, and as near as he could tell, he was the only one of Buffalo's defenders still on his feet. Logic dictated that he get the hell out of town, meet up with Tomasz in Syracuse, tell Phoebe some comforting lies about her childer having fought well, and then move on. Those were his marching orders, and he'd seen enough to know that there was something fishy going on. From the briefing Tomasz had given him, Dustin had expected dozens, if not hundreds of opponents—war ghouls thundering down the street, packs of hunting *antitribu* flushing out havens and setting buildings on fire, chaos in the streets—and he'd intended to use the plant sprayer only as a last resort to get him out of a tight spot.

Instead, he'd seen about a dozen invaders, total. Clearly, someone had monkeyed things up somewhere along the way. Nothing jibed, and while it wasn't his job to figure it out, Dustin had a sneaking suspicion

that it *was* his job to get that information to someone who could put two plus two together and get
something other than "math is hard."

Dustin looked around. In the distance he could
see the smoke from multiple fires rising into the night
sky. Sirens whined from every corner of the city. A
shotgun barked, once, well off to the northeast. The
fight was clearly over. It was time to go.

"Right, one last check on those two to make sure
that they're most sincerely dead, and then I'm blowing town." The night refused to comment on his
witticism, and Dustin sighed. He pondered ducking
down into the sewers for safer travel, but decided
against it. He figured he'd spend more time moving
the fricking manhole cover at each end of the route
than he'd save by taking the quote-unquote short-
cut. Besides, it was damn difficult to lift up a massive
slab of metal in the middle of the street discreetly
and quietly.

With that in mind, he simply closed his eyes for
a second and imagined himself to be invisible, then
started pacing down the street past the abandoned
cars (and one extremely incongruous black sports car
that had no damn business being in this neighborhood without being up on blocks). Tomasz claimed
to use a different technique for vanishing, but this
was what worked for Dustin. Mind you, vanishing
didn't make him feel any different, but he could see
its effects on the world around him, and he liked it.

He especially liked it when vanishing gave him
a way to get the drop on dickweeds like the pair of
hunter-gatherer types he'd flambéed a few hours back.

Grinning and self-satisfied, Dustin turned the
corner to the place he'd left the smoldering forms of

his victims. Unfortunately, there was someone already there.

She was slender and scarred, with long black hair and a headset receiver on. She wore black, of course, and had a face that clearly said "here is a woman who has been pissed 24/7 since the day she was born." She was squatting by a pile of blackened flesh that Dustin immediately recognized as one of his victims, and she was calling out to someone who was out there but not showing himself.

Dustin wondered if he was up against a fellow Nosferatu, and remembered any number of clichés about the better part of valor. Besides, if he waited a minute, the vampire in the street's partner might get tired of her screeching and show up just to shut her up.

He had no such luck, however, and after an eternal minute or two, he began walking toward the woman. She was clearly one of the enemy, and clearly about as bright as a sack of sand. Even better, there was no sign of her buddy, which meant that he could toast her and get out with no one the wiser.

The other option, of course, was that her buddy knew he was coming and was hiding, waiting for Dustin to show himself. It, and variants thereof, were basic Nosferatu strategy, but that was unlife in the big city. He decided to risk it. She was standing now, still cursing the air. Dustin moved in and flicked the sprayer nozzle into position. The woman was completely oblivious. She had no idea he was there. He brought up the lighter and took a last look around for his other prey. There was not a soul on the street. Grinning, he dropped his shroud of invisibility—too excited to concentrate anymore—and let the flames roar into life.

What was left of Mary smoldered in the middle
of the street. It might have been still moving, or perhaps that was just the shriveling effect of the fire on
the husk of her corpse. Adele spotted her first, spat a
curse and ran to her. "MacEllen?" she called, but the
ductus had vanished. Not wasting any more time on
that chickenshit—who'd clearly run when he saw
that he might get hurt, she reflected bitterly—Adele
knelt by Mary's side to get a closer look at what had
been done to her. A crunching sound underneath her
feet announced that she'd found Sheldon's remains
as well. She looked over Mary's cadaver with an ap-
praising eye. Her professional assessment was that
whatever had hosed her down hadn't been a flame-
thrower but wasn't a bad approximation of one. In
other words, they were dealing with a brutal, clever
amateur.

She looked around for her missing ally. "Damn
you, MacEllen, get over here. You should see this."
Only silence answered her for a long minute, then
she resignedly got to her feet. She still had the headset on, and decided to call in one or two of the others,
just in case the nutjob with the napalm fixation was
still around.

That was when the flames hit her. She threw
herself violently to the left, but didn't quite make it
to safety. The fire washed over her right arm and part
of her back, and a scream forced itself out of her throat
as she fell to the ground. Behind her, she could hear

her assailant cursing, his footsteps slapping on the asphalt as he moved in for the kill. She rolled desperately in an attempt to put the flames out, then gave in to sheer animal panic and started howling in earnest.

"Shut up, you stupid bitch," Dustin said, then whirled and sprayed a burst of flame in a semi-circular arc behind him. Deep within the shadows cast by an abandoned house, MacEllen let out a roar of inchoate rage and dropped to the ground.

"Screw you, asshole. I *use* that trick, you think I'm dumb enough to fall for it?" Dustin was already on the move, fading into invisibility as he went. MacEllen scrabbled for his pistol and let off a few shots in the vicinity of where the Nosferatu had vanished, but hit only brick, glass and metal. Adele, her head wreathed in flame as her long black hair caught and blazed, continued screaming. Her right hand left smoking palm-prints on the asphalt as she crawled toward the end of the block.

The flames over his head gone, MacEllen climbed to his feet warily. The Nosferatu was still out there somewhere, with a flame-thrower no less, and he needed to be at his best. Adele's frenzied howling distracted him, so after a second's deliberation, he put a bullet into her head. She gurgled once and collapsed. Suddenly, the only noise on the street was the soft crackle of the flames eating away at her prone form, mixed with the hiss of burning fat.

"Son of a bitch," said MacEllen very clearly as he began to circle away from Adele's remains. His pistol was in his hand, his eyes straining for any sign of his opponent. Briefly, he considered a tactical retreat. He could grab some of the others and come back. With help from someone besides the utterly useless Adele, he could flush the bastard out and put the clamps on him. Then this little operation would be over with and he'd come out of it smelling like a rose—all of Buffalo subjugated in a single night.

As quickly as the notion arose, he dismissed it. There was no way in hell he was going to ask for help. This was his operation, his command, and bringing anyone else in would be setting himself up for a challenge. No, better to handle the risk—and the benefits—solo.

And then there came a sudden sound behind him, and MacEllen knew that he was very, very dead.

Friday, 13 August 1999, 2:25 AM
Baltimore Street
Buffalo, New York

Talley stepped into shadow about forty feet from where Adele was burning. Not far past her, MacEllen was firing randomly into the night. One of the bullets nearly winged Talley, and mentally the templar made another black mark against his estimation of the man's competence.

Dispassionately, he watched as the thug silenced the screaming Adele. That was simply a waste of resources. Had MacEllen been thinking, he would have attempted to smother the flames in shadow, or found some other way to try to save his reasonably useful second-in-command. But the ductus was lost in his own little fantasy trip at this point, acting from gut instinct rather than reason, and it had cost him.

MacEllen stepped away from the corpse delicately and began a series of spinning maneuvers presumably designed to make sure that no one was getting the drop on him. In actuality, they made him look ridiculous, like a fat man in fatigues missing targets at a rifle range, but Talley didn't care. He was too busy scanning the street for the author of the carnage.

It took only seconds to locate the Nosferatu with an awkward bulge beneath his coat. Confident in his invisibility, the vampire made no effort to take cover or otherwise protect himself. Instead, he was laughing, and mimicked one or two of MacEllen's more ridiculous *faux-jetées*. He seemed to be having a grand old time. Unfortunately for him, Talley was old enough and powerful enough to see through his efforts to veil himself. "You're never the last link in the chain, lad," Talley murmured to himself. "If you'd remembered that, you might have gotten out of here."

Talley was tempted to leave MacEllen to the fate he deserved, but if the Nosferatu took out the ductus, Lucita might never show her face, and the trip north would be wasted.

Talley knelt down and picked up a pebble. It was a shard of cement, perhaps an inch across and with jagged sides. No doubt it had been torn out of a sidewalk somewhere nearby through rough usage or harsh weather, but that was of no importance. Talley looked at it calmly. It would serve.

Out in the street, the Nosferatu had ceased his capering and took careful aim at the nearly spasmodic MacEllen. Another second and the positioning would be perfect, and slowly he turned his back on where Talley stood to follow the gyrations of his target.

Talley tsked. He placed the pebble in the palm of his left hand and squinted, making sure that his aim was true. Lifting his hand, he concentrated for a second and then flicked the pebble right at the center of the Nosferatu's misshapen back.

The sound the pebble made when it went through the tank might have been mistaken for a gunshot. The sound it made when it exited through the Nosferatu's stomach was indescribable. The results, however, were easy to discern. The vampire flicked into plain view, clutching his stomach with one hand. He spun, looking for his assailant with an expression of shock on his face, and staggered. Gasoline or something like it made a wet stain on the back of the creature's coat and dripped to the ground; a bloody mixture poured from between his fingers.

MacEllen finally noticed what happened (seconds too late, Talley noted dispassionately) and turned with a roar. Talley merely stooped and picked up another pebble. In the street, the Nosferatu broke into a stumbling run, trying to shed both his coat and the leaking tank on his back. MacEllen sprinted after him, screaming imprecations.

Talley ignored that and instead took his aim again. He aimed, not at the fugitive, but rather at the cracked asphalt just behind him. The pebble took off with a whoosh, and struck the street precisely where Talley had wanted it to. The impact, as such impacts are wont to, created a spark.

The results were impressive. The flame scurried up the Nosferatu's coat in a matter of seconds, inspiring a wail of terror and pain. The vampire stumbled on a few more steps, then the flame reached the tank.

What happened was not precisely an explosion. Rather, it was a burst of flame that more or less took off the upper third of the Nosferatu's body, and sent minuscule bits of the tank whizzing about. MacEllen narrowly avoided getting singed, and flattened himself to the street as the tank went up.

From a safe distance, Talley permitted himself a humorless smile. That quickly vanished as MacEllen pulled himself up and cautiously advanced until he was nearly straddling the still-burning corpse. He kicked it, once, cautiously, and the flaming remnants of what had been an arm flew several feet. MacEllen jumped back, startled, and cursed again, at which point Talley decided that it was time to make his presence known lest his assignment suffer the vampiric equivalent of a burst blood vessel. He stepped out into the yellowish light of the street lamps, and waited for MacEllen to notice him.

"—er just exploded. Never seen anything like that without a Tremere around, never seen anything like it at—what the fuck are *you* doing here?"

Talley bowed, precisely, from the neck. "Saving you. Against my better judgment."

"So it was you—"

"Indeed. It was me. Now is the time, Ductus MacEllen, when you stop stammering and thank me."

MacEllen stalked closer. "Son of a bitch. It was you. You were here the whole time."

Talley nodded. "We've already established that. In fact, I have been watching you since the operation began, including tailing you through the steel factory, observing your conversations with your late second-in-command, and so on. I must say I was impressed by the turn of speed you managed in getting here. If you'd moved a little more slowly, I might have been able to protect Adele as well. Incidentally, I think she's about out. You may want to stamp on her bits to make sure."

"So you saw everything." MacEllen took a few more steps, sparing only the briefest of glances for what was left of Adele. "Why are you here? Are you spying on me for Polonia and those assholes? Is that it, you're here to make me look bad?"

"No, you idiot, Lucita is in this city! Do you want to face her alone?" Talley shifted his weight into a fighting crouch. Impossible as it seemed, it looked as if MacEllen might actually attack him. Whether or not the man had succumbed to his inner demons, he was clearly unhinged and might well decide to try to get rid of any witnesses to his self-assessed humiliation.

MacEllen's chances of actually hurting Talley were comical, but the situation was sticky enough as it was. So Talley, being the efficient sort of vampire that he was, simply locked eyes with his would-be assailant and extended his will against MacEllen's. Unsurprisingly, the resistance was minimal.

"Sit," Talley said, and obediently MacEllen sat where he was. "Behave yourself," Talley said, suddenly irritated for no reason that he could fathom. MacEllen nodded with pathetic eagerness, and Talley exhaled in disgust. This short-tempered idiot, who clearly couldn't handle himself in any situation more stressful than a game of darts, was going to get himself killed sooner or later regardless of what Talley did. For a brief instant, he considered handing the man off to Lucita as a bribe not to bother any of the three archbishops. The idea had a certain appeal, he had to confess.

He turned back to MacEllen in disgust, prepared to frog-march the man back to the putative field HQ, when suddenly, everything became very, very dark.

Friday, 13 August 1999, 2:28 AM
Baltimore Street
Buffalo, New York

Lucita had observed the entire affair from a rooftop across from where MacEllen now squatted in the street. She'd watched it with some amusement—the whole chain of Kindred, each convinced that he was both invisible and invincible, made for a certain sort of low comedy. She'd seen vampires hunting vampires before, but the combination of factors—the bizarre little Nosferatu's choice of weapon, the blustering swagger and cowardice of MacEllen, Talley's nonchalant approach to the problem—all combined into something profoundly risible even as it was terrible.

Seeing Talley had surprised her at first. She'd received word from her first employer that the Hound had been imported. Rumor had it that her own sire had sent the man to safeguard his beloved archbishops. But Talley being in Buffalo, while the archbishops were presumably safe elsewhere, didn't make sense.

Unless he was after her.

The thought caused Lucita some concern. Talley's presence was an unexpected complication. The Hound was good, very good, and would change her plans for dealing with her target. MacEllen himself was nothing. He'd nearly been taken out by the childe with the flamethrower, and clearly was well below Lucita's level in terms of talent, power and intelligence. But Talley was a different matter, a very powerful and determined one.

Lucita had crossed paths with the Hound once before, some eighty years prior in New York City. She'd been there on pleasure while he was on business; they'd intersected in the notorious Five Points. Talley had

Talley had been sent by Monçada to rid the city of a troublesome vampire named Karl who'd been noisily disrupting certain of the archbishop's long-range plans. Unfortunately, Karl was also the Kindred responsible for much of Lucita's amusement at the time, and she took exception to the attempt to remove him before she was finished. The duel had been long and bloody, sparking a brawl in the tenements and speakeasies to rival the infamous Dead Rabbit Riots. At the heart of it, the two ancient children of shadow had torn at each other with unimaginable fury, cloaking an entire city block in impenetrable darkness. The newspaper reports talked of broken power lines as an explanation, but in truth, it had been Lucita and Talley hunting each other in the dark, fueling themselves with the lives of the hundreds trapped within their battlefield.

Lucita had won, barely. Karl had been wounded but slipped away during the fury of her counterattack. She'd later learned that he'd fled the country, and had been destroyed by Talley in Vancouver, in 1934. By that time, of course, she'd long since ceased to care. Talley himself had left the scene exhausted but relatively unscathed, leaving her with a mocking bow and an expression of regards for her sire. And she had stumbled out of the tenements, weary but more or less triumphant, and thoroughly convinced that Talley was, if not her equal, then at least one of the more frightening opponents she'd ever faced.

And now here he was across the street, muttering to himself. No doubt his professional sensibilities had been thoroughly offended by MacEllen's performance. No doubt he was just the slightest bit irritated, and that meant that he was the slightest bit distracted, and that meant that if she moved very quickly, everything would work out just fine.

She reached out, across the street, to the shadows that so recently had hidden Talley himself. They responded to her call, eagerly shaping themselves into ropy arms that stretched forth to envelope the templar. Talley, to his credit, did not hesitate, but rather ducked and rolled to his left, out into the street. One shadow tentacle did grasp his arm as he moved, but with practiced ease he simply tore it to shreds. Lucita smiled and sent more tendrils of blackness after him. The idea was not to kill Talley, or even to wound him, but rather to keep him off balance and drive him further and further from the still-dazed MacEllen. Then, when it was too late, she'd simply terminate her target and stop harassing the templar, leaving without any fuss.

Of course, that plan relied on keeping Talley on the defensive, and that was going to take everything she had. She frowned, and another tentacle of shadow burst forth from beneath a manhole cover in the middle of the street. The metal disc went thirty feet in the air and nearly caught Talley on the way down, even as he dodged of the way of his new assailant. Slowly but surely, he was moving into the middle of the street, which was blanketed in illumination from multiple streetlamps. Lucita's shadows stretched themselves thin to reach Talley here, and he avoided them with ease.

"Lucita," he called out, glancing about in an attempt to pinpoint the attack. "Good to see you again! Your sire asked about you, in case you were wondering." He ducked another swipe, then drew on shadow himself and tore Lucita's servant to shreds. "He mentioned you might be in the States; so glad to see he was right!"

Lucita cursed and called up more shadows from

the now-open manhole. They geysered upwards, then plunged down on Talley like a hammer of night. The templar sidestepped, and the shadows' impact on the street cracked the asphalt with a sound like thunder.

"Lucita, you're not going to get me like that! Come on out, so we can talk. At the very least, you owe me a rematch!" All the while he dodged and struck, called forth shadow tendrils of his own and moved with a laughing grace that was hypnotically smooth. Huge clubs of darkness smashed the surface of the street, leaving enormous holes and sending debris flying everywhere. In the middle of the carnage, Talley laughed, and Lucita saw for the first time the pure, unadulterated joy the man took in his work.

It was as good a cue as any to finish matters. She called forth a last arm of darkness and brought it screaming down toward where Talley stood. He avoided it easily, and she split it into three smaller entities. Two continued to pursue Talley, while the third arrowed straight for where MacEllen still sat, oblivious.

Talley saw what was happening and desperately summoned shadows of his own in a vain attempt to deflect Lucita's. Even as he did so, the first two tendrils struck him like hammer blows. He cried out, the first time Lucita had ever heard him do so, and his control of his shadows faltered.

As Talley fell, Lucita's last shadow tendril reached MacEllen, wrapped around his neck, and with ungentle pressure, tore his head off. There was silence for a moment, and then the pack ductus's body topped to the street with a barely audible thump. Blood pumped from his neck into the gutter, pooling amidst the trash and dead leaves. His head came to rest a few feet away, face down.

Talley slowly and silently picked himself up as the arms of shadow that both vampires had created dissipated into nothingness. Lucita dusted herself off and took two steps back from the ledge, acutely aware that she was dangerously low on blood should Talley decide to continue their disagreement.

"Lucita," he called, in a more reasonable tone of voice. "Nicely done, my gracious señorita. I'll be on the lookout for that in the future. It seems that this time *you* are the hunter, and I the protector. I think it only professional courtesy that I advise you to let it end with this one." He gestured toward MacEllen. "Otherwise, I—*and* your sire—will be greatly displeased."

With that, he executed a sketchy bow and walked off. Lucita debated following him, but the gnawing hunger in her stomach told her that it would be foolish, if not suicidal. Instead, she went down the cast-iron fire escape at the back of the building she stood on and loped the three blocks to where she'd parked. Ideally, she'd find someone to eat on the way out of town, hole up somewhere in secure Camarilla territory, and relax in order to plan the next job.

She came out of the alley she'd entered across the street from her car. Wonder of wonders, it was still there. Even more miraculously, the tires had not been slashed. She climbed in and started the engine; it responded with a warm purr.

Some nights, she reflected, things actually did all go your way. It was unfortunate that the city was doomed anyway, but in the end, that wasn't really her concern.

With a smile, she slammed the car into gear and roared off into what was left of the night.

Talley stood in front of the abandoned steel plant. It would serve as well as anyplace for a temporary haven. The survivors of the assault had straggled back over the past several hours. They were mostly up-beat; they'd crushed the pitiful resistance Buffalo had offered. A couple of the ghouls had bullet wounds, but mostly everyone was unscathed. They laughed and joked and told stories about how they'd dis-patched various of the idiots sent against them. If anyone missed Sheldon or Mary, or even Adele or MacEllen, it wasn't evident from what Talley heard. The troops were just happy the fight was over and that they'd kicked ass.

All in all, he found it hard to disagree with them.

As the last of the survivors entered the building, Talley gazed out at the streets. The charred corpses had been unceremoniously hurled in dumpsters. Fires and vampire-initiated firefights had distracted the police and other mortal annoyances sufficiently that there had been no interference with their efforts.

As for MacEllen, he was no great loss as far as Talley was concerned. The trip north had been about as successful as he'd expected it to be. He'd warned Lucita. If she failed to abide by his advice…well, he'd have no compunction in dealing harshly with her the next time they met.

Having accomplished that intermediate goal, Talley was ready to return to Washington and direct his attention to the question that, to Monçada, was more pressing even than the personal well-being of the archbishops: Who had hired Lucita?

For now, Talley walked inside the steel plant, then, and shut and locked the door. Outside, the sun came up sluggishly over the Sabbat city of Buffalo.

part three:
pillars
of smoke

Saturday, 14 August 1999, 11:18 PM
Hyatt Regency Capitol Hill
Washington, D.C.

My Most Eminent and Beloved Cardinal, the letter began, *While I have no inkling of what I have done to
displease you so greatly that you have decided to sentence
me to penance among this den of madmen, brutes and
liars, I would most humbly beseech that you would tell
me so that I might make amends and thus be done with
this entire matter.*

Talley paused and put his pen down for a moment. It was, he thought, perhaps a bit strong, but he
was not in a mood to be delicate. Besides, Monçada
valued him and his service too highly, he hoped, to
get overly upset over a letter. And if Monçada was
right and there was a God inclined to rain miracles
down upon the unworthy, this missive might even
serve to get Talley out of here.

He shook his head to clear it and took up the
pen again. *The offensive on Buffalo was a qualified success. While the city was taken, as you no doubt have
heard, the casualties were a bit heavier than expected.
The intelligence Archbishop Vykos's spy provided was
mostly correct, but as you and I both know, the Devil
himself lurks in the details.*

*One of those details was Lucita, who made an ap-
pearance. For whatever reason, she was intent on dealing
with the ductus whom Polonia had put in charge of affairs. It seems odd to me that Lucita's talents would be
wasted on such a—and pardon me for saying so—pathetic excuse for a Lasombra.*

The paranoid in me bears in mind your mention of a

potential traitor. Of those I have observed among the high command here in the New World, only the archbishops would have access to the financial resources required to entice your prodigal childe. Polonia and Borges profit from drugs, graft, et cetera, in their respective cities; Vykos has had centuries to hoard its treasures. There are others, of course, in the Sabbat Internationale who would have the interest and the means to destroy an archbishop—the regent springs to mind—but you have narrowed the field to my unhappy triumvirate, and in this I trust your impeccable judgment.

I cannot believe, however, that any of the archbishops would have required the services of an assassin, particularly one as expensive as Lucita, even had one of the three harbored a desire to dispatch this MacEllen. Borges would have crushed him; Don Polonia would have simply clutched the man's neck and twisted—from what I understand, he nearly did so at a war-council meeting just prior to my arrival—and Vykos would have turned the fellow into a nice footstool or endtable. None would have faced recrimination.

The matter smells of outside influence. I suspect this is no longer simply a family affair. Not that a third party arranging MacEllen's demise—if such truly is the case—exonerates our beloved archbishops of designs upon one another.

Speaking of the archbishops, they are a fine set indeed. Vykos, when not busying herself with the siege of the stubborn Tremere (which continues apace without notable result), is the perfect hostess, deferring to Don Polonia in most matters of strategy and concentrating on her duties as archbishop of this fly-ridden city. She seems in little hurry for the offensive to continue north, now that her territory and status are fairly secure. With Washington embedded between Miami and New York as it is, she stands to benefit should a tragedy befall either Borges or Polonia, as would they if something untoward happened to her.

As for Don Polonia, he is a bit more of a cipher. His devotion to the sect seems single-minded and his strategies are excellent. But little things about the man still rankle. Why does he take such delight in baiting Archbishop Borges? Sheer perversity? Certainly Vykos is the more formidable threat to Polonia's ascendancy to a position of prominence over the American Sabbat. Why, then, does he risk driving a potentially powerful enemy into his rival's arms? It makes little sense to me, but in the meantime we have suffered no major setbacks in the field, and no losses of any Cainites of consequence.

Finally, we have Archbishop Borges, who seems intent on challenging his fellow archbishops at every opportunity, generally to the advantage of Polonia or Vykos. Borges may have bludgeoned his way to the top of that rubbish heap that is Miami, but he lacks the subtlety of his rivals. What were Les Amies Noir thinking when they extended to him the highest honors the clan can offer? His forte is the bullish, straight-ahead assault; he spends most of his nights feverishly scrutinizing reports from the field, looking for evidence that his people have done something praiseworthy. Perhaps he is intimidated; much of his support is scattered in the wake of the offensive, while much of Archbishop Polonia's is close at hand. I would not be surprised to discover him either the object or the instigator of Lucita's attentions.

Beyond that, there is little to report. Vallejo seems to be edging toward Polonia's service, presumably because service with a Tzimisce disagrees with him. He is often away on business of his own, which seem to be trips into the field to observe some of the more efficient packs in action. Perhaps he is looking for potential recruits.

On the whole—aside from the unmitigatedly disastrous assassination attempt on the Ventrue, Pieterzoon—the operation stands somewhat satisfactorily. Information flows on a steady basis. However, since the surprises at Buffalo (which, besides Lucita, included a clever little fellow of a Nosferatu who stayed behind long enough to make an extreme nuisance of himself), it has been decided that such intelligence should be supplemented by more extensive field reports from scouting details. A half-dozen or so have been dispersed, including some of Borges's and Polonia's favorite subordinates. Supplies continue to flow freely, though the antitribu Munro overseeing the operation is as unpleasant to deal with as he has ever been.

Other than that, the captured territories are being scoured and Buffalo fully invested. Several smaller cities nearby—Rochester, the ironically named Syracuse—have also been taken, to little fanfare. Again, the resistance was minimal. The enemy seems to be concentrating in Baltimore. One wonders precisely to what end. A counteroffensive to relieve the Tremere in Washington? Sensible, but unlikely; this whole thing smacks of the Americans' Civil War, where opposing capitals glowered at each other from a few dozen miles away while war raged everywhere else. Atlanta? Nonsense, it's too isolated and too far away from any other theater that matters. Still, I have made recommendations to the various archbishops that we prepare for the Camarilla's resistance to stiffen. Even a dying dog has one last bite in it.

As for myself, I generally stay within the city, attaching myself to one archbishop or the other. Borges is resentful, Vykos distant, and Polonia utterly unconcerned. There has been no sign of Lucita since Buffalo, though I expect she will make her presence known shortly. Beyond that, there is no news to report. Decisions will be made soon on the Giovanni presence in Boston and the next target for assault—I would expect the so-called New England to bear the brunt of it—but now all I have is idle speculation, with which I would not waste your time.

May this letter find you in good health, and please keep me posted on the resolution of the chess game you had begun with Don Ibrahim. I have been playing in my mind with the board I saw, and think I may have found a way for black to triumph after all.

Yours in Utmost Respect,
Talley

The Hound glanced at the finished result and frowned. It was hardly literary, but it would serve to keep Monçada informed. Hurriedly, he stuffed it into an envelope and addressed it; one of the couriers constantly winging back and forth from Europe would convey it shortly. Hopefully, the messenger would be clever enough not to open and read it en route. Good couriers were, after all, very difficult to find.

Lucita had been to the Holy Land several times, and she could say with reasonable certainty that it was not located on a hill overlooking I-84 in central Connecticut. Still, "HolyLand USA" was what the sign on the dilapidated gate read. Above her, on the summit of the slope, a huge cross outlined in yellow and white fluorescent lights cast a sickly glow over some of the sad-sack displays from the life of Jesus that dotted the hillside.

Once upon a time this place had been a curiosity, an inspirational amusement park for the good people of Waterbury. But that had been years ago, and now it was a ruin of overgrown weeds and broken-down fiberglass and chickenwire displays. The disenfranchised youth of Waterbury had long ago found their way here, and the park's tumble-down remnants showed the effects of their long occupancy. Graffiti defaced the surviving figures of Jesus, Mary, Joseph and the disciples. Some of the latter were without heads; Lucita was fairly sure she'd stepped on part of Peter after hopping the ineffective fence. Some of the displays had simply been smashed or otherwise desecrated, and at least one had been carved by a particularly enterprising youth with a rough inverted pentagram.

Lucita stopped for a second and gazed at that, surprised that a mild twinge of anger still roiled in her gut at the sight. She had long ago left the Church behind—her sire's attentions had seen to that—but found this petty sacrilege irksome. She'd seen evil—to some, she was its very personification—and this tribute to what some idiotic child thought was naughty belittled what she'd seen and done. She made a mental note that, when her work here was finished, she should find the author of this indignity and show him precisely what he was making pathetic reverence to.

But that would come later. Now it was time for business. Talley and Monçada be damned—she had a contract.

Broken glass, cigarette butts and other, less identifiable things were scattered everywhere on the ground. A less cautious hunter would have been betrayed by the crunching of the omnipresent glass under her feet, but Lucita had taken certain precautions. She smiled. Even if she hadn't known that her prey was here, she would have guessed that he'd pick someplace like this to go to ground.

The traffic from the highway below was steady and insistent. It did a good job of masking whatever noises Lucita's target (and any company he had) might make. The constant flow of cars added another concern, however—everything she did on this hill was highly visible to the mortals below, and that meant that her arsenal was limited. The tactics she'd used to distract Talley from MacEllen wouldn't work here. Monstrous tentacles and forms of shadow silhouetted against a twenty-foot cross might be seen by her employers as a breach of the Masquerade, and part of the terms of any contract with the Camarilla was abiding by its rules.

She looked around. Nothing stirred on the hill. Lucita pursed her lips in an almost-frown, the yellow light from the icon above her making her appear almost jaundiced. She'd have to flush Torres out. Oh, he was here. Of that she had no doubt. There was evidence of him here if you knew where to look— tracks in the high weeds that were made by someone dragging off a body, odd spatters of blood on the ground, a discarded shoe along the side of the path that looked too new to have been there more than a week. Actually, from the amount of evidence, Torres definitely had company.

Well, there was no time like the present to begin. Lucita dropped to her haunches and concentrated. The light from the cross, far from being the bane its manufacturers would have expected, instead helped her. Shadows sprawled behind every rock and bush, and crawled out from each of the surviving displays of crumbling piety.

It was very simple, really. Torres was nowhere in the light. He couldn't move, for fear of being spotted. That meant that he was hiding somewhere in the shadows. And no matter how tough or learned Torres might be, it was certain that the shadows would not hide him from Lucita's attentions.

She closed her eyes and listened *through* the darkness. The sounds of the rushing cars and of the wind skirling between the displays faded. Instead, Lucita's world filled with darkness. She cast her consciousness about, from one place to another, seeking the faintest noise, the slightest movement....

There. And there. And over there. There were three of them, all doing their very best not to be seen. It meant that they'd seen her coming and probably had a good idea of who she was. It would make her work more difficult. She pulled back from the shadows even as she sensed the three moving to the attack, and spun to meet them.

There were already two knives in the air as Lucita stood. She dodged to the left, vaulting over the miracle of the loaves and fishes, and was rewarded by a pair of muffled crunching sounds as the blades cut into the fiberglass behind her. She could see all three of them, with the two she didn't recognize leaping to the attack and Torres hanging back. He looked as if he couldn't tell whether to help his friends out or run, and that indecision was exactly what she needed.

The two moving toward her were fairly nondescript, as far as vampires went. One was tall and lanky, with a straggly red beard and stragglier red ponytail, while his partner was shorter and broader, and had dark hair. Both wore what she'd heard disparagingly referred to as "Sabbat uniform"—black biker jacket, jeans, boots and leather gloves. The tall one already had another knife out, while the shorter vampire rushed her position with a scream. Farther back, Torres seemed to have finally made up his mind. He ran.

Lucita smiled. As the shorter vampire closed on her, arms wide and fangs bared, she simply dropped to a knee and rammed her fist into his gut with enough force to crumple a car door. The man's scream abruptly transformed into a gasp as she felt something in his entrails *give*, and he suddenly sat down hard with a stunned look on his face. He tried to scrabble to his feet, and Lucita lashed out with a kick that collapsed his cheekbone and eye socket. He fell over with astonishing speed.

Even as she rose out of the crouch, the other vampire threw his knife and reached for yet another one. It was a good cast, and the spinning blade caught the light from the cross in bands of yellow and gold.

Lucita didn't duck out of the way. Instead, she merely extended her left arm, palm out. Beside her, the man she'd punched whined in pain. She ignored him.

And the knife smacked neatly into her hand, the blade slicing through her palm and out the other side. Lucita gritted her teeth, but made no other show that the impact affected her. Thick blood dripped down her hand onto the ground, but she ignored it. Perhaps fifteen feet away, the vampire who'd thrown the knife paused, mid-cast, as she removed it from her hand.

"Care to try again?" she said, as the hole in her palm knit itself shut. The knife in her right hand was slick with her blood, but it was weighted well, and sharp. The blade was leaf-shaped, about three inches long, and it had been polished to a high shine. Idly, Lucita wondered precisely how many more the childe had on him.

The vampire snarled something that might have been a curse, and let fly with his remaining knife. His aim was off, however, and the throw missed her by a good foot to the right. She laughed, taunting him, and he leaped over the display in front of him to come after her. Lucita circled right, placing his downed friend between the two of them, and feinted first left and then right with her stolen blade. Her attacker backpedaled, clearly not ready for a taste of his own medicine, and in that instant she rammed the knife down on the crippled vampire on the ground in front of her. The point of the blade went into the back of his neck as easily as if it were going into thin mud, and the man spasmed once before collapsing completely.

The other vampire didn't care about his friend, or perhaps simply saw that Lucita's knife was now stuck between a pair of his cohort's cervical vertebrae. He charged in, reaching out for Lucita with the obvious intent of tackling her and using his superior size and weight to bear her down. Behind him, Lucita could see Torres making for the fence. The sight sobered her. It was time to finish this, and to see to her real target.

The lanky vampire charged, and Lucita shoved the body of his ally at his ankles as hard as she could. As Lucita could lift small cars if she put her mind to it, the cadaver went flying at her assailant fast enough that he had no time to leap over it. Instead, he crashed to the ground as the dead weight of his friend took his feet out from under him. The man's jaw hit the hard ground with an audible crack, and before he could scramble to his feet, Lucita brought her booted foot down on the back of his head.

The vampire's skull collapsed messily, as Lucita's boot went through his skull and nearly out the other side. She stared down at the corpse for a long second, then shook her foot free and took off after Torres.

He was over the fence by now and headed for the highway. Lucita summoned the strength of the blood within her (less than she thought she'd had, as healing the knife wound had taken some doing) and surged forward. Torres saw her coming and panicked, leaping the rest of the way over the fence and stumbling forward as fast as his legs could carry him. Within seconds, Lucita saw, he'd reach the highway. There was light traffic, and with a little luck Torres would make it across the road and into the maze of buildings on the other side. She might catch him there, or she might not. And if he got away, he'd go to ground so deep that she'd probably have to spend weeks to find him again.

It had to end now, witnesses be damned. She

stopped running and seized hold of a shadow on the far side of the fence.

Torres was a bare twenty feet from the road. The headlights of eastbound cars illuminated him in flickers. Lucita concentrated and, under her breath, muttered a prayer.

The tendril of shadow shot out and wrapped itself around Torres's foot. He screamed and fell, hard. Lucita smiled and made a "come-hither" gesture. In response, the tentacle of blackness started dragging the howling vampire back away from the road. Torres clawed at the dirt, which came up in his hands. He clung to weeds, which broke under the inexorable pressure Lucita's servant exerted.

A car coming around the curve slowed, a face peered out from the window. Lucita cursed, and called more darkness to hide the scene. No other vehicles gave evidence of any observation, and Lucita smiled. Torres was ranting obscenities, but the sound of the passing cars drowned them out. He was as alone and lost as if he were in the middle of the Sahara.

"My most sincere apologies, Rey," she said, not particularly caring if he heard or not. She blew him a kiss, and another shadow tendril joined the first. His screaming could be heard now over the din of the traffic, mixed in with curses and pleas. The shadows had tugged their victim nearly back to the fence by now, and Lucita idly added another tendril to the mix. The three hauled Torres to the chain-link fence, and Lucita made another gesture.

The third tendril wrapped around Torres's chest and hauled him upright. The others still held his ankles, pinning him against the fence. He struggled, but to no avail.

Lucita strode purposefully down to where her prisoner waited. She walked up to the fence and prodded him in the small of the back with a single finger. "A pleasure to see you again, Rey."

Rey spat. "Go fuck yourself, Lucita. What the hell are you playing at?"

"I could ask you the same thing, no? This place is a long way from your usual nest."

"I'm a tourist. This is my vacation. Any other stupid questions?"

Lucita made a great show of considering the lie, even though Torres couldn't really turn his head far enough to see her. "Oh, I see. How could I have been so mistaken. Here I stood, thinking that perhaps you were here scouting, and I think that you're trying to preserve your worthless skin a few seconds longer by attempting wit, which has never been your strong point. And furthermore, I think that I really have no inclination to stay in this city any longer than I have to, Rey, so I do not think your little delaying tactic is going to work very well."

"Oh really?" There was bravado layered over desperation in his voice. "So what's keeping you here?"

"You're not dead yet," she said. "But this can be remedied. You'd be surprised how little they're paying me for your life. And did you know something else, Rey? I forgot to eat before I got here. Imagine that."

When she finished supper, Lucita dusted her hands of what was left of Rey and headed back up the hill. She left the two corpses of the younger vampires arranged neatly in front of the remnants of the Last Supper. It seemed, she thought to herself, entirely appropriate—at least as far as Rey was concerned.

The phone rang precisely thrice before someone picked it up. There was a moment of fumbling noises, then finally someone rasped "Hello?" into the receiver.

"Do I have the pleasure of speaking to Mr. Schreck's personal secretary?" Lucita was in a good mood. She was headed eastbound on I-84 with the top of her convertible down, the wind in her hair and a completed assignment behind her.

The Nosferatu (for now Lucita recognized the voice as belonging to the "woman" from the basement in Baltimore) on the other end of the connection chuckled briefly. "If that's what you want to call it for the moment. Good evening, Lucita. How's the convertible holding up?"

"The car is lovely, thank you. Most satisfactory." The Nosferatu made as if to say something else, but Lucita cut her off. "Are you finished with the pointless chitchat so that I can make my report, or do you wish to continue pretending that you actually enjoy talking to me?" On the right, a sign marking the turnoff for I-691 and Middletown flashed by in the night. Lucita ignored it, cut into the left lane and looped around a rig that was doing a mere eighty-five.

There was silence on the line for a second. "And here I thought all of you Lasombra appreciated the social graces."

"Courtesy, yes. Breeding, yes. A sense of propriety, yes—even if one is no longer welcome within the loving arms of one's clan. Assumed, unearned familiarity is another matter entirely. Do not presume on a business acquaintance, and do not pretend you know me or my kind. Now, do you want the evening's report, or shall I hang up and simply enjoy driving this wonderful car you've given me?"

The wind made it hard to hear the Nosferatu's response, but Lucita was certain it was something quite rude. It was followed by an expectant silence, so she shifted the phone to her left hand, tucked it under her chin, and rattled off the evening's details.

"Torres is dead. Your spotter's information was good, and once I was in Waterbury I was able to find him easily. Your man did not mention that Torres had runners with him, but I expected as much. They have been dealt with as well, but their bodies were left as a message."

"You didn't get that?" The Nosferatu sounded surprised. "That should have been in the last transmission."

"It doesn't matter at this point. Both are dead." She blew her horn as she nearly ran up the tailpipe of an Infiniti, which took a moment to wobble over to the right lane. "And no, I did not hear that. Interesting."

"Curiouser and curiouser. Well. Damn. You said you got both?"

"I did. Out of the goodness of my heart, I will not even add them to the bill." She paused. "I must admit, I was surprised to find Rey here, of all places."

"It was a lucky break," the Nosferatu admitted carelessly. "We knew that they'd sent out scouts, so we put people out to watch the main roads. One of our roving spotters on interstate detail caught him by accident in Duchess County and called it in. From there, it was just a matter of getting people on the right roads to look for him. Are you still on for the last two targets?"

Lucita's expression melted into a frown. The next mark was insignificant, but as for the archbishop, she'd been contracted not once but twice to take out that target, and Talley, damn him and his "professional courtesy," would oppose her. The money was frankly unimportant. It was the principle of the thing. No one kept her from what she had claimed for her own. No one.

Not anymore.

"Lucita? Are you still there? Lucita?"

"Hmm? Yes. Just…some difficult traffic."

There was a deliberate pause at the other end of the line. "Are you sure that you can handle Talley?" the Nosferatu asked, as if reading Lucita's mind long distance. "We can send in help if you need."

Lucita's brow darkened with anger. "Good night," she said, and broke the connection. In the near distance, the lights of Hartford obscured the stars and turned the night sky a sickly purple. The city was still in Camarilla hands, for the time being. She'd stay here for the next few nights, regrouping, and then press on. One more simple assignment, and then it was on to the big one.

Not to mention, she thought, *Talley*.

Wednesday, 18 August 1999, 3:17 AM
A subterranean grotto
New York City, New York

Calebros handled the long, wooden match with considerable deftness despite the gnarled talons that served as his fingers. He lit the final candle on the candelabra—a device he kept as far as possible from his desk, piled high with papers and folders, while still close enough to benefit slightly from the flickering illumination. His former desk lamp had flickered once too often for its own good, and Calebros had reacted…well, violently. Thus the candelabra.

At least candles were *supposed* to flicker. Calebros had enough sources of tension in his unlife without cantankerous desk appliances. He'd long since thrown in his lot with the Camarilla, unlike many of his clanmates here in the Big Apple, and right now everything was going the Sabbat's way. Perhaps Calebros had put too much faith in Pieterzoon, but if a childe of Hardestadt couldn't save the day, so to speak, what hope remained?

Calebros returned to his work, taking a several-nights-old report from his desk and exorcising his agitation with a red pen.

15 August 1999

Re: Sabbat advances

FILE COPY

End of curfew in D.C. has allowed
Sabbat to solidify hold of city;
Prince Garlotte and Prince Vitel
already pulled as many strings as
possible to get Maryland National Guard
there (more manageable) instead of
federal troops; points south now firmly
Sabbat-controlled since blitzkrieg.

Buffalo gone---failure of Pieterzoon's
plan or (our intelligence?)

No hint of Buffalo offensive from
Ravenna/Parmenides; out of the loop?
sold out? Spending most of his time at
siege of Tremere chantry, away from
Vykos according to Courier.

Or treachery?
Attack force surprisingly small;
seemed to expect Tzimisce defense.

That leaves Baltimore, part of NY,
and Hartford of any value.

Thursday, 19 August 1999, 3:49 AM
Wisconsin Avenue
Washington, D.C.

Four vampires could often do safely what no mortal in his right mind would even attempt, in this case wander the streets of Washington, D.C., after dark without the slightest fear for their personal safety. The fact that three of the four were archbishops of the Sabbat, and the fourth was a bodyguard who could, on any given night, give each of the three a run for his money didn't alter the situation that much. It simply meant that the quartet was impossibly formidable, instead of just being extremely nasty.

Currently the four—Archbishop Sascha Vykos of Washington, Archbishop Domingo Polonia of New York, Archbishop Borges of Miami, and the ominous, silent Sir Talley, who strode four paces behind them— were taking their ease on Georgetown's main drag, walking past closed pizza joints and used-CD stores. The homeless, who normally dotted the street after the students and tourists and Eurotrash had gone home, took a look at what was coming down the street and, one by one, withdrew into doorways or side streets or alleys, shivering there until the four predators had gone.

They needn't have worried, however. Three of the four were after bigger prey, and the last wasn't after anyone in particular at all.

"It seems that we have two problems," said Vykos, who had slipped her arms through those of the Lasombra flanking her. Borges flinched at her touch, while Polonia accepted it without hesitation.

Talley, stalking behind, noticed this as he noticed everything else. Mostly, however, his gaze was on everything but the three vampires in front of him. Instead, he kept an eye on the rooftops, the doorways and the alleys, and especially the shadows. He knew better than to expect his warning had served any purpose, other than to allow him to say he'd made every attempt to comply with the letter of Monçada's instructions not to harm the cardinal's childe.

Talley didn't *think* Lucita would be brash enough to try anything here, but then again Lucita had been brash since before her sire had brought her from life into unlife. Surely she couldn't be rash enough to try to attack all four of them…but then again, deciding that she couldn't possibly do something meant that you stopped defending against that particular eventuality.

Lucita, he knew, was very, very good at finding out where you'd let down your defenses. So, Talley decided, the best course was to assume nothing, prepare for everything and use that as an excuse to ignore the discussion the three vampires he was escorting were having. It was, he found, surprisingly difficult. His eye kept being drawn back to the obvious tension ahead of him. To the casual observer, the trio might look like three friends on a night out, possibly students or, given their exotic features, attachés from one of the nearby embassies.

But Talley could read the body language of those three like he could read a map, which was to say with but a quick glance, and what he read bothered him. Polonia's movements were graceful by human standards, but compared to the archbishop's usual feline grace he was positively wooden. Clearly, his mind was elsewhere.

Vykos, by comparison, was almost too ostentatiously at ease. She laughed too loudly and too often. Her walk was still predatory, but overexaggerated.

As for Borges, he moved under tight control. Every brush against Vykos, every laugh or comment made him stiffen.

"So we have two problems," he heard Polonia say. "First, there is the matter of the most noble and notable Theodore Bell, who seems to be behind many of our problems. Pieterzoon appears to be leaning on him heavily. I would very much like to see what would happen if we removed that crutch, and would be very pleased if the Ventrue toppled as a result."

Borges spat. "Should we even be discussing this here? This is neither the time nor the place to be planning serious matters."

"On the contrary," Polonia's voice was smooth and a bit amused, "it is the perfect time and place. For once there are no idiot Panders banging on the table, no ghouls snacking in the corner and no pack priests needing to be disciplined just so we can all agree that fire is hot. We, and Mr. Talley behind us, are the real powers here. What we decide is what happens. The rest is mere shadowplay, a puppet show to make the others follow us more willingly. For the moment, however," and a note of surprise crept into his voice, "I find myself a bit weary of playing to the crowd.

"So, we have a problem. Two, actually, but I think we should deal with Bell first before moving on to the other."

Borges harrumped. "I think I'd rather hear what

you think our other problem is, Don Polonia. We keep on trying to tackle things piecemeal, and I worry that we are spending too much effort and time by doing so. Perhaps one of our problems can help solve another, yes?"

Vykos gave a silvery peal of laughter. "Why, Archbishop Borges, that's an excellent notion." Borges almost skipped a step and Talley could see his shoulders tense in a way he'd seen in wolfhounds about to leap to the attack. "What else do we have on the agenda, Archbishop Polonia?"

Polonia gracefully disengaged from Vykos's arm and made a gesture that was more or less equivalent to a shrug. "I don't see how it will help in this instance, but the other concern I have is Boston."

"Boston?" Borges snorted disbelief. "What about it? It's been ripe for the taking for years. It's a rotten fencepost. All we have to do is lean on it and it will fall over."

"As far as the Camarilla is concerned, yes. However, there's another power there that concerns me far more. The Giovanni are strong there, and getting stronger, and unlike the Camarilla they don't play by any rules."

"True enough," Borges chimed in. "Half the time, you can trust the Camarilla's own Traditions to hamstring them in a fight. The necromancers are under no such compunction. Unfortunately, they fight to win."

"Indeed. And their allies among the dead make them more formidable than their numbers would indicate." Vykos sounded a trifle concerned, though Talley admitted to himself that it could just be wishful thinking. He'd known Vykos a long time, known *of* Vykos for even longer, and had only heard the Tzimisce sound afraid all of twice in all that time. He liked hearing Vykos afraid. It let him know how, should it become necessary, he could take the freshly minted Archbishop of Washington down.

Then again, there was quite a distance between "possibly mildly concerned" and actually afraid, and Talley knew better than to confuse the two.

"…Saying we should ignore the Camarilla for the moment and just strike full force at Boston?" Polonia's voice was incredulous.

"Not ignore it. Keep up harrying attacks at the cities on the front. Wait for Archbishop Vykos's friend to tell us where they'll be weak and hit there with small units. Such tactics brought us Buffalo, did they not? And in the meantime, go after the Giovanni sons of bitches so hard with everything else we've got that Venice sinks another six inches in sympathy." Borges was flushed with excitement, his left hand tracing maps in the air as he outlined his plan.

Vykos frowned and interjected. "It's a good notion, but how do we put it into practice?"

Polonia sidestepped a pile of trash in the middle of the sidewalk and nodded. "The difficulty is in getting men there. We can't come down from Montreal because the territory in between is hostile, rotten with lupines. We'd lose most of our forces before we got within shouting distance of the city. Heading north from New York forces us to strike out across Camarilla territory, which negates the whole point of your excellent strategy, Don Borges. The same holds for any move east from Buffalo. And the Giovanni have a very firm hold on the airport and docks, so sea or air maneuvers are unlikely at best."

lasombra

"Are you so sure of the latter, Archbishop?" Vykos asked.

"Quite. I've had occasion to use their services." That almost broke Vykos's stride, and Talley gave a quick laugh that he swallowed in a cough. "Oh yes, they're excellently professional."

"Dare I ask why you placed yourself in their hands?" The laughter and coquettish tone were gone from Vykos's voice. "A whim? Surely not."

Polonia laughed. "More of a fact-finding mission. I wanted to see first-hand how they were managing to smuggle so many Ventrue into New York. I came away slightly waterlogged and very impressed. They have a superb, almost enviable operation."

"And did you learn how to end the flow of Camarilla vampires into your city, Archbishop?" Borges's tone was deceptively mild, implying that the whole thing was a trifling affair and that anyone of reasonable competence could be expected to handle it with a minimum of fuss.

"No," said Polonia softly, "but I did learn some other *very* interesting things." The implications hung in the air a moment, and Talley watched the other two very carefully for their reactions. Unfortunately, he was predictably disappointed by what he saw.

"Ah," replied Borges, dismissing Polonia's comment. "Well, sooner or later they won't have anywhere to come from, no?"

Talley could almost hear Polonia forcing his face into a smile at the insult. "The man with snakes in his garden has more to worry about than the man with uninvited guests, Don Borges. You'd do very well indeed to remember that."

Borges bristled, and for an instant Talley thought

he'd have to intervene. Fortunately, Vykos did so before he had to. "The truism is quaint, but I still haven't heard what you intend us to do."

Polonia took an extra step forward, spun on his heel and bowed deeply. The entire procession ground to a halt as he did so. "The noble archbishop is, of course, correct. May I beg your indulgence one moment, then, to explain my humble plans?"

Borges frowned. "Butter wouldn't melt in your mouth, Polonia."

"Nor in yours, dead man. Now hold your tongue for a minute, before it flaps out too far and gets cut off." Pushed too far, Borges descended into angry sputtering, which Talley was quite certain was what Polonia had wanted all along.

"As I see it, the key is still Bell. Pieterzoon leans on him, relies on him. He is the means by which the damned Ventrue integrates himself into the machine of the American Camarilla. Soon, the two of them will function in harmony, coordinating their efforts and maximizing their results. It is at that precise moment that we must remove Bell, once and for all. If we do so, we succeed twice over. First of all, by destroying Bell, we take a dangerous piece of the enemy's off the board. Even better, we hamstring Pieterzoon, who must suddenly start to function without his ever-reliable crutch. It will take him more time to rebuild his operations than it did to build them, and in the meanwhile the advantage is all ours."

"Ambitious," murmured Vykos.

"A simple law of statecraft," replied Polonia. "It is axiomatic that one expels the spy after he has taken over the local network, rather than before. It disrupts all of his half-achieved plans, and makes it take that much more time for the next spymaster to settle in, after all." He gave a short bark of laughter. "If you wish to know who's been spying, my sire used to say, look to see who's been deported."

Vykos nodded. "Still, you've given reasons why Bell should be removed, not plans for how to do it."

"Patience, my dear Archbishop. Here is what we will do, combining our problems as Don Borges suggested earlier. We will kill Bell. With him removed, Pieterzoon's operation collapses into temporary chaos. During that opportunity, we drive toward Boston across the heart of New England. To prepare the way, we send out a pack as advance scouts during the first part of the operation, and in the confusion they can slip through the Camarilla cordon into Boston proper. Then they go to ground and begin laying the groundwork for a full-scale operation against the Giovanni." Polonia smiled, and not kindly. "As you seem to be a bit short-handed on personnel, Don Borges, I will even volunteer one of my packs to run the gauntlet into Boston; I can think of one already who's been doing so off and on for years, and which has established something of a safe haven there. You, my honored peer, can have the honor of leading the guerrilla operation instead, with Sir Talley at your side."

"Hmm." Vykos waved a finger in the air lazily, as if conducting an orchestra no one else could hear. "I think I see one flaw in your plan, Archbishop."

"Oh?"

"You said 'kill Bell,' as if it would be that easy. Do you have any ideas as to how this might be accomplished, or were you just trusting Jove to send down a convenient thunderbolt?"

"Tsk tsk, such blasphemy. Your patron would not appreciate it. Besides, I thought I might indulge in your favorite political tool."

"Ah. I see." Vykos's face was expressionless. "That tack failed once already, you know."

Polonia waved the objection away. "We failed with the master, now we try the man. I doubt he'll be as difficult a target. Besides, the Camarilla has a unique blind spot in their tactical vision. For some reason, they think that if they foil a stratagem once, it could never possibly work again. No doubt Pieterzoon and Bell and Vitel and all of the others are sitting around, congratulating themselves on the fact that they've outsmarted the assassins we sent after the Dutchman. Surely we would not be so gauche as to try the same trick again. They won't expect it, not at all."

Vykos steepled her fingers and frowned. "I hope you are right, Archbishop. Am I to assume that this portion of the operation is mine?"

Polonia bowed from the neck. "You assume correctly, Archbishop. And even if we fail here, we succeed. We shake the Camarilla's faith in what they 'know' about us. We decrease their trust in their safety. We make them worry. And a worried enemy, as you both know, is a beaten one."

"I'll think on it," said Borges brusquely, and he turned and walked off. Polonia raised an eyebrow, and Vykos nodded and went after him. As the sound of their footsteps on wet cobblestones faded, the Archbishop of New York looked at Talley, who remained before him.

"Excellently played, Archbishop," said Talley mildly.

Polonia regarded the templar with disinterest. "You would be referring to…?"

"Your baiting of Archbishop Borges. You goad him toward…rashness. You drive him to acts that could cause him harm."

"And that offends your sensibilities, my dear Templar?" Polonia asked casually. "Tell me, if you feel Archbishop Borges to be in such danger, why are you still here with me?"

Talley spread his hands. "I assure you, Don Polonia, I am merely doing my job."

"Ah. I see. And that job is?"

"Keeping Archbishop Borges, among others, functioning. Would it surprise you to hear that my actual orders from Cardinal Monçada are slightly different from the ones that were communicated to you?"

Polonia inclined his head slightly. "Not at all. Walk with me, Templar." Without looking back, he headed down the street, in the direction opposite that which Borges had taken. Talley frowned, and then followed.

"So," Polonia said, "what *are* you doing here? Or does the cardinal not wish that to be known?"

"More or less what you expect. I am to protect you and your fellow archbishops—because while we have very good evidence that one of you has been marked for assassination, the details are still a bit unclear—and generally to make my presence very publicly known." Talley's voice was expressionless, his eyes everywhere but on Polonia.

"Known to whom?"

"To whomever is employing Lucita, Your Excellency."

Polonia sighed. "And that brings you to me?"

Talley sidestepped a garbage can. "Call it a pre-ventative measure, Don Polonia. Rey Torres, one of Borges's most loyal associates, has been sent away and cannot reach the archbishop in case of trouble. Don Borges himself is the target of constant goading, and sooner or later he'll erupt in a fashion that I can't contain. It behooves me to go to the source of this problem and try to eliminate it."

Polonia turned with one eyebrow raised. "I had no idea that Torres was such a matter of concern."

Talley nodded. "By himself, he's not. He's a coward and a braggart, but right now I'm more concerned with where he fits into the larger puzzle."

"Fit in the past tense, I expect, at this point. But that is neither here nor there. Hmm. Had I known that you were so suspicious of my motives, I would have insisted that Torres not take point. No doubt Borges would have objected to my stealing his people's chance for glory, however, and…" Polonia's face curved into an expression of contempt for a second, then he looked up. "Again, that is of no consequence. Say what you have been waiting to say, before we walk ourselves out of the city."

Talley stopped and sat down on a concrete step. "If you insist. Tell me, Don Polonia, why do you want Archbishop Borges dead?"

"That is easy. I do not."

"No?" Talley almost snorted in disbelief. "Then please, explain to me how it is that so many signs point to you."

Polonia gave a thin smile. "Allow me to explain something to you, Don Talley. Borges is an impetuous man. He is a man of strength and passion, but he has little control or subtlety. He can be led much like the bull is led in the ring, coerced into a rage and then turned at a target. In that, he is useful while the war lasts, and I do not discard tools while there is some use in them. This fight is not yet over, and for all his faults, Archbishop Borges would be a hard man to replace. Besides, I suspect that Borges's temper will kill him long before I decide it is necessary to bring his name before *Les Amies Noir* for judgment or execution. So I do not wish Borges dead; or instead, let me say that I do not wish him dead any more than I have for the last two centuries, and possibly less so at the moment.

"If I wanted Borges dead," Polonia said softly, "he would have been dead before the gracious cardinal sent you here. Do you understand me, Templar?"

Talley almost caught himself flinching. He was older than Polonia, and probably more powerful, but the man had an air of veiled menace about him that chilled the blood.

"But of course," Polonia came to a stop as he paused, "you ask me if I've hired Lucita to destroy a fellow archbishop. What else would you expect me to say?"

With that, the Archbishop of New York continued on his way, leaving Talley to stand alone in the night.

"I am curious, Cardinal. Tell me: What game are you really playing?"

Cardinal Monçada spread his hands beatifically. "Why, chess, of course. And I will allow you to take back that last move, unless you truly do wish to sacrifice that bishop."

"I thought you were sacrificing an archbishop," grumbled Don Ibrahim. He peered at the board. "Let the move stand. I would rather lose than take charity and score a tainted victory, *bismallah*."

"If you insist." Monçada reached ponderously over the board and swept the bishop aside with a knight. "I admit, the symbolism of the move is a bit cloying. One can read too much into such things, Don Ibrahim. As I told Talley before I sent him away, the chess metaphor is a weary one."

Ibrahim crossed his arms and sat back. "If it has gotten weary, that is because it has given honorable service upon so many occasions. So what game *are* you playing, Cardinal? Sate my curiosity. You know I have no stake in these American squabbles, and no interest who lives or dies."

"None whatsoever?"

"Talley will come back."

"I should hope so." Monçada heaved his immense bulk from the chair and stood, blinking. "And Lucita, as well. Vykos? Probably. It is old and powerful, and while it is in danger, it is skilled at survival. As for the others, well, if Lucita survives, one of them will not. It is simple logic." He began a slow circuit around the room, rubbing his hands and sighing. "As for what my game is, well, I confess to you that I have none. I am protecting my assets and trying to flush out a traitor. There are too many subtle signs of wrongness emanating from this entire escapade. There are too many powers in one place, too many agendas. Sooner or later it will all thin itself out, and I want to make sure that it does so in an orderly fashion. I don't expect Talley will succeed in his stated mission, in truth. I simply expect his presence to eliminate waste and unnecessary carnage."

Ibrahim nodded and studied the board, then moved a pawn forward to threaten Monçada's knight. "Sensible. Eminently sensible. But what do you do when the smoke has cleared?"

Monçada stopped and gazed up at a tapestry that was almost as old as he was. It depicted the opening of Jesus's tomb on the third day, and it had a curious stain down the left side. "We shall see what we shall see when it does, Don Ibrahim. Someone may require punishment, if he has been too avid in following his own agenda and not the greater one that God has allowed us to set for him." The latter was said mildly, in a matter-of-fact tone that might deceive any who did not know the cardinal. Don Ibrahim, on the other hand, had a very good idea of how Monçada defined "punishment," and suddenly felt a bit anxious himself.

"What if it's one of your archbishops?"

Monçada frowned. "Then I will punish an archbishop."

Ibrahim nodded. "I am pleased to hear that. Some of them grow too confident in themselves if left too long to their own devices." A sudden thought struck him. "But what do you do if Talley actually succeeds?"

The cardinal turned, an unguarded, unwholesome smile on his face. "Against my daughter, Don Ibrahim, do you really think he will?"

Don Ibrahim said nothing for as long as he dared, then turned back to the board. "It is your move, Cardinal," he said quietly.

"Indeed it is, my friend. I thank you for reminding me. Indeed it is." And he settled himself back into his chair and stared at the board, concentrating once again on the game at hand.

"What we have here," said Angela with a plastic smile, "is a failure to communicate." The man she was speaking to didn't answer, possibly because his mouth was filled with blood and fragments of his own broken teeth, but that didn't seem to be an acceptable excuse to Angela. She reached down and grabbed him by his stained shirt front, then hauled him to his feet. He kicked feebly, once or twice, but to no avail. Overhead, the occasional car rumbled across the Jamaica Way overpass; in the near distance an early Orange Line train screeched its way into Forest Hills station. Other than that, however, the night was deserted, which struck Angela as something of a pity. A witness, in her mind, would make a convenient excuse for more exercise than her current victim was providing.

He was a small man, with black hair and swarthy features that might have been almost handsome before Angela had gently applied a tire iron to his lower jaw. He wore a shirt that had once been white but now was stained with dirt and blood, a black vest and black slacks. There was a ragged and bloody patch on his scalp where Angela, in her enthusiasm, had torn out a hunk of his hair, and a trail of blood leaked from his ruined mouth. When he breathed, bubbles of pinkish foam formed and burst on his lips.

Angela figured he had maybe five minutes, ten at the outside. There was plenty of time for her to get the answers she needed and have a little fun besides. She thought for a second, then grabbed her victim and turned him over. He spat gobbets of half-congealed blood onto the cobblestones. "You have one chance to make this painless," she said. "Tell me where your boss parks his car, and I end this right now. Play stubborn, and you end up like them." She pointed straight up with her off hand.

The man followed her gaze. Directly over them was the overpass that took the Jamaicaway over the southern terminus of the Orange Line subway: four lanes' worth of concrete and steel stretched thirty feet straight up. On the underside of the construction were corpses, at least a dozen. They were impaled on spikes that jutted down from the overpass, and crudely but securely manacled and gagged. A stench of rot drifted down lazily, to mingle with the garbage and urine smells that were thick on the breeze. "Hmm?" Angela asked.

The man laughed. Startled, Angela dropped him. "What's so funny, you little shit? What's so funny about that?"

The man spat more blood, choking on it even as he tried to rein in his amusement. "Man, you just don't get it, do you? That's what you're threatening me with? Man, you don't know a damn thing." His voice was thick and slurred, but his mocking tone came through regardless.

Angela looked down at him, tapped his jaw with her foot once, and waited.

"Lemme explain something to you, okay? You're gonna kill me? Great. You're gonna break every bone in my body? Fine. You're gonna make me hurt like no one has ever hurt before, and eventually you're going to kill me. Fan-fucking-tastic. Do it. I'll scream as much as I can, even, if it makes you feel better. But what you don't get is that in the end, it's all gotta end. You're gonna kill me, and I'll be dead and then you can't hurt me any more." He coughed once, a rattle in his chest that hadn't been there before. "But once you kill me, it's over. If I sell out, well, I die anyway and then the hurting really starts. And you know what? Once my boss gets his hands on my soul, I'm gonna hurt *forever*." He spat and grinned bloodily. "So do your worst, you bitch. I'm not going anywhere." He started laughing again, loud enough that it could be heard over the thunder of the eighteen-wheeler passing overhead.

Angela stared at him thoughtfully for a long moment. "Hmm. That's a good point. Unfortunately for you, you've missed what's really going on here. Look up again. Look very carefully at the people up there. Then count how many are still moving."

The man looked up once again, and his eyes got very wide. "Oh," was all he said.

Angela smiled, not unkindly. "The sun never, ever gets under here, you know, and we just drape a tarp across the whole thing and make it look like there's someone doing maintenance. It's worked for years."

"Years?"

She nodded. "Years. That's how long I've been visiting town on Polonia's orders. That's how long Arnold's been up there…you remember Arnold, right? I think he had your job before you did, then he disappeared.

"Even your boss didn't know what happened to him, did he? Well, here's the story. He wouldn't talk, either, so I decided to let him hang around until he changed his mind." She leaned over and kissed his forehead with an almost maternal gesture. "Don't worry, Danny. You're going to be hanging around, too."

It was nearly dawn when Angela finally got the tarp back in place, with a little help from an early-rising phone crew she flagged down and pressed into service by dint of one of her better-developed vampiric abilities. Danny was up there, his mouth still open in that stupid little "oh." He hadn't talked yet, but Angela was sure he was going to, soon. And when he had, she'd leave him up there anyway, as a little payback for laughing at her.

Already, the first commuters were straggling along the path to the train station. Some looked blearily at Angela, no doubt seeing her as a late returnee from a night of partying (never mind that Boston rolled up its sidewalks at 1 AM). All of them walked right under where Danny now rested, two feet of sharp steel through his sternum. None of them even bothered to look up; there were times when the vampire felt that the tarp covering her little menagerie was a wasted effort.

Angela felt herself smiling, and broke into a brisk walk. The temporary haven where the others were waiting with their news was only a few blocks away, so there was no need for her to rush. She felt good, however. Soon the Giovanni's chauffeur would break, and they'd know everything they needed to in order to deal with the man's master. Then that knowledge could be passed back to Archbishop Polonia, and he could get it to those who needed to know.

It was going to be, Angela decided, an absolutely beautiful day.

"You're late." The voice echoed hollowly through the empty room. The only piece of furniture in it was a straight-backed wooden chair, occupied by a short, black-haired man in an immaculate, and squeakily new, biker jacket. His boots were planted squarely on the floor and his hands were folded neatly in his lap. He was silhouetted against the moonlight that poured through the bay window behind him, but nothing in his posture betrayed the slightest tension or fear. The great wooden doors at either end of the room were barred from the outside, and the walls were featureless white. A single candelabra, marred by the wax drippings from countless tapers, swung silent and black from its chain.

Lucita walked out of the shadows like Venus rising from the waves at Cyprus. The darkness flowed off her, leaving her facing her prey alone. She wore her usual working clothes, and her hair was tied back with a simple black leather cord. There was a broad-bladed knife in her left hand, but her right hand was free. "I'm disappointed in you, Munro. The briefing my client provided said you'd be difficult to deal with, yet here I find you, waiting for me. Tired of existence?"

Munro chuckled for precisely two seconds, then cut himself off. "Hardly. Though I do confess to waiting for you. Have you been looking for me long?" His voice bore traces of a Scots burr, long since washed away by years away from his homeland.

"Not terribly, no. In most things, my employer is quite accurate. In this case, he told me where I'd likely find you and when, what defenses I'd encounter, what the floor plan looked like and the likelihood that you'd be wearing that jacket. It has been," and she nodded primly, "a most satisfactory professional arrangement."

The man in the chair blinked. "For a satisfactory professional arrangement, you're going to destroy me? That hardly seems fair."

Lucita waggled a finger. "Of course not. I am going to destroy you because I've been paid a great deal of money, as well as certain other considerations, to do so. The fact that I think you're ridiculous, and that my employer is wasting his money by having me do this, is entirely beside the point. You never should have strayed, *antitribu*. The Sabbat doesn't suit you."

Munro deliberately crossed his legs but made no other motion. "Until tonight, I was happy with the choice." He tugged at the creaky leather of his sleeve. "The wardrobe is a small sacrifice."

"A poor one to make. You look like a clown, Munro." Lucita began tossing the knife in the air and catching it with her off hand. The fifth time she did this, the knife never came down. She didn't seem to notice. "It matters not, though. Your story ends here. I will let you pray for a minute, if you wish. You were wee kirk, yes? My sire has spoken highly of your devotion."

Munro gave a tight smile. "Not necessary, I think. Besides, Lucita, I'm not quite ready to die yet. Are you?" He clapped his hands once.

Nothing happened, save that Lucita finally decided to look up after her knife. It hung, suspended in midair, with its blade reflecting the moonlight into a diamond shape on the wooden floor. "Hmm?" she said. "Were you expecting someone?"

Clearly angry, Munro clapped again. There was

again no answer but silence. He leapt to his feet, knocking the chair over backwards with a loud clatter, and screamed, "God damn it, where are you? Get in here! She's in here with me!"

Lucita turned to him, her eyes wide with mock innocence. "Oh, don't tell me. You are calling for those twenty men you had waiting outside, yes? The ones who were supposed to charge in here when I approached you and then overwhelm me by weight of numbers, yes?" Munro turned to her, his mouth hanging open in shock. "I'm terribly sorry, Munro. They had a little accident." She paused and appeared to reconsider. "I must correct myself. The ten through that door," and she pointed to her left, "had a terrible accident. The ten through that door," and she swung her arm around to the right, "I killed. Now, does that clear everything up? I think the next step is for you to attack me in a blind rage, and for me to kill you. Then I leave, collect my payment and take a few nights off before preparing for my next target. Yes?"

Munro glared at her with pure hatred for a moment, then turned and dove for the window. Lucita, surprised, was frozen for a full half second. Then she simply pointed at the fleeing vampire. The tendril of shadow that held the knife darted out and, with whiplike speed, slashed the back of Munro's calves. He collapsed as the knife dropped to the floor. Lucita gave a cluck of disapproval, then walked over to where her prey writhed on the floor, still struggling to reach the window.

"You disappoint me, Munro," she said. "Showing your back to the enemy? A poor tactic, even for a fool like you." She stooped to pick up the knife and, after considering her options, drove it through the man's hand and into the floor underneath. "Now, what to do with you?"

The bubbling noises coming from the floor might have been curses, or they might have been pleas. Lucita ignored them in either case, pondering. Finally, after a long minute, she leaned down close to Munro's ear, and whispered. "Peter," she said, "I want you to know something. It does not matter to me at all that you die now, save as a contract fulfilled with a minimum of fuss. I have been told that your death is necessary to limit the Sabbat's ability to obtain certain firearms and other toys, but honestly, I do not care. What I do care about, little man, is this: You have wasted my evening with your posturing. You make a terrible villain. The role never suited you and you would have done better to stay where you were." She dropped to her haunches. "You are also naïve, and a coward, and I dislike both of those things intensely. That is why I am taking this moment to speak to you, rather than putting you out of your misery immediately."

With a snarl, Munro tore his hand free from the floor and clawed for her throat. Lucita danced out of the way, easily avoiding the strike. The knife clanked to the hardwood and Munro reached for it, but she kicked it away and it skittered to the far end of the room. He flipped himself and got to his knees, but as he did so she struck his nose with an open-fist punch. The man gurgled and nearly fell over backwards, fear in his eyes as Lucita took a step toward him. She raised her hand for another strike, and he toppled as it caught him in the throat.

She stared down at him, disgusted by the ruin of his face. Blood ran everywhere, but it didn't interest her in the least. Munro's vitae, she was sure, would be as thin and distasteful as he himself was. "Good-bye, Peter," she said softly. "I won't play with you any more." Munro's eyes, wild with terror and hatred, stared up at her as his ruined legs flopped desperately. He threw up an arm to defend himself, but she slapped it out of the way. Then, with slow deliberation, she cupped her hand below her mouth and blew him a kiss.

Munro gaped. Nothing happened for a moment, and then she exhaled as if she were blowing out a candle.

Munro's face, for all intents and purposes, exploded. Lucita failed to blink as bits of it spattered on her legs, but she made a mental note to have these togs burned as soon as she could. Munro was precisely the sort of whiny soul who tended to linger as a ghost, and she intended to give him as few anchors for bothering her as possible. Without a second glance for what was left of her target, she walked to the door to her left and unbarred it. The carnage outside was, if possible, even more brutal than what she'd inflicted on Munro. Bits and pieces of hired thug and low-grade vampire were scattered across the room, from the curiously immaculate piano to the gore-spattered sofa. She ignored it all and kept walking, right to the kitchen and out. The stove was a massive cast-iron antique, squat and ominous. More importantly, however, it had four gas burners. Lucita turned each on in turn, then snuffed the pilot light with a breath. It was a pity to destroy such a lovely old house, she felt, but more of a pity to leave Munro's corpse around to pollute the night.

Two minutes later she was on the road to Hartford, dialing the contact number for her client to let the mysterious Mr. Schreck know that three of the four targets were dead, and that the last one's nights were numbered.

"So what do you think?"

"I think that if Lucita is after you," said Talley carefully, "I am your only chance of getting out of this intact, Your Excellency. Mind you, I will bow to your expert analysis of the situation if you disagree, because you are an archbishop and I'm but a lowly templar. Never mind, of course, the fact that I've been doing this sort of thing for approximately six centuries and have acquired a certain familiarity with the ground rules of operations, while you were a by-blow of that ridiculous treaty signed in 18—"

Archbishop Borges held up a meaty hand. "Enough. Thank you. Yes, I trust your analysis. I've been given your services by the cardinal, and it seems prudent to make use of them. Now, what do you suggest I do about it?" he asked, levering himself out of his black leather desk chair and rising to his feet. Behind him, a screen saver busied itself in drawing pictures of plumbing across a monitor.

"You know, of course," said Talley as he began taking slow steps forward, "that the assassin I'm supposed to be guarding you from is Lucita." Borges visibly paled at the mere mention of her name, and Talley's grin bared his fangs for the first time since he'd arrived in America. "Ah. I see you've heard of her. She's a lovely woman, extremely talented and one of the most skillful killers I've run across. Oh, did I mention that she's the cardinal's childe, and that he's very, very fond of her? Yes, that's right, Archbishop. Changes your assessment of the situation, doesn't it?"

Borges put a brave face on things. "Bah," he said, with a dismissive wave of his hand. "I'm aware of Lucita's lineage—who is not? The childe does not always follow the sire's path, else we'd still be skulking around Lasombra's castle in Sicily waiting for Montano to fetch us peasants for dinner. Is there any particular reason you're trying to scare me with old news, Templar?"

Talley made a mocking bow from the neck. "Ah, I should have known that you'd be well informed. But don't you think it's curious, Your Excellency, that Archbishop Vykos came here as Cardinal Monçada's envoy, yet it was Archbishop Polonia who received word from the cardinal that I—the cardinal's gift to the three of you—would be arriving? Furthermore, for what purpose do I arrive? Why, to protect that illustrious trio from the cardinal's own wayward daughter." He stepped closer to Borges until he was right in the man's face. Patches of shadow still masked Borges's eyes, and Talley got the definite feeling that Borges was not so much seeing as sensing him. "Fascinating, isn't it, that all of the surviving players in this little tableau are somehow connected to the esteemed cardinal—except for you?"

Talley suddenly spun, and faster than the eye could follow he was seated in Borges's just-vacated chair. "Does that make you feel…isolated? Nervous? Worried? Well, it should." He leveled his gaze on his client, now pacing about the room. "You're alone with me, Your Excellency, and I don't think anyone other than Vykos and Polonia knows our whereabouts," he said in a very quiet voice. "If this were all a plot by the cardinal, you'd be in a great deal of trouble."

Borges fixed him with a tired glare. "Sir Talley, I have no idea what you are attempting to accomplish here, but whatever it is, I resent it. If you have finished trying to frighten me and have nothing new to say, get out. If, however, you've decided to get serious about fulfilling your duties, then do so. Do I make myself clear?"

Talley nodded. "Perfectly. I must say, it's nice to see you deal with a stressor without immediately trying to throttle it. I was beginning to despair of you, but this gives me hope. If you continue in this vein, you have a chance. A slim one, but a chance."

With a snort, Borges settled himself on top of the marble surface of the table behind him. "You don't exactly sound confident, Talley. I thought you were the famous Hound, who could do anything his master set him to?" The archbishop's expression was rather sour, and for an instant it struck Talley as humorous.

It was only an instant, however, and then the templar was all business once again. "Your Excellency," he said wearily, "an unknown party has gone to great trouble and expense to set an extremely talented and professional assassin on what is most probably your trail." Talley scrutinized Borges with a trained eye, watching for changes of expression, an unexplained tic, the slightest telltale sign of duplicity. Talley's speculative scenario, after all, was designed specifically for effect. "Lucita's been warming up with subordinates on this operation—at least, that's how I read her exercises on MacEllen and Torres."

"Rey, dead?" said Borges with sudden interest.

"That hasn't been confirmed."

Talley was carefully noncommittal. "He's missed the past three arranged call-times. Two bodies, the descriptions matching those of the two he took with him, were found in Waterbury, Connecticut. It's one of the cities he's supposed to be scouting." He paused for a minute. "I saw the news footage of the bodies. It's her work. You get to recognize styles after a while."

"You say there were only two bodies found. Rey could have gotten away." There was an unexpected tinge of hope in Borges's voice, one that quickly faded as Talley raised a quizzical eyebrow.

"Torres might be remarkably talented for his age and lineage," said the templar, "but on his best night and Lucita's worst, all he could do would be to extend matters another few minutes. Without help—and I saw what happened to his help—he had no chance." There was another moment of awkward silence. "I'm sorry. If I'd been there, I could have saved him—but there's no guarantee that Lucita wouldn't have moved on you instead in my absence."

"Dammit, Talley, when did this become about you?" Borges slammed his fist down on the table. The famous temper was on display again. "My second-in-command is missing and presumed destroyed, two of my best soldiers are curiosities for the local coroner to poke at in his spare time, and you're apologizing because you couldn't be in two places at once? Good God, you arrogant son of a bitch, do you think that I was given the blood yesterday, that I would be helpless without you? That I am archbishop because I won a popularity contest? By all the saints, Talley, you have no sense of whom you are talking to!"

Talley blinked, once, deliberately. "Your Excellency," he said with cold formality, "whoever seeks your death has gone to tremendous lengths to ensure that you—if you are indeed the target—have no hope of survival. He has purchased the services of the one assassin that your ultimate patron in this affair cannot move against."

"He's not my patron."

"Monçada is the patron of this entire affair, Borges, and you are just a small part of it. Be thankful he considers you worth preserving. My services are not assigned lightly, nor am I usually a watchdog. They call me the Hound for a reason. I hunt. If I am leashed to you, it is because the situation is most pressing indeed. Now listen to me; listen very closely. There is a pattern here, one you should fear. You are the one whom my instinct tells me most specifically to guard, and the one who has the least connection with the cardinal. Whoever has set this assassin on your trail—unless the whole thing is a ruse, and the cardinal has been fooled as thoroughly as I have— knows the cardinal well enough to know his weakness regarding Lucita, and has the resources necessary to make use of that knowledge. The implication, then, is that it is someone who knows Cardinal Monçada and knows how he works—but as yet, there is no telling who it might be."

Abruptly, he stood and began pacing. "I find it highly unlikely that your indirect assailant is of the Camarilla. Archbishop Vykos would be the obvious target in that case, seeing as the Camarilla seems to fixate on destroying Tzimisce; it must be the Tremere influence. On the other hand, Archbishop Polonia would be the *sensible* target, as he is the commander and chief tactician, and surely the enemy knows it.

But no, the target I feel the need to watch most carefully is you—the Lepidus in this little triumvirate." Borges bristled at that, and Talley ignored him. "Furthermore, Lucita's services are too expensive to acquire just for a feint, and she'd hardly consent to be a diversion. She has quite the sense of her own importance, you know." He flashed a brief, humorless smile. "Still. It doesn't add up. Nothing here says Camarilla, and yet the other options don't make sense either. You simply don't matter to the independents, except the snakes, and they have their own people to take care of matters without going to the expense of hiring Lucita. That leaves our own side, which would explain how the cardinal heard about it, but not who, or why. There's been no notion put before *Les Amies Noir* for your destruction; and frankly, it would seem more likely that you'd hire Lucita to eliminate Archbishop Polonia."

"I need no assassins!" blustered Borges, but Talley wondered about the thoughts behind the shadowy façade. One did not become archbishop of anything if one were a total fool, and Talley suspected that at least some of Borges's worst behavior was just an act.

"Indeed. I never said you did. What evidence could possibly point at you, Your Excellency? Now, Don Polonia might be another matter. If he was the one to send Torres on that recon—"

"I insisted," said Borges.

"Ah," Talley said. "No doubt wanting to garner some plaudits for you and yours. You played right into your enemy's hands, you know. You sent your best man out where he could be isolated and destroyed efficiently. Someone wants to cut you off. Presumably, that someone also encouraged you to send Torres out. If not Polonia, then Vykos?"

"No, no." Borges shook his head. He drummed his fingers on the tabletop. "Vykos wanted him for something different, another of her fool schemes. Polonia said something suitably condescending, what was it? Ah, 'Good officers shouldn't be wasted on foolish missions,' or something of that ilk. You know how he is," he added irritably.

"I see," said Talley softly. Inwardly, his frustration was mounting. He was having little success pruning his respective lists of targets and traitors: Each was still three names long. That being the case, he had little choice but to continue to prepare to protect all of the archbishops. "Fine," he began again irritably. "You, Your Excellency, are going to keep your remaining people on a short tether. You will not let anyone get your goat and trick you into doing something rash, no matter what. I can prevent other people from killing you, but I can't keep you from getting yourself killed. Furthermore, you are also going to follow my instructions any time we're in a situation that I deem dangerous. Do you understand?"

"You are presuming a great deal, Templar," said Borges in a low, dangerous voice.

"You know something? I am." Talley had suddenly had it with all of the damn touchy archbishops and their foibles that just made his job that much harder. "I am not doing this because I like you, Archbishop Borges. I don't like you. But that doesn't matter. I have been told to keep you from the Final Death, and that is what I will do—if you allow me to do it. If not, fine. I will declare my mission a miserable failure, return to Madrid and tell the cardinal what an uncooperative bastard you were. Mind you, the key word I use is 'were' because I have no doubt that without me to defend you, Lucita will fulfill her contract and be off spending her ridiculously large fee by the time my plane touches ground in Europe. At that point, I am sure that the cardinal will tell me that he's very disappointed in me, and then he'll ask me what I think of the latest move in his chess game, and if I am truly lucky, he will ask me to take confession. Then we will undoubtedly sit and talk, and wait for the official news of your demise."

"I see." The tone of Borges's voice indicated quite clearly that he approved of neither Talley's tone nor his manner, but there was a certain persuasiveness to the templar's argument. "And if I cooperate, I have some minuscule chance of survival?"

Talley nodded.

"Ah. It appears, then," said Borges, "that I have no choice but to put myself in your capable hands."

Talley bowed, from the waist instead of the neck. "If you don't mind, Your Excellency, I will take my leave. This room is, to the best of my ability, secure for the moment. I recommend, of course, bright lights throughout. If you need me, I will be down the hall." He went out, shutting the door behind him with an audible click.

Archbishop Borges sat for a moment, then got up and turned off all the lights instead. Humming tunelessly to himself, he sat down in the dark to wait.

The vampire who signed his name "Lucius" was, for lack of a better term, disgruntled. The recent council deliberations had not gone the way he'd wanted them to, not at all. Oh, the others had agreed readily enough that they were not quite ready to make a stand (a stance he intended to perpetuate *ad infinitum* until such time as the entire American Camarilla was backed onto the tip of Long Island or some other equally hopeless place), but then things had fallen apart. Lucius had voted for abandoning Stamford and the Connecticut coast, under the premise that the population density was too low to make the shoreline defensible. That argument had been shot down from multiple directions. The Bridgeport ferry was access to Long Island for a possible counterassault there. Stamford had financial importance beyond its size. Groton's nuclear submarine factory could not be allowed to fall into enemy hands. Blather blather blather, talk talk talk.

In the end, Lucius knew he was beaten. Ideally, his plan would have cost the Camarilla its main approach to New York, and isolated Hartford, Worcester and Springfield for the taking whenever Polonia got around to it. Instead, the Camarilla had chosen to consolidate its forces along the coast, abandoning Hartford and indeed all of central New England. Hartford itself would be defended by a skeleton force *á la* Buffalo, as the lone ghoul to survive that attack had reported relatively heavy enemy casualties. Unfortunately, he'd also reported that the enemy forces were surprisingly sparse, almost as if they knew the city would not be heavily defended.

Lucius knew where that line of logic went, and did his best to discourage it subtly. He also took a moment to fudge as much of the ghoul's memory as he dared, for the others would no doubt be looking for that sort of thing. Hopefully, that would turn suspicion in other directions. Lucius himself contributed the idea that the half-hearted attack on Buffalo meant that the Sabbat's troops were clearly building up for an imminent assault somewhere else, and he had briefly whipped everyone into a fine frenzy of panic. That had passed, however, and as things stood Lucius simply wanted to be away from everyone and everything. He stalked out of the inn, brushing lesser vampires and ghouls out of his way with a word or sometimes even a look. They scurried off, compelled by the power of his will and his blood.

Eventually, he reached his haven and, with disgust, he slammed the door behind him. The Cainites he was forced to work with here, with their petty politicking and clinging ghouls, disgusted him. However, it wasn't as if the Sabbat were any better these days. He'd handed that ungrateful wretch Vykos every tidbit he could pass to her. She'd learned troop dispositions, strategies, tactics—everything. But did she show gratitude? Did she offer the barest crumb of courtesy?

No. Instead, she'd threatened to expose him if he didn't supply even more than he already had.

Lucius was the sort of Cainite who kept a very careful eye on his debts and credits, and from where he stood, by threatening him, Vykos had exhausted her credit line with him. It was too late to back out of the arrangement—the die had been cast, after all—but Vykos needed to be reminded that power still flowed in two directions. Grinning in a way that would have made a sane man flee, Lucius went to his desk, pulled out a piece of stationery, and began to write. He wrote quickly, though not necessarily neatly, and several times he had to resort to blotting paper to clean up the excesses of his enthusiasm.

The letter was brief and to the point, though a handwriting expert might have blanched at the style of what Lucius's hand had scrawled. Carefully he folded the stationery and placed it in an envelope, which he addressed to "Sascha." Then he flipped the envelope over and sealed it with wax, eschewing any particular seal in favor of an anonymous blob.

"Jack," he called as he watched the wax cool. "Jack! You're needed!" Bare moments later, the door to the suite swung open to admit a younger vampire, dressed in what Lucius could only assume was the casual wear of this decade.

"Another letter?" Jack's tone was laconic, but his service had thus far been exemplary.

Lucius handed the envelope across the desk to Jack, who took it by one corner, as if he were afraid to smudge it with his fingerprints. Perhaps he was. "The delivery is a little different this time, Jack. Are you ready?"

"Oh?" was all Jack said, with no discernible enthusiasm whatsoever. For all the world he looked as if, in a moment more, he'd fall asleep where he stood.

"Yes. Vykos has been disrespectful of late. I do not appreciate such things. Therefore, it behooves me to teach her that such disrespect has a cost."

"Oh."

"Therefore, Jack, you must deliver this letter and a message." He leaned forward with a hungry gleam in his eyes. "Find her chambers. Make my displeasure known. Show her that anywhere she holds sacred, my servants can go. Anyone she values, I can destroy. Do you understand me, Jack?"

Jack nodded, slowly. "Of course. Back in three hours." He sketched a quick bow and walked toward the door.

"Oh, and Jack?" Lucius called after him.

"Yes?"

"Don't forget to deliver the letter."

With a pained expression on his face, Jack left.

The corner of a letter stuck out from under
Vykos's door as she returned from her evening con-
stitutional and meal. "Hector? Ilse?" she called out,
cautiously. Neither of the ghouls assigned to her door
were present. That was odd. They knew better than
to abandon their posts, on pain of her extreme disappointment. Furthermore, each had seen the
ramifications of her extreme disappointment before,
and as such had presumably learned not to disappoint
her.

She stared down at the letter for a minute. The
deliberate placement was a taunt, but the question
was whether or not there was a trap attached to it as
well. Clearly she was supposed to do something to
the envelope, presumably drawing it forth and thus
triggering whatever might be attached to it. She
frowned and delicately pressed her ear to the door.
Nothing stirred within. Even straining her inhuman
faculties to the utmost, all she could hear was the
quiet wheezing of the air conditioning, the gurgle of
water in the pipes and the vague confusion of voices
from other rooms and other floors.

All of which meant nothing, of course. If a
Cainite assassin, properly trained, waited behind the
door, then of course she'd hear nothing. If there were
some sort of electronic device tied to the letter, it
would not betray itself through sounds she could recognize. The corner of the letter jutted from beneath
the door, taunting her. She could not go forward, but

could not just leave it there. Ordinarily, she'd call for a ghoul to deal with the matter, but none of her ghouls was responding to her calls.

Suddenly, the crunch of footfalls on carpet startled Vykos. She'd forgotten she hadn't restored her hearing to normal levels, and hastened to do so before the intruder spoke. A normal conversational tone would be painful, while a shout might deafen her.

"Good evening, Your Excellency." Talley's voice carried ahead of his presence. "May I approach?"

Vykos smiled. This was a stroke of luck. The templar, as her protector, was among the very select few to know of this haven. "Of course. You're just the man I wanted to see, Don Talley."

"Just Talley, please." He strode forward, a hint of confusion on his face. "Your Excellency, where are your guards? I had been led to believe that your protection was provided for by your servants. I don't see them here." Indeed, Talley and Vykos were alone in the hallway. There were no signs of even the briefest of struggles, no scuff marks on the paint or bloodstains on the cream-colored carpet. There was just one damnably insolent envelope sticking out from a door that it had no business being under.

"I was just pondering that same question myself, I must confess. I return from an evening's work and find, not my servants, but this letter waiting for me. I am not pleased."

Talley suppressed his urge to smile. "Have you read the letter?"

"Of course not," Vykos responded irritably. "What sort of fool do you take me for?"

The templar made a vague gesture of obeisance.

"Forgive me, Your Excellency. In my current line of work, one must ask even the foolish questions." He touched his index finger to his chin, frowned, and pointed at the letter. "May I?"

Vykos backpedaled gracefully. "I should prefer to be elsewhere if you did." Talley laughed.

"You wound me, Your Excellency. I do have resources of my own, you know." And with that, his form melted into a pool of shadow that, after a moment's hesitation, oozed under the offending door. Careful not to touch the letter, the shadow wafted past it. There was silence for several minutes while Vykos stood patiently outside, content to let Talley risk whatever unknown dangers lay within. Vykos was more than reasonably certain that she could overwhelm or endure practically anything that might be waiting for her, but an incendiary device or some such might be extremely painful, and she disliked pain, at least her own. So she stood and waited, and half-amused herself devising suitable punishments for her missing ghouls.

The letter slid back beyond the door with a rasp. Vykos was suddenly alert again. She heard the sound of tearing paper, and then the bolts on the door clicking one by one.

The door opened and Talley stood there, the open letter in his hand. "Your Excellency," he said almost apologetically, "you may want to see this." Without waiting for a response, he turned and walked to the inner door of the suite. Here there were signs of struggle, long scratches in the woodwork and bits of paint and plaster from the wall on the carpet.

Talley reached the door and rested his hand on the knob. "Were you fond of those particular ghouls,

Your Excellency?"

"They were ghouls, Templar. Stop wasting my time," responded Vykos. "Are you telling me that my ghouls are dead? If so, say it and get out of my way so I can see what happened."

"If you insist, Your Excellency." And with that, Talley opened the final door.

The ghouls were in there, neatly laid out on the room's single table. There was no blood anywhere, not even in the bodies, which had been cleanly dismembered and then reassembled. Nothing else in the room was even disturbed.

Vykos did not gasp. She did not reel in horror, nor did she angrily swear vengeance. She had seen worse, indeed she had inflicted far worse herself, in her laboratories and donjons over the centuries.

She was, however, furious over the insult. "Lucita?" she hissed through clenched teeth.

"I would think rather one 'Lucius.' Would you be so kind as to verify this handwriting? The letter is rather familiar in its tone, so I would assume you'd know his script."

It was not often that Vykos lost control, but on those rare occasions when she did, the occasional survivor inevitably described the sight as "terrifying." She snarled, impossibly deep in her throat, and tore the letter from Talley's fingers. The beautiful woman, the artlessly crafted shell, slipped away for a moment and in that second, the templar found himself face to face with Vykos's true self—a ravening, formless obsession, an ancient rage that wore flesh and blood only because they were the sole materials at hand, and that would gladly set aside all bonds of sense and loyalty to destroy Talley at this moment because

Talley had taken, briefly, something that was hers.

Talley did not move, though in the split-second between his recognition of the threat and the time when the letter was pulled from his hand he went from relaxed to battle-ready. The room was full of shadows and the draped windows offered the perfect escape if he needed it, but he sincerely hoped that neither would be needed. If Vykos attacked, there would be no way anyone could reach the room before one or both of them was dead.

"Your Excellency," he said in a low, tight voice, "calm yourself. Read the letter if you must, though I recommend waiting. Yes, I read the letter, to make sure that the envelope itself was not trapped and to see if there was a clue as to what had occurred here. I am sorry if that offended, but I prefer to fulfill my office and see to your safety properly." He raised his hands, slowly. Behind Vykos, the shadows coiled eagerly, silently, awaiting the order to strike.

Vykos stared at Talley through mad eyes. She said nothing, but with infinite slowness, sanity crept back into her gaze. Her loose, monstrous flesh slowly collapsed in on itself, revealing the elfin features of Elizabeth Bathory that Vykos had been wearing since her arrival. "Give me a good reason not to destroy you, Templar," she whispered, voice shaking with the effort of control. "No one does this to me. No one sees me like this. No one tells this tale."

For an instant, Talley considered offering up the fact that the fight would be no sure thing as a reason not to pursue it, but thought better of the idea. There was no sense in prodding the Tzimisce's tender ego, not if he wished to calm her down.

"Because," he said in a soothing voice, "I don't

think that our mutual patron would appreciate that, Archbishop, and because we are both old and wise enough to know that tempting the cardinal's displeasure is a foolish thing to do. Because it would no doubt make this Lucius very happy to goad us to fighting amongst ourselves. And because," and he very gently smiled, "my estate would not be able to pay for the damages no doubt we'd incur." He took a step back, not coincidentally toward the window. "Do you agree, Your Excellency?"

Vykos's eyes were sane now, but there was an icy hatred in them. "Fortunately for you, I do." She glanced at the letter and threw it on the floor. "Lucius will pay for this."

"I would expect nothing less of you. He has, if I may say so, chosen perhaps the wrong Cainite to try to 'teach a lesson.'" Talley pulled up a chair a respectful distance from the table and sat.

"He has the power to enforce his will, if he truly feels the need. His ego is such that, at the moment, he is content with small demonstrations." She walked over to the table and flowed into a chair. Her elbows rested on the tabletop, bare inches from Ilse's naked and abused cadaver. "This was by way of a demonstration that he feels I am not properly appreciative of his efforts on our behalf. It's rather petty, really." She gazed at the dead and drained ghouls, her expression now distant.

"It would seem, yes." There was a minute of silence. "So it is to be Hartford?"

Vykos nodded absently. "The enemy prefers to protect Stamford, it would seem, and the other resources of the coastline. Hartford is being held with the same sort of screen we saw in Buffalo. It is ripe for the picking, and it is a big enough prize to take. Besides, it opens the door to Boston faster than even Archbishop Polonia anticipated. I wonder what they are up to."

Talley licked his dry lips. "In truth, their overall strategy does not concern me, except as it relates to my assignment."

"Do you really expect me to believe that, Talley?" Vykos's voice was surprisingly mild. "I find it hard to accept that the notorious Hound has no interest in conquest and the chase."

The templar shrugged ruefully. "You'll have to believe it, Your Excellency, because it's the truth. I loathe this continent and most everyone on it, and look forward to the end of the war simply because it's the only end I can see to this assignment. So who gets to earn immortal glory at Hartford?"

"Archbishop Borges, most likely. I still have the Tremere chantry to deal with before I can move on, and Archbishop Polonia has too many other things to deal with. The pack leaders and Panders can shout and demonstrate about wanting to run amuck, but after MacEllen's destruction, Hartford needs to be taken efficiently and without loss. An archbishop taking personal command of the operation lends a certain gravity to it. Don't you agree?"

The Archbishop of Washington waited a solid three minutes after Talley had left, then turned on every light in her suite. She carefully gathered the first few chunks of Ilse's body and brought them into the bathroom. Singing tunelessly, she worked the cold clay of the ghoul's flesh into a clotted liquid that fell into the toilet, then turned and repeated the procedure. Within a few minutes, the bowl was nearly full. Dispassionately, Vykos flushed it, then went back for another load.

Sometimes, she mused, mindless work was the best thing for a stressful evening. Besides, she might need the table later.

Talley shook his head as he made his way back to the Hyatt. He was a hunter, a tracker, a killer. His stock in trade was ending existences, not preserving them. And now he was faced with the prospect of Archbishop Borges leading a war party to Hartford. Talley didn't approve of Borges going outside, much less to Connecticut. But the archbishops weren't about to make their plans to suit a mere templar. This assignment was giving him a bad feeling in his gut. He was not being told everything, of that he was sure, and it would be impossible to do this right without knowing as much as he could. Damn all of them and their secrets. Damn Borges for being a fool and a blusterer, but not being enough of one to be controllable. Damn Lucita for being good. Damn Polonia for his arrogance that contributed to this madness. Damn Vykos for her games and her airs, and for causing problems with "Lucius" at exactly the wrong time.

"And damn you, Cardinal," he muttered under his breath. "Damn you for not disciplining your childe, damn you for sending me into this, and damn you most sincerely for giving me no way out."

Washington had slipped into a deceptive nighttime calm, but Talley felt as if he would explode.

"Damn them, " he said to the darkness. "Damn them all."

Monday, 30 August 1999, 2:32 AM
Main Street
Hartford, Connecticut

Hartford was not a kind city to its resident Kindred. The city itself was relatively small, with a confused welter of streets making the downtown area an inescapable labyrinth for any first-time visitors. Proximate but distinct, East Hartford and West Hartford stubbornly refused to amalgamate into a single city, presumably for fear of lowering their property values. I-91 and I-84 trundled through the city, more or less, making for an eternal traffic bottleneck from construction, as well as a steady stream of accidents from improperly constructed interchanges. The Charter Oak Bridge arched across the Connecticut River from the city, hurrying traffic over to I-84 and the Massachusetts border, but most of the façade the city presented to the river was dingy, gray, and architecturally confused. In short, Hartford was hard to get around in, not well designed for feeding and generally confusing even if one had a map.

Lucita, there on her third visit, considered it entirely appropriate that one of the main traffic arteries was called "Asylum Avenue."

She'd spent the evening studying her final target. Lucita had long since digested the provided material on the archbishop's habits, favorite stomping grounds, abilities and resources, and had stepped out into the night to clear her head before planning the operation. Thus, she found herself strolling through the core of the city well past midnight, watching the occasional late-night reveler stagger off to his car. Under other circumstances, she might have indulged herself, but she needed a clear head tonight, and a second-hand drunkenness would hinder her thinking later. There was still an edge to her hunger, but a discreet encounter earlier in the evening had taken care of the worst of it, and she'd find someone else after the night's labor was done.

In the meantime, however, any number of insurance executives, ad-copy writers and other denizens of central Connecticut passed under the shadow of death and moved on, never knowing how close each had come to destruction. Lucita prided herself on being able to move among mortals without them noticing anything untoward about her. Most young Kindred were in a tremendous hurry to acquire an aura of danger that would set them apart from the herd, while most older ones acquired that same air unconsciously. As soon as one stepped into a room, the kine knew that there was a wolf in the flock, and reacted accordingly. For that reason, humans always made excellent early warning systems against incursions by other Kindred. They were canaries in the mine, a superb if perhaps wasteful means of detecting the approach of invisible peril.

Lucita could blend into the crowd, however, and it made her that much more dangerous. She could still be detected for what she was, of course, but only if someone knew to look for her. The warning sign many Kindred used when deciding when and how to search, though, was the reaction of the mortals around them. It made Lucita's job that much easier.

She strolled along past what had been a G. Fox department store, then in front of a raucous restaurant that advertised fresh beer brewed on site. Around the corner, cars began to line up anxiously as the Hartford Stage opened its doors after another performance. Beyond that, an overpass conducted 84 from West Hartford to the river. She could see that there wasn't much beyond that save construction, and so she made a smart turn on her heel, sniffed the air, and started back the way she had come.

Presumably, that would give the man who was following her time to catch his breath.

He'd been following her for several blocks, and doing a reasonable job of it for a human. He didn't get too close, used the terrain to his advantage, and was remarkably adept at finding shadows to hide in.

Unfortunately for him, using shadows was not the best way to get a leg up on a Lasombra.

Lucita resisted the urge to smile. Her sudden turn-around had panicked the man, and he'd scrambled for cover. At the moment he was crouched down in an alley that ran along the side of the brew pub, trying hard to blend in with the darkness next to an overflowing dumpster. Presumably he was waiting for Lucita to go past, and for the last of the theater traffic to turn off so that he'd have a clear field to operate. If he were smart, he'd try to drag her into the alley and go to work there.

No doubt that sort of thing would work extremely well against a mortal woman. Alas for the spirit of street-level free enterprise in Hartford, Lucita was hardly an ordinary woman. A tinge of hunger reminded her that she hadn't fed terribly well that evening, and with slow, deliberate steps, she sauntered back past where her would-be assailant waited.

Down the block, traffic cleared. A light changed from green to red, solely for the benefit of the night. Lucita paused, and bent down ostensibly to adjust the buckle on her left shoe.

The mugger, surprisingly, failed to pounce. Lucita held her position a moment longer, then turned and stared into the alley. Faintly, she could hear sounds of a scuffle, followed by a metallic clanging that could only be a human head being repeatedly bounced off a dumpster lid.

"Son of a bitch," she breathed quietly, and stepped into the alley. Ahead of her, she could see two figures. One was moving, one was not. The one who was turned to her and hissed. Its visage was a horrific mass of scars and boils, and its eyes shone red. It dropped the body of the mugger on the alley floor and took a step toward where Lucita stood. Long, wicked claws curved out from the fingers and caught reflected light from the red neon sign out front.

"I'm not impressed," said Lucita. "You're sloppy and slow."

"What the hell?" said the Nosferatu, dropping his aggressive pose. "Crap. You're Kindred. Who the hell are you? I haven't seen you present yourself… wait. Lucita?"

Lucita counted to ten, first in Spanish and then in Latin. "You will explain how you know my name, yes? Then you will explain what you are doing here, and why I should not do to you what you have done to my supper."

"Him?" The hideous little vampire looked down at the broken wreck that had been the mugger. "He was yours? Damn. Should have figured that out, I guess. Saw him following a pretty lady, and prince's orders are to keep downtown neat because he's been trying to attract investment, and…" His voice trailed off lamely as he caught the expression of pure disdain on Lucita's face. "Right. Whatever. I'll get you another one. Over by the bus station is prime feeding ground."

Her annoyance palpable, Lucita began tapping her fingers on the brick wall of the alley. "You are still not answering the questions I have asked you. You have ten seconds to do so. Nine. Eight. Seven."

"I know your name because I work for Schreck. Well, I work with people who work for Schreck, at least at the moment—all right, all right! I've got a message for you from Schreck. I was supposed to deliver it to your hotel but I was going to wait until later. Then I saw this guy out here, and—urrrkk!"

The last came as Lucita simply grabbed the vampire by his throat, squeezed, and lifted him against the wall with impressive force. His feet kicked wildly, two feet off the ground, but to no effect. With desperate strength, he clawed at Lucita's hands, but her grip was unyielding.

"Stop that," she said curtly, "Or I let the shadows hold you instead. Would you prefer that?" The Nosferatu shook his head violently to the negative, at least as much as he could in his current position. "Good. Now at some point, I will have to sit down with Mr. Schreck and remind him not to employ idiots. If you have a message, you deliver it. Immediately. You do not speak about confidential matters anywhere but in confidence, and this alley does not qualify. You do not accept identification without proof—how did you know I was Lucita? Because I looked like a picture you saw? And what if I were a fleshcrafter, what then?"

She dropped him. He collapsed in a pile near the mugger, reflexively gasping. Lucita made a short, sharp gesture and the shadows of the alley began closing in on him. "Tonight you are lucky. I am exactly who you think I am, and I will take that message from you now. What is it?"

The Nosferatu looked at the encroaching shadows and gibbered, doing his best to curl himself into a small ball. "I'm supposed to tell you to stay in Hartford, that the target might be coming here! They're folding the city the way they folded Buffalo, and they think that will lure him out for you." One of the shadows, more daring than the rest, brushed against the withered flesh of his arm. "Oh God no, make them go away, I've told you what I was told!"

Lucita considered for a moment. She had no desire to stay in this place any longer than she had to—even under normal circumstances, Hartford was not precisely her favorite sort of city. On the other hand, Schreck had suggested two nights ago that Lucita head toward Hartford; now he was urging patience. Thus far, the Nosferatu's intelligence had proven reliable. If the prey were being lured to her, she could afford to sit tight.

Besides, she had another source she could check to confirm her prey's whereabouts, one that she was almost certain led back inside the Sabbat itself.

Her mind made up, she turned back to the quivering little Kindred, now almost completely enveloped in shadows. "I see. Thank you for your courtesy in delivering the message. I'll make sure Mr. Schreck learns that you carried out your assignment."

With that, she closed the fingers of her right hand into a fist. The shadows contracted as she did so. There was a brief, sickening crunch, and then the darkness melted back to where it had first come from. Lucita considered the cadavers, considered the overfull state of the dumpster, and then, with all due dignity, walked away.

Tuesday, 31 August 1999, 1:31 AM
Hyatt Regency Capitol Hill
Washington, D.C.

"Precisely how much information about the defenses did your informant on the council give you, Archbishop?" Borges's voice betrayed an edge of irritability, but that was all. Talley glanced over at him and said a silent prayer that the man's temper would fray no further, at least not tonight. There was too much work to be done.

Vykos pushed a small sheath of papers across the table with a noncommittal expression on her face. Thankfully, the map of Hartford on the tabletop did not so much as wrinkle. "Everything I was sent is here, Archbishop Borges. We know as much as they do when it comes to their numbers and strength. Most of the city's Cainites will be evacuated by tomorrow night, leaving only raw childer and suicidal ghouls to serve as a rudimentary defense."

Borges glanced over at Talley, who nodded once, then reached for the papers. For several minutes, there were no sounds but the rustling of pages, and various noises of approval or disapproval that Borges made, seemingly without knowing he did it.

"Hmm. Twenty newly Embraced vampires, a dozen ghouls, and nothing else?" Borges finally said. "We could sweep the city with a single pack." He looked smug as he put the papers down on the desk.

"We could," said Vykos, "and by doing so we'd confirm for them that, again, we knew exactly what we were going to be facing. It's a short step from that to uncovering my source, and the loss of one of our most important assets." Her face showed no trace of the disgust that colored her voice ever so slightly.

"Indeed. And that is why we must strike with overwhelming force. We must wash them away in blood, drown them in foes!" Borges was on his feet, face flushed as he imagined a victory not yet won. "No losses, like we had in Buffalo. With strength and with numbers, we shall eradicate them!"

"I couldn't agree more," added Polonia. "The attack must be overwhelming, and rather than entrust it to a lesser, an archbishop should take personal command. You," he said directly to Borges, "are the perfect leader."

Borges, his thought processes apparently having caught up to his bravado, took pause at the suggestion. He retook his seat. "Personal command, in the field?"

"That is *not* a good idea," said Talley at once. He'd been expecting the suggestion from Vykos, but from Polonia as well…?

"There is no glory without risk," Polonia pointed out. "And with you at his side, Don Talley, I'm sure Archbishop Borges will have nothing to fear. In any case, I must attend to matters in New York—I've been away far too long—and Vykos is busy with the Tremere here in Washington."

Talley scowled. Borges, shifting uncomfortably in his seat, seemed caught between conflicting thoughts of Lucita on one hand and crushing his enemies on the other.

"Vallejo can oversee the Tremere siege as well as I can," Vykos spoke up suddenly. "If it will ease everyone's minds, I will accompany Archbishop Borges, merely as an observer to his command, of course. With two archbishops, who by their very presence define the word 'overkill,' and a sizeable force, we should allay the suspicion that the fix is in, especially if we delay the attack this time." Vykos's voice was mild, but amused.

Borges turned to glare at his peer, then glanced at Talley's dispassionate face. "Even so," said Borges, "we shall bring numbers, and we shall make sure that you and I, Your Excellency, are prominently visible. I don't expect the evening to be much of an exercise for either of us, but even so, as you say, it will do your informer good to have us seen on the field." Borges inclined his head, bird-like, at his bodyguard. "And I trust that Don Talley will keep us safe as we do so."

Talley gave a quick frown. "I can if you don't expose yourself too much, Your Excellency. I say that now so I am not forced to remind you of it later."

Borges nodded and fanned away the objection. "Yes, yes. I understand. Rest assured that I will take no unnecessary risks, and I trust Archbishop Vykos to do the same."

"Very well." Talley sounded resigned, and not at all convinced. Borges ignored him.

"Archbishop Vykos," Borges continued, "would you like to involve any of your people in the operation? Perhaps the Little Tailor has some pets he wishes to field-test? Or surely some of your adherents are growing restless and would enjoy a night's exercise in the field. I was thinking that perhaps three packs, plus our own presence, would be sufficient? Perhaps we could use the university, the capital building, and that intersection there," he pointed at the civic center on the map, "as good places to start."

"We don't know where the enemy will be deployed, Archbishop. Why don't we wait until my contact tells us that?" Vykos's voice was weary; she clearly regretted agreeing to be part of this.

"The foe is Camarilla. All we need to do is set a few fires and endanger their precious Masquerade, and they will come running to us." Borges tapped his finger on the map, twice. "I like the notion, now that I think about it. If we make them assault our positions, they lose whatever benefit preparing defenses might have given them. It works well. Now, on to the timing of the affair...."

Talley simply tuned Borges out, and considered ways in which he could hustle him or Vykos out of danger when things began to degenerate. The plan was passable but clumsy, failing to take into account any number of possibilities. The worries were endless: Lucita's presence was studiously avoided in discussion—Talley tried to bring the point up several times, and Vykos and Borges had taken turns changing the subject; Lucius might have decided to teach Vykos another lesson by sending false information and letting the Sabbat offensive run straight into a Theo Bell-shaped buzz saw; Vykos's involvement in affairs, as well as Polonia's convenient absence, was still troubling. And so it went.

But the archbishops, deafened by their own arrogance and sense of superiority, did not seem inclined to listen to Talley. No, the best thing to do, he decided, would be to wait until things looked dangerous and then remove the target from the scene if Lucita showed up—*when* Lucita showed up. The rest of the attack could succeed or fail on its own merits, but his job was what concerned Talley.

"Don't you agree, Don Talley?" The templar emerged from his reverie to find both archbishops looking at him quizzically, though perhaps for different reasons.

"Of course, Don Borges. It is, in this case, as you say."

Vykos looked mildly surprised. Borges looked smug.

And Talley just wished that the fighting would start already so he wouldn't have to listen to this any longer.

Lucita stood on a corner in West Hartford, looking across at the entrance to the University of
Hartford campus. The lawn was brown, the sign was
ugly, and beyond it stretched what could only be described as acres' worth of parking lots. This meant
that there was no cover anywhere in the vicinity,
which was how Lucita liked it. She pulled out her
phone and dialed a pager number that had been given
to her, long ago when this escapade began. No doubt
she'd need to abandon yet another cell-phone number when this call was complete, but Schreck seemed
to be perfectly happy to supply her with all she needed
to avoid being traced.

Besides, Schreck's lackey had told Lucita to stick
around Hartford. That had been over a week ago,
and there was no sign of her target yet. Maybe her
other employer would have better information.

The call connected and there was a series of
clicks. After the requisite number of beeps and whir-
ring sounds, a guarded "Hello?" came over the line.

"Good evening."

"Ah. Doña Lucita. It is pleasant to hear from
you." The voice of the vampire on the other end of
the line was smoothly polite. "May I be of assistance?"

"A trifling matter, really. I am wondering if you
might be able to spare me the barest hint as to where
my target might be roaming in the upcoming nights?"

There was a pause. "How would I know that,
Doña Lucita?"

"Because whoever pulls your strings knows, yes? I'm not too blind to see what is in front of me. Who is it? Polonia? Vykos? One of the fat fools down in Mexico City?"

Another pause. "I am afraid I have no idea what you are talking about, Doña. I am truly sorry."

"You are a truly sorry liar, and that is all. So tell me: Where will he be?"

"Within two weeks, you may find Hartford a profitable place to hunt. I trust that is sufficient information?"

"I will not lie to you: No, it is not, but it will have to do. Very well. I thank you for all of your courtesies."

"The pleasure is mine." There was a click, and the line went dead.

Lucita folded up the phone and put it away, then jogged across the street onto the campus. It was always good to know the ground one might fight on, and besides, she was hungry.

Hartford was dying in bits and pieces, but the symptoms were mostly well-disguised. There was a fire at the Civic Center, and another outside the CBS station downtown. The city library's exquisitely carved wooden doors had been smashed by a moving truck whose driver had lost control of his vehicle, but there didn't seem to be any injuries. Police who could be spared from the other crises overwhelming the city were on the lookout for the driver, who had apparently fled the scene on foot. There was gunfire in the Mt. Zion Cemetery, and a four-car pileup that blocked the Charter Oaks Bridge eastbound. A hit-and-run accident with fatalities tied up I-91 just north of the I-84 interchange. The ritzy mall at Corbin's Corners, just west of the city, had a rash of looting and vandalism, perpetrated by a gang of teenage boys that security claimed they'd never seen before. A party on the University of Hartford campus degenerated into a riot, and a bus broke down in front of the Asylum Avenue station so that no one could get in or out.

Somewhere, in the middle of this carefully contrived chaos, Talley had been allowed to become the Hound again.

The initial plan had called for the commanders of the operation—Borges, Vykos and Talley himself—to hang well back from the action, directing troops and staying out of the line of fire. Furthermore, by insisting that Vykos and Borges remain in close proximity, Talley had both reduced each's ability to act against the other (if that was what was planned), and increased his own chances of protecting either. In theory, Talley's presence would be enough to make both archbishops behave, though it was hardly an ironclad guarantee.

The problems began with a lucky shot. Some Camarilla partisan left to screen the retreat somehow sussed out the location of the Sabbat's command center and started sniping at the trio of behemoth war ghouls Vykos had brought with her as a precaution. One's head exploded with the second shot.

Her two remaining ghouls in tow, Vykos started off to sweep around and flank their assailant. When Talley objected in no uncertain terms, archbishop and templar nearly came to blows over the matter, their argument punctuated by the rat-tat-tat of the sniper's rifle. Over Talley's strong protests, Vykos insisted on going.

"Fine!" Talley spat after the Tzimisce archbishop. "If you want to get yourself killed, I'll watch over Borges." Talley turned to caution Borges to stay exactly where he was, or else.

Borges was gone.

Perhaps the freshly spilled blood from the ghouls had combined with the excitement of battle to drive him into frenzy, or maybe he was just in a mood to glory-hound it. It didn't matter. Either way, the man was gone.

Talley cursed, briefly but with heartfelt passion. He had two choices: Go after Vykos, who had spurned his advice and was accompanied by two war ghouls; or try to find and protect Borges, who had also ignored Talley's warnings, but who was alone and had been thrust into command, all too conveniently, by

Polonia and Vykos. The Tzimisce had demonstrated an ability for centuries to take care of herself; Borges, to be charitable, had not done quite so well.

In the end, it was no choice at all.

And so, Talley plunged off into the fire-lit night to find Borges. Killing everything that got in his way would simply be a bonus.

Tuesday, 21 September 1999, 1:36 AM
Park Terrace
Hartford, Connecticut

Talley was not the only hunter on the streets that night. Quietly, effortlessly, Lucita slipped from shadow to shadow, observing. She watched, dispassionate, as a roaring war ghoul smashed a ghoul wearing a policeman's uniform into a bloody pulp, then overturned the man's car for good measure. Flames licked the underside of the vehicle, lighting the entire scene in lurid yellow and red. She watched, wordlessly, as a pack of howling *antitribu* ran amuck in Pope Park, shooting at everything that moved and, almost coincidentally, annihilating the squad of freshly created Brujah who leapt out of the trees at them. She watched, frowning, as Vykos took a man who got in her way to pieces, simply for the crime of being in the wrong place at the wrong time. Neither of her sources had said anything about Vykos being here.

Nowhere, however, did she see Borges. She knew he was there; she heard his name called often enough. Not once, though, did the archbishop present himself. Evidence of his handiwork was everywhere—torn corpses, mostly, mixed with Talley's neater handiwork—but the archbishop himself was as elusive as smoke.

Fortunately, Talley wasn't. For lack of anything better to do—the defense of the city was not her problem, after all, at least not above and beyond the removal of the Cainite leading the assault—she began following the Hound as he moved from scene of carnage to scene of carnage. Occasionally he'd stop and examine what Borges had left behind, but generally he was on the move, swift and angry and deadly. Every so often Lucita caught him causing surprising amounts of peripheral damage as he loped along, and slowly she realized that she wasn't the only one looking for Borges. He'd slipped his leash and was on the loose in the city, God alone knew where.

She would have laughed if she dared, but that would have revealed her presence to Talley. Lucita knew she was lucky the Hound was preoccupied, otherwise he might well have noticed her. She had no doubts that Talley would consider stopping her infinitely preferable to rounding up the errant archbishop before he got hurt. After all, if she were occupied, who else in the city could so much as harm Borges, let alone kill him?

She knew the answer to that question, of course, but didn't waste time speculating on whether it was a valid concern.

In the meantime, however, it was increasingly clear that Talley himself was looking for Borges in the flame and the chaos. Lucita, as she saw it, had three choices. She could follow Talley back to Borges and hope she could strike down the archbishop before Talley could interfere; she could strike out on her own and hope she found Borges before Talley did; or she could abandon the entire exercise and wait for another window of opportunity.

It took a split second for her to decide that following Talley was her best course of action. She was sated and well rested. Talley occasionally had to deal with the various messes Borges had not quite finished off in his haste or his frenzy, and he was moving too fast on the archbishop's trail to stop and feed in order to replenish himself. Borges himself was leaving an impressive path of gore behind him, meaning that no doubt he was drawing heavily on the blood within him. Judging from the amount of vitae leaking into the gutters and splashed on the walls, the Archbishop of Miami wasn't stopping to feed, either. When Talley finally caught up to his charge, and Lucita caught up to both of them, the two men would be weak. Hungry. Unable to fend off a sustained assault. With luck, she might be able to deal with Talley permanently. Her dear sire would be unhappy if she broke one of his favorite toys, but Talley was too much the wild card to be allowed to wander around freely. If the chance for her to eliminate him presented itself, she would take it, and send Monçada a condolence card later.

A few blocks away, someone bellowed with rage. A scream of terror matched it, spiraling up with it through the night. Talley didn't even bother to stop and look up. Instead, he simply sprinted in the direction of the noise with an inhuman burst of speed. Lucita grinned wolfishly and, without a sound, followed.

Talley had been cursing under his breath for nearly an hour non-stop, ever since that idiot Borges had gone bounding off into the fray. Under normal circumstances he would have caught the fool in a matter of minutes, but these were not normal circumstances. Borges was a one-vampire wrecking crew all right, but that wasn't what the situation needed. Behind him, his troops floundered, lacking direction. Each time a pack overwhelmed the slightest opposition, they felt the need to celebrate, noisily, and set whatever was at hand on fire. This served no good purpose except obscuring Borges's trail and cutting off major traffic arteries, not to mention crisping a few Sabbat vampires who got too close or too wildly enthused. The resultant detours and roadblocks cost Talley precious seconds that stretched into minutes as he navigated chaotic city streets in an effort to relocate Borges's trail. Only the scent of blood on the air served to guide him, but fortunately, where the Hound was concerned, that was enough.

The other complication was the fact that not everyone whom Borges ripped through was quite dead. Some demonstrated a surprising amount of fight as Talley pounded past them in an effort to follow the itinerant archbishop. One played dead until Talley was nearly upon him, then put two bullets into the templar's left arm. Talley rolled to cover and sent a shadow tentacle out from under a mailbox to crush the man (Talley didn't have time to see if the victim was Cainite, ghoul, or gun-toting innocent bystander) to an unrecognizable pulp. Other victims simply moaned, and Talley took a second to dispatch each with a single blow. One never could tell who was faking, after all, and after that first surprise Talley wanted to make sure that there were no more. The last thing he needed was some would-be hero coming up behind him at a sensitive moment. Even the feeblest ghoul could distract him at precisely the wrong moment with a bullet or bull rush, and distractions were precisely what he didn't need if he were going up against Lucita.

More screaming and hoarse shouts of rage came from up ahead. Talley concentrated for a moment to knit the wounds the bullets had torn in his shoulder, then redoubled his speed in hopes catching up with Borges and hauling him bodily out of the fray. Hopefully the archbishop would resist, and that would give Talley an excuse to beat him senseless.

Talley considered bending Borges's will to summon the archbishop, but if Borges were caught in a serious fight, say if Lucita had found him, the psychic itch of a summons could be the difference between avoiding a blow and almost avoiding it. Talley didn't dare distract the man until he was safely in hand again. Even if Borges were not Lucita's target—still a possibility—the man had jeopardized the entire operation by flying off half-cocked, and might yet managed to get himself killed. Talley was certain that the Camarilla would gladly trade Hartford for an archbishop.

Even as he sprinted forward, the Hound made a little promise to himself. Once Borges was safely off the field of battle, Talley was going to beat the unliving shit out of that idiot. Borges was going to survive this battle, at least if Talley had anything to say about it, but he was going to wish he hadn't.

The shouting in the near distance died down, and Talley put his head down for a final sprint. With any luck, that was the sound of Borges coming down off his blood-inspired frenzy. If not, it meant that Lucita had just found him. Either way, Talley wanted to be there. Like a madman, he ran.

Tuesday, 21 September 1999, 1:43 AM
Putnam Street
Hartford, Connecticut

Archbishop Borges looked around with a satisfied smile on his face. There were at least three dead vampires sprawled out before him. All three were in various states of disrepair, and one was entirely without limbs. They'd fought well, with a desperate, unreasoning ferocity, but they had never had a chance. One might as well ask toddlers to fight a grizzly bear as to ask untrained, unskilled vampires fresh from the Embrace to tackle an archbishop at the height of his power.

The intersection was nondescript, and he had no idea why these three vampires had died to defend it. Perhaps it held some emotional significance, or maybe they'd just gotten lost. Either way, they'd had the bad luck to have Archbishop Borges in his full madness come upon them. One had actually managed to rake the Archbishop's face with rudimentary claws, but Borges had caught the boy's arm mid-stroke and snapped it like kindling.

As the first attacker had fallen, Borges moved on to the second one with inhuman speed. Even as his opponent made a clumsy swing, Borges dropped to a knee and punched straight forward with all his strength. There was a muffled crack and the vampire screamed in pain as he folded in a way that the human torso had no business folding. As the man went down, Borges came up with a sledgehammer blow that connected with the underside of his chin and nearly tore his head from his shoulders.

Behind the archbishop, the first one came forward, clutching the ruin of his arm and howling. Borges turned and caught the boy's head between his hands. As the vampire scrabbled impotently at his eyes, Borges turned the boy's head hard to the left and was rewarded with the sound of splintering vertebrae. He twisted to the right, got more of the same, and dropped the spasmodic, twitching corpse at his feet.

The third vampire chose that moment to attack, forewarning Borges by screaming as he did so. The archbishop almost laughed as he saw his assailant, a middle-aged man in a hideous brown suit, his face twisted by hatred and frenzy into a monstrous mask. The vampire sprang for Borges, who ducked, turned, and caught the man's ankle as he went past. The momentum of the neonate's leap was such that Borges was able to take it and use it to his own ends, swinging the man by his foot into the unforgiving concrete. Without stopping, Borges flipped his opponent over by his ankle, and continued turning. The crunch that followed was not entirely dissimilar in tone from the one his friend's neck had made, but it did allow the victim to give a thin scream. Borges roared in triumph and moved up to the man's knee. That snapped, too, and then everything had been lost in a red haze of remembrance....

Borges blinked. Talley slapped him again, hard enough to shatter the jaw of a weaker man.

"You utter, worthless, *pointless* moron," the templar said. "Why the *hell* did you run off like that— no, don't tell me. You've already painted a bull's eye on your back for Lucita, and I don't want you out here any longer than necessary. We are leaving, Archbishop. We are leaving right now." He grabbed Borges's hand and pulled him as one would pull a poorly behaved child out of a store. "And when I get you out of this, I want you on your knees and thanking God for a solid hour that I found you before Lucita did. Come *on*."

Borges broke his grasp, and Talley turned to face him in disgust. "You go too far, Templar," the archbishop said thickly. "I have won this battle, and you are trying to steal my glory for Vykos by removing me from the field! I will not stand for it!"

Talley could take no more. "Fine," he said. "You're exactly right. I've got two bullets in my shoulder because I give a rat's arse about which of you idiots gets credit for reducing a city that even the Camarilla didn't care enough about to defend. Brilliant, Archbishop, absolutely brilliant. Now say precisely nothing. You're coming with me." Bands of shadow burst from every corner to bundle Borges tightly; before the man could even shout in protest he was tightly bound, and silently he toppled to the sidewalk. Swiftly, Talley stooped to where Borges lay and tucked him under one arm. It was time to get off the field, and the only way the archbishop was going to move quickly would be as luggage.

Talley was suddenly, virulently sick of the whole business. The last few minutes, Borges's rant in particular, had strengthened a certain suspicion that the templar had harbored for some time now. He decided that he would safeguard Borges for the rest of the battle, find Vykos and wrap the affair up, then catch the next night flight back to Madrid. There he would tell Monçada himself what he'd learned, and that the cardinal should find another lapdog for this sort of assignment. Talley could go off into the Schwarzwald and hunt lupines for a month as a vacation, perhaps. Anything would be better than staying entangled in this poisonous web of jealousy and willful stupidity.

He continued on toward the pre-established rendezvous point, toting Borges as easily as a man might carry a folded-up newspaper. Lucita had not yet made her presence known, and Talley wondered, for the first time, if he'd been wrong and Polonia was the real target after all. Frowning, the Hound picked up his pace. Soon enough, none of this would matter. He could see the meetpoint up ahead and moved toward it. Soon enough, it would all be over.

And then a great wall of blackness came down around Talley like a century's worth of midnights all at once.

Lucita watched the brief debate between Talley and Borges and nearly laughed with joy. If this were no trick, she could not have asked for a better chance. Borges was bundled up like an infant and Talley seemed intent on leaving town as quickly as possible. All she had to do was wait for the right moment, and Borges would be hers, easily.

It was a matter of seconds until it would all be over.

Suddenly, Lucita hesitated. A thin scream, barely on the edge of hearing, skittered through the air. Lucita knew that sound; it was one of Vykos's favorite war ghouls, hunting, and it was nearby. Lucita offered a silent curse on her sire and the persistence of his tools, then unleashed the shadows. She could no longer afford to wait. A globe of blackness rose up from the sewer grates and enveloped Talley. The templar didn't even have time to shout before he was overwhelmed.

Borges fell to the ground, his prison unraveling in seconds. He stumbled to his feet and looked around. To his credit, he took the entire situation in at a glance. "*Me cago en su madre,*" he breathed, and took a step back.

Lucita didn't waste time. She leapt down from her awning perch, pillars of darkness behind her billowing out and reaching out for her prey.

Borges did the sensible thing. He ran. Channeling what little vitae he had left in him, the Archbishop of Miami took to his heels. Wordlessly, Lucita abandoned the shadows and sprinted after him.

Fear lent Borges wings. Lucita was more agile, a better runner and better fed than he, but sheer terror gave speed to his flight. He ducked into an alley, out the other side, up a block past some construction and then left. All the while, Lucita followed as surely and as swiftly as a lioness running down her prey. Block by block, she closed the gap, until she was a bare pace behind Borges.

The man looked behind him, nearly stumbled, and put on a final burst of speed. Lucita swiped for him, missed, and then reached out for a small tendril of shadow. One came to her, and she sent it to tangle Borges's feet as he ran.

The man stumbled and fell, skidding fifteen feet down the sidewalk as he did so. He tried to climb to his feet, but Lucita was upon him in an instant.

"My apologies, Archbishop," she said. "If it helps ease the pain, you will no doubt be remembered posthumously for having won a great victory." She drew back her hand for the killing blow, and felt something clamp on her wrist. Startled, Lucita turned and saw a band of shadow wrapped around her forearm, tugging her backward toward...

...*Talley.*

"Your fat father said that you weren't to be harmed, Lucita. I'm going to have to apologize to him after I kill you then, aren't I?" He jerked the tendril back, and Lucita was yanked willy-nilly from her position atop the recumbent archbishop to land on her back in the street. A fresh bloodstain spread on the templar's shoulder, but he ignored it.

Borges half staggered, half crawled away. "Run,

Borges," said Talley. "Run very far and very fast, and pray you never see me again." He made another motion, and the band of darkness on Lucita's wrist tightened with bone-crushing strength.

Lucita did her best to ignore it. With her other hand, she reached down to her right ankle, where she kept a spare throwing knife at all times. Crying out with pain, she launched the shiv at Talley. The throw was off-line, but Talley took a split second to judge the knife's trajectory. During that split second, he wasn't paying attention to Lucita herself, and that was all the time she needed.

A shadow of her own tore Talley's to shreds, and she rolled left even as Talley unleashed another on her. Her hand caught a piece of debris and she flung it at him. The shadow tendril knocked it out of the air, but it bought her another precious second, as he came to her feet and prepared to counterattack.

A half-dozen shadows reached out from sewer grates and beneath cars to wrap themselves around the templar. He snarled and dissolved into a pool of darkness himself to escape, but even as he did, Lucita turned and ran after Borges.

Luck was with her. He'd managed to stumble off, but not to get far. One of his ankles was shattered from the shadowtrap that had brought him down; it would be a poor end for one of his station. He saw Lucita coming and hobbled faster, fear plain on his face. Shadows half-formed around him and faded to nothingness. Fear and pain rendered him unable to control them.

Lucita didn't try to catch him. Instead, she summoned darkness, paying no heed to the growing hunger that gnawed at her. A pair of tendrils arrowed after the wounded archbishop, only to be batted aside by others that had to be controlled by Talley. Not even pausing to watch, Lucita sprinted forward after Borges. Something wrapped itself around her ankle and she fell, hard. Bloodied, she managed to flip herself over and see that a staggering Talley had managed to snag her with a lone strand of darkness.

Lucita's face flushed with anger. Talley was clearly spent; he had nothing left. She was tiring, but she still had enough to deal with him and then pursue Borges. If nothing else, she could probably take the archbishop apart with her bare hands. Closing her eyes, she stopped resisting. The tendril dragged her, foot by foot, closer to Talley, wrapping up more and more of her leg as it did so. Talley was deadly, she knew. Even Fatima had spoken of him with respect, and Fatima had little respect for any *Franj*. Lucita knew his skill, knew his determination. But now he was angry as well. He might be weary, empty of blood and wounded. But he was still the Hound.

Lucita clenched her fist. A shadow slithered out from under a car and came to her. She fed it strength, then told it to smite Talley. In its own way, it understood and went to obey. Black as night and as terrible, it reared back to strike.

A full-throated roar erupted from behind Talley. He resisted the temptation to look, instead dodging the shadow tendril as it arrowed toward his heart. Lucita cursed as he flattened himself on the pavement and the shadow passed overhead. There was another scream, then, and one of Vykos's remaining war ghouls crashed to the ground a yard from where Talley lay. Its face was smashed into an unrecognizable ruin by the force of the shadow's impact but still, somehow, it moved. Another war ghoul thundered past, bellowing defiance at Lucita as it did so.

"Stop her!" Vykos shrieked at her gruesome pet from somewhere in the distance.

Talley sprang to his feet, looking around for the Tzimisce archbishop, but to no avail. Up ahead, the ghoul hurled its misshapen bulk on Lucita even as Borges scrambled away. There was a sickening crunch, and for a moment Talley thought that the monstrosity had achieved the impossible. Then Lucita's fist emerged from the creature's back with a wet sound, and the ghoul whimpered in agony.

Talley could pay no more attention to anything but his mission. He leapt for Lucita, but moved a fraction of a second too late as she shoved the limp bulk of the ghoul at him. Its weight toppled over onto him, and he was forced to take a precious instant to hurl it aside. In that moment, Lucita turned and pounced onto Borges, who raised a feeble hand to defend himself. With animalistic savagery, Lucita tore at him, eschewing anything more complicated than her talons and fangs as she shredded the archbishop's arm, chest and throat. A thin, high-pitched wail emerged, impossibly, from him as he frantically tried to push Lucita away. Then there was terrible silence.

Talley dropped his shoulder and plowed into Lucita's back with bone-crushing force, a moment too late. She went over and sprawled on the asphalt, but Borges's features were already rotting away. The Archbishop of Miami was finally, irrevocably dead.

Lucita scrambled to her feet, but not before Talley was on her again. He caught her face in his left hand and tore across, leaving a trail of bloody furrows before she wrenched out of his grip. Talley howled rage and frustration then, a sound to chill the blood as she came to her feet. He lashed out with a fist, which she parried, but the man's second blow caught her in the knee and nearly buckled it. Talley smiled wolfishly and circled to the left, looking to exploit the weak knee. Hobbling, Lucita turned to face him.

With a grim countenance, Lucita assessed the situation even as Talley feinted a kick at her injured leg. She dodged, painfully, and then had to duck a vicious swing that would have taken her head off had it connected. Borges was dead. She was far weaker than she wanted to be; too many shadows had been required to kill Borges and distract Talley. And the Hound was about to earn his reputation all over again. It was time to go.

With strength born of desperation, she launched a spinning kick at Talley. He dodged it, but she used the seconds to force healing blood to her knee. Talley lashed out with another combination of blows, but she weaved out of the way of each and then turned her last dodge into a full-fledged sprint. Talley gave a bellow of inchoate rage and started after her. If she remembered the city properly, the river was not far away. She just had another row of buildings to pass, then the highway to cross, and she'd be safe. Behind her, the templar came charging after, his weakness masked by bloodlust and anger.

Lucita made for an alley between two warehouses. Talley bellowed and reached for a shadow to stretch across her path, but his strength was fading, and the barrier disintegrated as she reached it. As she ran, Lucita threw trash cans, boxes, anything she could find behind her to slow Talley down. He waded through the obstacles as if they were nothing.

Beyond the alley was the highway, elevated on this side. Southbound traffic was light, but north-bound was still snarled from the earlier accidents. Lucita whispered a prayer of thanks, climbed the embankment, and leapt over the guard rail. She dodged a black Bonneville that was half on the right shoulder, stumbled and sprinted onward. Calling on almost the last bit of blood she had in her, she moved out and across the first four lanes of traffic. Behind her, Talley reached the roadside and continued forward, machine-like in his persistence. Traffic veered around him, horns honking. One car clipped him with a bumper. He spun, but kept moving relentlessly.

Monçada's childe didn't look back. Instead, she leapt onto a car trunk and picked her way across the stalled traffic as fast as she could. Within seconds she was across the road and into the tall grass by the riverside. Talley, exhausted or no, was hot on her heels.

Lucita risked a last glance at her pursuer. The Hound's visage, clearly visible just a few steps behind her, was the essence of implacable hatred. There was only one way out.

She blew Talley a kiss, then, and dove into the muddy waters of the Connecticut River. Almost instantly, even the ripples of her passage had vanished. She was gone.

Arriving bare seconds too late, Talley stared after her. He could pursue, but trying to find her in the sludge that passed for river water would be nigh-impossible. Besides, he reflected bitterly, he had what he had really come for. Monçada had been right; Borges had been, in the end, expendable so long as the truth of his death was known. And Vykos? Vykos had shown remarkably good timing this evening, knowing just when to disappear and then when to show up. It was a fascinating coincidence, or it would have been, if coincidence was in fact what it was. Somehow, he didn't think so.

Talley suspected that he knew enough to end this miserable assignment. Disgusted, he sagged down onto the riverbank and waited for company. It didn't take long to arrive.

Vykos looked suitably concerned when she joined him. The Hound turned and stared at the Tzimisce with weary hatred. "So what exactly were you thinking back there?"

Vykos stared back. "I was thinking to change the odds for you, Templar. I assumed that you would not object to assistance."

"I object to nearly being trampled without warning, and I object to hindrances being foisted upon me. Come now, you've been in the field long enough to know better than what you showed tonight. You've gotten clumsy." Talley's tone was bleak, though deceptively mild.

"There was no time to do otherwise, Talley. Don't forget your place and presume to lecture me." There was an edge to Vykos's voice. Talley ignored it.

"I forget nothing, Archbishop. Nothing at all." Both were silent for a moment. In the city proper, sirens whined and fires shot up into the soot-filled air. Borges's men were building him quite a funeral pyre, even if they didn't yet know he was destroyed.

"She got away?" asked Vykos softly.

Talley nodded. "She got away, as if that surprises you. Into the river and no doubt down to the sea. I won't be surprised if she swims all the way to Florida and goes to steal Borges's cigars."

There was another pause. "We have won the city," said Vykos at last.

"*You* won the city. I wish you joy of it. I now get to return to our patron and explain to him everything that happened here." He smiled, then, and not pleasantly. "Everything. Including how Lucita knew precisely where to be in order to find her prey."

Vykos smiled back, as empty and plastic as a Halloween mask. "I'm sure the cardinal will be understanding, considering the impossible nature of what you were asked to do."

The templar hoisted himself to his feet and stared deliberately at the Tzimisce, still seated. "I am leaving, Archbishop," he finally said. "And I'm sure you're right. I have no doubt that the cardinal *will* understand." With infinite care and dignity, he turned and made his way back toward the city.

In the distance, the sound of a car exploding split the night—and it was almost loud enough to drown out Vykos's single, soft peal of laughter.

Lucita fished herself out of the river two miles downstream. She'd planned on such as a potential escape route earlier for a worst-case scenario, and was profoundly thankful she'd done so. She stripped herself of her wet clothes and threw them back in the river. They floated for a moment, then sank and presumably began their journey to Long Island Sound. Nothing she abandoned had been with her long enough to be useful to an enemy who might use thaumaturgical arts against her; she had made sure of that.

Briskly, she walked to where she'd cached a new set of clothes, as well as everything else she needed. The black bag was where she'd left it, duct-taped to a high bole of one of the many trees planted alongside the river. Agile as a cat, she climbed the trunk and rescued her wares. She dropped the bag to the ground and jumped down lightly after it. Quickly she unzipped it and pulled out a fresh change of clothes. Shrugging into them, she didn't notice the cold from the breeze off the river. Truth be told, changing was unnecessary, but wet clothes were uncomfortable and Lucita detested discomfort. Besides, water would do unpleasant things to the leather seats of her car.

Fully dressed, she reached into the bag again. With minimal fuss she pulled forth keys, a wallet, a handful of knives, and various other sundries she'd stowed the night before against just such an eventuality. Everything had gone, and was continuing to go, according to plan.

The bag emptied, she looped the carrying strap over her shoulder and headed for the road. She'd parked the BMW a few blocks off 91, which still ran parallel to the river here. Traffic was lighter and easier to dodge here, so she strolled across the highway, up the ramp and to a soft-serve ice-cream place set well back from the road and moated by more parking than it would ever need. It was here that Lucita had stashed her car. She'd had a rental ready to move in Hartford as well, but something had told her that she'd be wanting the fast car here. As the night's exertions began manifesting as aches and pains, she found herself glad she'd listened to her hunch; she would have hated to abandon the BMW in Hartford.

As she approached the convertible, Lucita noticed something tucked under the windshield wiper. It was bright orange, and at first she thought it was a parking ticket. Another few steps brought the object into sharper focus, and the laughter she'd been suppressing suddenly died in her throat.

It was not a ticket. It was not a piece of paper at all. It was an orange scarf, neatly knotted around the windshield wiper blade as a reminder.

Fatima had been here. Lucita had thought of the other woman earlier; now it didn't seem like such a coincidence. Lucita stood, motionless. How long had Fatima been watching her? How much had she seen?

Had she been there tonight? And if so, was she waiting for Lucita now?

One of the parking-lot lights chose that exact moment to flicker and die, and that made up Lucita's mind. She reached down for a knife she'd taken from her cache, pulled it out, and walked over to the car. Without a sound she sawed the scarf off the wiper blade and let it fall to the ground. She then gave the vehicle a quick inspection for bombs and traps, not really fearing any—Fatima would never kill her that artlessly—and, her curiosity satisfied, she opened the door and got in. The motor purred quickly to life and, with almost unseemly haste, Lucita peeled out of the parking lot. 91 southbound beckoned a few blocks away; behind her, Hartford sent thin straggles of smoke into the darkened sky.

Mr. Schreck is going to get a phone call very soon, Lucita decided. So was her mysterious other client. She was going to take their money and everything else they'd offered, tell both of them that they could go to hell, and leave this miserable country.

Perhaps it is time to take confession again, whispered something that might once have been Lucita's conscience. *Time to go see your sire*.

Lucita frowned and tapped the accelerator, even as the notion resonated. The car leaped forward eagerly, as eagerly as Talley had leapt for her not so long ago. But all of that was over. She was done.

And she might even be going home to give her sire a piece of her mind.

Wednesday, 22 September 1999, 7:45 PM
Iglesia de San Nicolás de los Servitas
Madrid, Spain

It was very dark in the confessional. Rumor had it that Cardinal Monçada had crushed any number of Cainites to death in the booth with his fearsome mastery of shadows, but Talley discounted the stories. Monçada was strong enough to have no need for trickery. He heard the cardinal's huge bulk sliding into the booth on the far side of the partition. There was a click as the shutter between the two chambers went up, and the cardinal said, "Yes?"

"Bless me, Father, for I have sinned," he murmured. "It has been four hundred twelve years, three months and six days since my last confession."

Monçada clucked disapproval. "That is a very long time, my son. You had time for a great many sins. Still, it is good you have come back to the Church. Speak to me, then. Tell me with what sins four centuries have stained you."

"I have killed, Father. I have lied, I have coveted, I have stolen. And I have failed my cardinal." Talley bowed his head. The shadows somehow seemed to press in more closely, though the templar told himself that was just a trick of the imagination.

There was a rustling of cloth. "Tell me more."

"Archbishop Borges is dead. At the hand of your childe."

"Tsk. That is grievous news indeed, my son. How did such a thing come to pass?" Around Talley, the shadows pressed in more closely.

Talley sketched out the details of the past nights.

fasombra

It took a surprisingly long time, and he found himself silently hoping he wasn't boring Monçada.

When the templar finally wound down, the cardinal's voice rumbled from the confessional. "Fascinating. And most understandable, perhaps, considering the circumstances. Much about this is odd, especially the end game." The shadows pulled away from Talley, and he let out a breath he did not know he'd taken. "Still, murder, theft, the others—these are serious sins. Waiting four centuries to confess them has given them time to stain the soul deeply, my son. Your penance will not be light, I think, nor will it end soon."

Talley bowed his head. "Whatever you prescribe, Father."

Monçada chuckled. "I shall have to think on it. In the meantime, do five novenas each morning, five Hail Marys every night, for the next fifty years. Do them without fail. You have many sins to wash away, Talley. *In nomine Patri, et Filii, et Spiritu Sancti, ego te absolvo.* You may go."

"Thank you, Father," Talley said, and made to duck out of the booth. He paused, though, and returned. "Your Eminence?"

"Yes?" The cardinal's voice was a barely audible rasp.

"I believe I know why Borges died, and who was responsible."

"Of course you do. I was startled that you did not include it in your confession."

Talley shrugged silently. "The sin was not mine, save perhaps one of pride."

Monçada chuckled. "You sound like a Jesuit, all trickery and sophism. Speak."

"Polonia should have been the one to die, but he is too strong. Even the Courts of Blood would fear to move against him. Borges, on the other hand, was not strong alone. Standing at Polonia's side, however, bound by shared lineage or hatred of others, promised glory and power and blood, he could have been formidable indeed. Polonia did not seem inclined to take Borges as an ally, but still, the possibility was there."

"Fascinating."

Talley nodded. "Wisdom would have dictated having him killed in battle, or maneuvered into being destroyed for some infraction or other, but wisdom is in short supply. Vykos wanted suspicion as far from her as possible, to sow discord and cover her role. Who would dare assume that she, your servant in these matters, would tempt your wrath by hurling your childe against your other servitors? It is a madman's plan, or a genius's—but there is no wisdom in it."

"Vykos? A pity."

"Vykos. It was she who created the diversion that drove Borges into frenzy and forced me to pursue him. Had I stayed longer in that miserable excuse for a city, no doubt I would have found evidence that the shooter who assaulted our command post was in Vykos's service in some fashion. It was Vykos who distracted me at the critical moment. Polonia's opportunism didn't help matters; but as for the traitor, all roads lead to your Tzimisce, Your Eminence."

Monçada let loose a heavy sigh. "I feared as much. You have done well, my faithful Hound. Well indeed."

"Not that well. Borges destroyed under my watch, and Lucita escaped. I suspect there was more than just Vykos at work, as well. The other killings did not carry her scent. A bluff, or perhaps something entirely unrelated. I do not know, though I suspect that your childe and I will never share civil conversation again."

"A pity, that." Monçada shifted his massive bulk within the confessional and coughed once, softly. "I am very glad you are well, Talley. And I am well pleased with you. Go, now. Hunt what prey you choose. I will not need you for a very long time, I think. Go, and take my thanks with you."

Talley blinked, once. "Of course, Your Eminence. Thank you." He stumbled out of the booth. Cristobal Garcia, a ghoul who'd been in Monçada's service for at least a hundred years, was waiting for him, and with suitable grace and humility conducted Talley to his quarters. In the evening, he'd depart with tangible evidence of the cardinal's gratitude, but for now, all he wanted was a day of slumber without dreams.

Still within the comfortable walls of the confessional, Cardinal Ambrosio Luis Monçada wrapped a cloak of shadows around himself tightly, and then another one. The darkness, he found, gave him comfort, and he found precious little of that in the world these nights. Crooning a tuneless song to himself, he closed his eyes. Here God and the darkness would preserve him, as they always had.

"Amen," he murmured, and gave himself to slumber and the embrace of the night.

About the author

Richard E. Dansky is the Developer of **Vampire: The Dark Ages** and **Kindred of the East** for White Wolf Game Studios. He has written for magazines ranging from **Folk Tales** to **Lovecraft Studies**. A graduate of Wesleyan University with an M.A. from Boston College, Richard previously developed **Wraith: The Oblivion** and **Mind's Eye Theatre** for White Wolf. **Lasombra** is his first novel, but hopefully, not his last.

The Vampire Clan Novel Series ....

Clan Novel: Toreador
These artists are the most sophisticated of the Kindred.

Clan Novel: Tzimisce
Fleshcrafters, experts of the arcane, and the most cruel of Sabbat vampires.

Clan Novel: Gangrel
Feral shapeshifters distanced from the society of the Kindred.

Clan Novel: Setite
The much-loathed serpentine masters of moral and spiritual corruption.

Clan Novel: Ventrue
The most political of vampires, they lead the Camarilla.

Clan Novel: Lasombra
The leaders of the Sabbat and the most Machiavellian of all Kindred.

Clan Novel: Ravnos
These devilish gypsies are not welcomed by the Camarilla, nor tolerated by the Sabbat.

Clan Novel: Assamite
The most feared clan, for they are assassins of both vampires and mortals.

Clan Novel: Malkavian
Thought insane by other Kindred, they know that within madness lies wisdom.

Clan Novel: Brujah
Street-punks and rebels, they are aggressive and vengeful in defense of their beliefs.

Clan Novel: Giovanni
Still a respected part of the mortal world, this mercantile clan is also home to necromancers.

Clan Novel: Tremere
The most magical of the clans and the most tightly organized.

Clan Novel: Nosferatu
Horrific to behold, these sneaks know more secrets than the other clans—secrets that will only be revealed in this, the last of the **Vampire Clan Novels.**

The American Camarilla is under siege. The Sabbat offensive is sweeping the East Coast. The Eye of Hazimel, an ancient and disgustingly powerful artifact, has resurfaced and even now wreaks havoc.

Have we got your attention yet?

There's more to come. Victoria, Vykos, Ramona, Hesha, Jan, Lucita and the others all have greater roles to play. Anyone who *survives* has a greater role to play.

Astute readers of this series will begin to put clues together as the series progresses, but everyone will note that the end date of each book is later than the end date of the prior book. In such a fashion, the series chronologically continues in **Clan Novel: Ravnos** and then **Clan Novel: Assamite**. Excerpts of these two exciting novels are on the following pages.

CLAN NOVEL: RAVNOS
ISBN 1-56504-808-3
WW# 11106
$5.99 U.S.

CLAN NOVEL: ASSAMITE
ISBN 1-56504-809-1
WW# 11107
$5.99 U.S.

Khalil Ravana sauntered pleasantly down the streets of Brooklyn. Two nights of real travel—catching buses, cadging lifts from sympathetic lorry drivers (*Truck drivers*, he corrected himself), telling the tale to lonely sales reps driving late—had settled the Ravnos's nerves. He'd fed well, he'd amused himself, he'd come up in the world. His clothes broadcast money, and class of a sort…though none of them fit him as well as they had their original owners. Amazing, these Americans…they'd give you the shirt off their backs just for asking (he smirked) and even the clumsiest Calcutta cutpurse could make a good living off the unguarded wallets in this country. A clever *shilmulo* like himself could make a fortune.

He still carried his 'casket.' It had been a convenient prop for his pose as a stranded tourist. When the traveling-musician idea came along, he'd conjured the image of a broken saxophone into it, and picked up sympathy and a little cash from fellow 'artists.' Bus passengers needed luggage. Business types carried cases. It held his wardrobe and growing cache of valuables by night, and his sun-shy body by day. What a gift Hesha had given him…he'd have to thank the Setite properly.

As soon as possible, Khalil decided. He began whistling.

A sudden urge drove him down a dark alley and out onto a clean-swept, well-lit little patch of sidewalk. "All right," muttered the walker. "You don't need to hit me with it."

I wasn't sure you would hear me over your own boasting. The voice felt dry as drought tonight. *This is the place.*

Khalil slowed casually. He set down his luggage without a glance around, and felt in his pocket as if for keys. With one eye on the lock and one on his bag, he pulled two bits of wire from his right coat pocket. From his left, the forcing pin...all three entered the keyhole at the same moment. Any ordinary observer would have sworn the young man, coming home very late, or to work remarkably early, had grasped his keyring with both hands and was having trouble with a rusty, cantankerous lock.

"You'd better be right," he whispered. "The sun's rising any minute now."

Trust me.

Oh, yes, thought Khalil to himself. *Sure.* The old Yale gave way beneath his probing picks, and the door handle turned in his fingers.

by kathleen ryan

Saturday, 3 July 1999, 3:18 AM (local time)
Caves of Ten Thousand Sorrows
Near Petra, Jordan

Elijah Ahmed, caliph of Alamut, walked silently through the darkness toward his destiny. His sandals were left miles behind, neatly arranged before the threshold of the caverns. His feet, the soles of which had not felt the fire of sun-scorched desert sands since the first days of the Holy Prophet, did not so much as displace a single pebble or disturb a granule of dust from its resting place upon the sandstone.

Elijah's mind was quiet. Calming scripture arose from his soul like the cool evening breeze blowing from the north. *He, Allah, is One. Allah is He on Whom all depend. He begets not, nor is He begotten, and none is like Him.*

The darkness was complete, yet the caliph stepped with surety. Countless passages branched off from the winding tunnel he followed, but Elijah's deliberate pace did not once slacken. Never before had he traversed this path, but the twists of the rough-hewn corridors were as familiar to him as the weave of his simple muslin robe. He could not deny that which drew him forward. He could not lose his way.

The passages wound this way and that, seemingly without reason; sharp, spiraling curves that nearly met themselves, broad arcs to the northwest, squared turns to the south, zigs and zags leading tangentially eastward but never directly toward the rising sun. Among the sculptured chaos, however, Elijah Ahmed's steps carried him always down, always deeper toward the heart of the earth.

He, Allah, is One. Allah is He on Whom all depend. He begets not, nor is He begotten, and none is like Him.

When finally Elijah had taken his last step, he stood not in one of the corridors of the past hours but in a vast chamber. Darkness opened before him like the void, but not even the absence of light could hide from his eyes the presence of the herald.

It sat upon an arrangement of mammoth stones, an unadorned throne crafted from bedrock. The herald, too, was unadorned—its naked, childlike body resembled a sculpture of hard-packed coal, each fissure, each crack in the kiln-hardened surface actually a jagged scar streaking like black lightning across the blackest midnight sky—black except for a crescent and a handful of matching bone-white stars. The crescent moon of this midnight was a necklace of bone that lay draped across the chest of the herald's perfectly motionless body. The stars were bone as well, though no mere accoutrements; they were the bones of ur-Shugli, visible where the midnight skin had peeled back or cracked and fallen away; they were the sheaths of the herald's essence, and his marrow was vengeance.

Thus was the being Elijah Ahmed faced.

Elijah Ahmed, caliph of Alamut, one of the tripartite *du'at*, looked into the deep emptiness that should have been the herald's eyes. The sockets were set beneath sharp ridges of bone, and the gaping nothingness was like an accusation of wrongdoing and injury thousands of years old, as if Elijah himself had gouged out the eyes in sport or cruel jest.

And yet the herald looked upon Elijah, and the herald did see.

"Elijah Ahmed," spoke ur-Shugli.

At once, Elijah prostrated himself before the herald. The sandstone, which should have been cool within the womb of the earth, burned the caliph's forehead. But he did not stir.

"Childe of Haqim," spoke the herald. "Blood of his blood of his blood of his blood." Ur-Shugli's voice filled the chamber like the south desert wind. His words stung like the first pricks of the sandstorm that gnaws flesh from bone.

"Rise, Elijah Ahmed."

The caliph obeyed, as would he have even had he desired otherwise. He rose to one knee. The sandstone had become the wide desert floor at noon. He needn't look at the palms of his hands to know that his own dark skin crisped—the left knee, on which his weight rested; the sole of his right foot; the top of the left. Head bowed, eyes downcast, Elijah ignored the fire of his body and paid silent homage to the herald of his master.

But a storm was rising.

The desert winds, an open furnace stoked by the rage of ancients, tore at him. His thin muslin robe quickly burned away, as did his hair, his eyebrows, and lashes. The caliph closed his eyes against the heat, but his eyelids soon curled back like singed paper. He had no choice but to look upon his reckoning.

In that instant, Elijah Ahmed knew fear. It was a mark of his wisdom. For who does not fear the power of heaven unleashed but the fool? In that instant, Elijah knew also the unvoiced question given form in that fiery desert wind:

Who gives you life, Elijah Ahmed?

Elijah could no longer reason, so great had become the heat, but he didn't need reason in the face of this challenge. The question was not new to him; it had dogged him as long as he remembered, since before wise Thetmes Embraced him into unending death, since Elijah's mortal days following behind in the footsteps of the Holy Prophet. From deep within Elijah's soul, the answer rose full like a gourd dipped in an oasis well.

Allah gives me life.

The fiery wind grew to a raging maelstrom. It

roared in Elijah's ears, those fragile shells of flesh that began to melt and run down the sides of his face. His naked eyes, too, were assaulted by the storm. His tears dried before he could cry them.

And then the herald was no longer sitting far across the chamber upon his great throne. He had not moved, but now ur-Shugli stood motionless before Elijah, mere inches from the caliph. The herald's craggy, coal-black skin shone amidst the violence of the vortex.

"Young Allah," said ur-Shugli. "Are you certain, Childe of Haqim?"

Elijah's face was now upturned, though he did not remember moving. His eyes became pools of blood, as the tender flesh disintegrated beneath the fury of ur-Shugli. The caliph's skin cracked and peeled away. As the last of vision fled, Elijah was not aware, could not be aware, of the eternal moment in which he re-sembled nothing so much as the herald before which he knelt. Elijah wanted to open his mouth, wanted to speak, but the muscles of his jaw were beyond use and his tongue was shriveled away to a smoldering lump.

As flesh burned away, one belief resounded from the core of Elijah Ahmed's being: *Haqim has stretched my existence, but it was Allah gave me life. He, Allah, is One. Allah is He on Whom all depend. He begets not, nor is He begotten, and none is like Him.*

"Very well," said ur-Shugli. His words found their way through Elijah's ruined ears, within the mind that was beyond pain. "In the name of the Eldest, I re-claim that which is rightfully his."

No sooner was it said than the blackened form that had been Elijah Ahmed, caliph of Alamut, vomited forth the blood of Haqim into a large earthen pot.

Many hours later, the winds settled, and all was again silent stillness of the void.

by gherbod fleming

next: rounds